Good

Life Sentences

Life Sentences

A NOVEL BY
Elizabeth Forsythe Hailey

Delacorte Press / New York

Published by
Delacorte Press
1 Dag Hammarskjold Plaza
New York, N.Y. 10017

Manufactured in the United States of America

Fourth Printing—1982

Designed by Richard Oriolo

Library of Congress Cataloging in Publication Data

Hailey, Elizabeth Forsythe.
Life sentences.

I. Title.

PS3558.A327L5   813'.54   82-7388
ISBN 0-440-04924-5   AACR2

For my daughters, Kendall and Brooke,
And for the daughters of us all

One

Lindsay knew when it was over that it was not over for her. Like a woman in love, she was convinced conception had taken place.

She was working at home that morning. One of the advantages of being an editor was that she did not have to sit at a desk to prove she was earning her pay. She answered only to herself which of course meant that she was working harder than anyone who worked for her.

On mornings when no meetings or appointments were scheduled, she would get out of bed just long enough to make a pot of coffee, then bring it back to her bedside table along with a stack of reading matter. She would work through lunch, happy to avoid the extended ritual that was part of a typical day on the job. At three o'clock she would arrive at the office clear-eyed and filled with the energy that comes from a sense of accomplishment. After a morning alone she welcomed the list of phone calls to be returned and often stayed at her desk long after everyone else had left.

Lindsay had lived alone since she moved to New York at the age of twenty-three. At that time her parents, concerned for her physical safety, sent her a monthly check to cover her rent in what was considered by New York standards a safe neighborhood —meaning that rape, theft, and murder, while not uncommon, occurred less frequently here than in other parts of the city. Her mother also insisted that she use an initial in place of her first name on her mailbox so it would not be evident to every passing stranger that she was a woman living alone. Opposed in principle to this subterfuge, Lindsay reminded her mother that in choosing her maiden name for her daughter's first name, she had unknowingly protected her from discrimination on the basis of sex—at least from strangers. As a child Lindsay was urged to join the Cub Scouts and later the Boy Scouts, as a teen-ager the YMCA solicited her attendance at summer camp, and the summer after she graduated from college her local draft board notified her to report for classification.

She knew people in the city who had been mugged in the street or subway or had come home to find their apartments robbed— some more than once—but it had never happened to her, a fact Lindsay attributed to the shell of physical invulnerability she wore like armor. Later, in reconstructing the incident, she realized that until it happened to her, she was as guilty as any man of thinking that a rape victim was somehow "asking for it." For was not the inverse of this attitude (feeling safe precisely because she was *not* "asking for it") just as prejudiced?

Her first thought when she looked up from her bed to see a strange man at the door of her bedroom was guilt: it was noon and she was still in her nightgown. She realized later that her initial confusion was caused by the way he was dressed. The man who crossed to her bed and pinned her arms above her head was wearing a suit and tie. His appearance carried with it an authority that kept her from screaming.

When he reached for his knife and held it against her throat, releasing her arms, Lindsay pointed toward her purse on the bureau, indicating it was his if he wanted it. In reply he slowly unbuckled his alligator belt.

Somehow Lindsay knew that her only hope of surviving the assault was to keep her eyes averted from his face. Her impression of him when he entered the room was of a middle-aged man with weary eyes. There was nothing desperate or unkind in his manner.

Despite his whispered injunction against movement of any kind, Lindsay instinctively raised her hands to protect her face, knocking her glasses to the floor as she did so. For once she was glad to be nearsighted. By deliberately avoiding his eyes as he bent over her, she hoped to will him into anonymity. Except for the red paisley tie that she watched rising and falling above her as he labored to a climax, her assailant had no distinguishing features. He could have been any prosperous man she passed on the street.

He did not loosen his tie until he stood to leave. He kept the knife at her throat while he fastened his trousers then took the tie from his neck and, turning her over onto her stomach, bound her wrists behind her. With the alligator belt he hobbled her ankles. Before he could stuff his hand-hemmed handkerchief into her mouth, Lindsay spoke for the first time since he had forced entry.

"I'm going to have your child," she said with a certainty that surprised her as much as it startled him.

She did not realize until later that she was striking a bargain —the unspoken clause of the contract being "if you let me live."

It was instinct that supplied her with the only weapon nature has given the female to combat the physical superiority of the male: the promise that she contains within her womb the seed of an uncompromised future.

His only reaction to her statement was to sheathe his knife— and to turn her over so that she lay on her back facing him.

"Please go. Just go," she begged. "If you leave now, I won't tell anyone."

Lindsay could not tell if he believed anything she was saying, but suddenly he stuffed the handkerchief back in his pocket then jerked the pillowcase from the pillow and pulled it over her head and shoulders.

As she lay there, inhaling her own breath, unable to see through the white linen enveloping her like a shroud, she thought she felt his lips between her legs. But the door slammed before she could be sure.

She lay in an agony of physical and mental submission, terrified that he would change his mind and return to silence her forever. The experience of being a victim was new to her, and she found herself immobilized by the surrender of responsibility that accompanied it. Her nightgown remained bunched around her waist, her lower half bare and exposed. Suddenly she began to shiver, and the tremors roused her enough to struggle free of the pillowcase that imprisoned her upper half. She looked down at the flannel granny gown she was wearing and saw that it was still buttoned at collar and cuff. The rapist had not seen the ring she was wearing on a gold chain around her neck.

After several minutes had passed, Lindsay felt certain he was not coming back. She struggled to stand, her ankles still hobbled by his alligator belt, and had just freed her hands from the red paisley tie when she heard the front door to her apartment open. In terror she half-lunged, half-dragged herself into the bathroom and locked the door. As she unbuckled the belt binding her ankles, she heard the building superintendent asking frantically if she was all right.

"Are you alone?" she asked cautiously from behind the locked door.

"Yes, but an ambulance is on the way. Wait in there if it makes you feel better. I'll stay here till they come."

This unexpected solicitude from a man whose services Lindsay had always taken for granted allowed her to experience the emotions she had held at bay during the attack. Behind the locked door, she began to sob.

"How did you know?" she asked when she finally emerged from the bathroom, wearing a woolen robe over her nightgown, face washed, hair combed.

"I got a call," he said, awkwardly putting a hand under her elbow to help her cross the room. Lindsay shuddered when he tried to guide her toward the bed, and indicated the door to the living room.

"Who called?" she asked, taking a seat on the couch as gratefully as if she had traveled a long distance to get there.

"A man. He didn't say who he was. He just said you needed help. And that he'd already called an ambulance."

"He didn't tell you what happened?"

"No. I asked, but he hung up. It's okay. You don't have to tell me anything. I'm just glad I got here in time to help. You have your friend to thank for that."

"My friend?" pondered Lindsay, knowing her life would never be the same again.

Two

When Todd Newman was five years old, a favorite aunt asked him what he wanted to do when he grew up. "Have children," he said without hesitating and was surprised when his aunt laughed and hurried to repeat his answer to the rest of the family. His ambition never changed, but he soon learned to supply answers that would be taken more seriously.

After graduating from college, Todd went into life insurance and was soon making a comfortable living. He then began searching for the woman who would share his real ambition: to raise a family.

This was the 1950s, so she wasn't hard to find.

Sarah Lewis, the girl Todd asked to marry him, seemed to want the same things from life that he did. Or at least she smiled in agreement when he told her what he wanted. At his insistence she put away the diaphragm for which she had been fitted a week before the wedding.

Six months later Todd took her out to dinner to celebrate the midpoint of their first year of marriage—its consummation joyously confirmed by her now visible state of pregnancy. Omnipotent with champagne and pride, Todd made love to her all through the night. Already pregnant, Sarah accepted his attention as proof that he loved her for herself and felt happier than she had since the night he proposed.

A week later their first child—a daughter—was stillborn. Todd blamed himself, though the doctor assured both of them nothing could have been done to prevent it and urged them to waste no time in trying again.

The next time his wife became pregnant, Todd suggested they refurnish the bedroom—with twin beds. He was, if possible, even more solicitous than before. Though he was usually awakened by the noises coming from the bathroom (once Sarah outlived the daily assaults of morning sickness, she was plagued by undependable and overworked kidneys), Todd never complained and used the time before his alarm was due to ring to make coffee and have breakfast for two waiting on a tray across her bed when she emerged, pale and sleepy, from the bathroom.

From the day her second pregnancy was confirmed, only the breakfast tray brought him into her bed. Sarah was ashamed to confess how much she still wanted him and never told him how lonely she was at night. She carried the baby—an eight-pound boy—to his full term, so neither she nor Todd were prepared when he died of heart failure in the hospital nursery twenty-four hours later. The doctor admitted to them in her hospital room he had detected an irregular heartbeat in utero several months earlier but saw no point in sharing his apprehensions.

When the doctor left the room, Sarah began to sob and would not be comforted. Todd assured her they were still young and healthy, and there was no medical reason for her failure to produce a normal child. He begged her to stop crying, not to grieve; they had a long and happy future ahead of them. She did

7

not tell him she was crying because all those lonely nights had gone for nothing.

The next summer he surprised her by renting a house on a remote island off the coast of Georgia. He took a three-month leave from his job and she happily abandoned the friends and volunteer work with retarded children that kept her occupied when he was at work. They rented bicycles and explored the island together. Raised in a Boston suburb, Todd had never experienced the exhilaration that comes from having a limited geographical area within one's grasp—knowing its terrain and climate, delighting in the amazing variety to be found within its precisely defined perimeters. He found equal surprise and pleasure in his wife. Except for the few year-round residents, on whom they depended for supplies and services, they had only each other for company.

Without consulting him, Sarah had packed her diaphragm. However, no one had explained to her that a preventive device fitted to a young virgin might be less than effective after two pregnancies. And so midway through the summer she realized she was pregnant again. She delayed going to a doctor to confirm what she had already guessed because she did not want to leave her husband's bed.

That fall when they returned to their house in Pond Crossing on Long Island, she did tell him and realized, when he was not surprised, that the summer had been planned for that purpose. He seconded the doctor's suggestion that she stay in bed to ensure an uncomplicated pregnancy and offered no objection when she announced that she was moving in with her mother until the baby was born. She remembered the last time and hoped that she would miss him less if they lived apart.

Sarah enjoyed being at home again—with her husband's approval—and began to think of her mother as a contemporary who, despite her age and experience, was often as uncertain about things as she was. This time, when she went into labor, her mother accompanied her, and Todd was not notified until the baby—a noisy female—was inciting a revolution of infant demands in the nursery.

Todd was delighted the next day when the doctor said he could take his wife and baby home. Sarah, who had not succeeded in quieting her infant daughter on the two occasions when the nurse brought her into the room and left them alone to get acquainted, was less than confident about her aptitude for child care, despite three certificates from the Red Cross prenatal training program (she sat through the course again before each child was born, hoping for new discoveries). But she accepted the doctor's decision and tried to feel as triumphant as Todd when they carried their screaming child over the threshold.

It had not even occurred to her to ask when the doctor told her six weeks later that it was safe to resume sexual relations. Nor did she tell Todd. She was exhausted from the intermittent snatches of sleep the baby allowed her and even when Todd got up in answer to the cries coming from the next room, she lay awake in her bed, wondering what they were doing wrong.

Then one night she awoke to silence. When she got out of bed, Todd stirred and, thinking she was crossing to him, held out his hand to her. But she hurried into the baby's bedroom and her scream brought him running to her side.

The doctor had no more explanation for their third failure than he had for the two earlier ones. He offered statistics on crib death, or sudden infant death syndrome as the medical journals labeled it, to try to provide an objective framework for their grief but no words of sympathy could convince either of them that they were not alone. They could not even convince each other.

Sarah moved out of the house, finding it more painful to face him in his grief than to bury her own in silence and solitude.

A month later she asked for a divorce. Todd consented only because he felt she deserved better. A year later she remarried—a man old enough to be her father. At least that was the way her mother described him the day Todd called to offer his best wishes.

When Todd finally started dating again, he was amazed to

discover how much women had changed in the decade of his marriage and divorce. He had been brought up to believe that a proposal of marriage—or at least honorable intentions—was required before a man could take advantage of a woman's innocence. But since women were no longer admitting to innocence, honorable intentions seemed irrelevant at best. A promise of marriage or financial support or even a second date no longer seemed necessary to make a sexual accomplice out of the most casual acquaintance. Indeed Todd found on the few occasions when he happened to mention marriage, in passing, that the woman on his arm invariably found a means of escape from the sexual encounter she feared would seem like acquiescence to a contract she could not keep.

Until he met Lindsay. She was the first woman to bring up the subject of marriage before he did—and only to say she did not want to deceive him into thinking their relationship had a future. But since the past continued to weigh heavily on him, Todd was more than willing to forget the future in favor of the present.

It was a relationship without promises and had been for twelve years. All that Lindsay had agreed to share with Todd were weekends, beginning Saturday morning. Knowing how important the illusion of spontaneity was to her, he never planned anything in advance. However, nothing could keep him from looking forward to the time they would be together—and counting on it.

They would talk by phone each Saturday morning, agreeing to meet at some mutually interesting destination—a play or a museum or, most often, a neighborhood movie. Afterward, they would walk and talk over the week's events, ending up at a restaurant in the part of town where their afternoon had taken them. From there they would go to the closer of their two apartments. Todd lived on the West Side and Lindsay on the East, so, more often than not, they spent Saturday night at her apartment. Still, the pretense of never being certain in advance of where they would spend the night relieved them both of the responsibility of having to be prepared for company.

In the beginning Todd was frustrated by the limited nature of their relationship. However, since there was nothing he could do to expand or change it (other women were no threat to Lindsay —she made it clear from the beginning she didn't want the responsibility of being the only woman in his life), he came in time to realize its advantage.

Lindsay greeted him each Saturday afternoon as if his presence were her sole reward for a week of hard work. She couldn't seem to get enough of him. She would touch his cheek as they stood on a crowded corner waiting for traffic to pass so they could cross the street, and she once kissed him at Bloomingdale's when they stopped to admire a model room. She would surprise him as they sat in a darkened theater watching a play or movie by placing her hand on his knee at a moment that had special significance for them, outside the context of what they were watching. He was often surprised later at the passion with which he defended something that was no more than ordinary by any objective critical standards because of the response it had evoked in Lindsay. Soon after they began to share their weekends, he stopped going places without her.

From the time they met on Saturday—after a week apart— the space they shared was charged with sexual anticipation. Every unexpected caress added to the promise of the pleasure ahead.

At times the tension would become unbearable and they would go to the nearer apartment before dinner. Their lovemaking was urgent and intense and quickly consummated. Dinner became then merely an interlude—a concession to more mundane appetites—and when they returned to the apartment, nothing could distract them the rest of the night from the giving and receiving of pleasure that was their single and shared purpose each weekend.

The joys, at once new and familiar, of the night extended into the following morning. It was the one twenty-four-hour period in the week when neither was answerable to the clock. Sunday unfolded with such languor that Todd, who had stopped going to church when he graduated from college and compulsory chapel attendance, felt he was celebrating the mystery of creation more truly or at least more actively than he ever had sitting in a hardbacked pew.

Sunday had always been Todd's favorite day of the week, even as an only child. The obligatory visit to his grandmother, which his mother loathed and used every means at her command to avoid or at least to curtail, provided his only access to the kind of large and boisterous family he yearned to have.

His parents brought him to his grandparents' house every Sunday afternoon. His grandmother, a staunch patriot in every other respect, had succumbed early in her married life to what she referred to as "my Tory weakness for afternoon tea," welcoming, Todd grew to suspect, the structure and purpose it imposed on the long hours between the time her husband returned to his office after lunch and arrived back home for dinner. During the week she was joined by friends for this ritual, but on Sunday the occasion was reserved for family.

Todd's parents were always the last to arrive and the first to leave, pleading a fatigue that at least in the case of Todd's father was quite genuine. He was one of those men who found a day with his family more tiring than six at work.

Todd always begged to stay behind with his cousins, a rowdy lot ranging in age from a boy ten years older who bullied him to a girl just learning to walk whom he could baby. The assorted cousins belonged to three sets of aunts and uncles whose company his parents took pains to avoid but who always seemed delighted to see each other. The aunts and uncles would volunteer in turn to bring Todd home after dark, sympathizing loudly with his plight as an only child. How hard it must be for a little boy to grow up without brothers and sisters. How lucky that he had so many cousins close at hand! His mother ignored their comments and thought to herself how happy she would have been *without* brothers and sisters, both as a child and every Sunday of her adult life.

Todd loved playing with his cousins outside until it got dark, especially in summer when they would catch lightning bugs in empty jelly jars begged from his grandmother's tolerant cook to light their way back to the front porch where his uncles had long since reinforced the tea cart with bottles of Scotch and bourbon. The cook would replace the platters of neatly trimmed watercress and cucumber sandwiches on thin white bread with thick ham and cheese on rye accompanied by bowls of potato salad and cole slaw. Thus afternoon tea turned into Sunday night supper without anyone ever noticing where one ended and the other began (including Todd's parents, who never stayed long enough to witness the evolution). Everyone ended the evening feeling much more content with their lives than when they arrived—especially the grandparents, who went to bed happy in the knowledge that what began as a duty visit had been extended without coercion into a social occasion whose participants forgot the blood ties that brought them together in the enjoyment of each other's company.

Sunday with Lindsay left Todd feeling equally content. They took turns making breakfast, depending on which apartment they were in, and ate it in bed with the Sunday papers spread out between them.

They seldom dressed until midafternoon—and then went out together for a walk or a concert followed by a casual supper before parting for the week. They had found early in their relationship that it was easier to say good-bye on a street corner —a quick kiss and the assurance from Todd that he was there if for any reason Lindsay wanted or needed to see him sooner than next Saturday. But she never did.

So he was not prepared when a call came at four o'clock on a Thursday afternoon. Lindsay wanted to see him as soon as possible. She wouldn't say why.

Three

Lindsay didn't tell the police anything beyond the immediate facts. They knew nothing of her life before the attack—and nothing of what she was certain would follow.

Only one detail of the case aroused their interest: Why did her assailant send help afterward? Was she certain there was no prior connection? How odd, Lindsay thought, that no one questions why a stranger would commit an act of violence, but an act of compassion arouses suspicion. And when both acts involve the same stranger and the same victim, it is only the act of compassion that requires explanation.

The doctor who examined Lindsay at the hospital asked if she was using an effective method of birth control. He apologized for having to ask an obviously well-adjusted modern woman what appeared to be such an unnecessary question in this sexually liberated age, but it was routine.

"Of course," Lindsay replied and assured him there would be

no unforeseen consequences. She did not think it necessary to inform him that, unlike friends who had felt freed by its discovery, she was not an advocate of the pill. She had tried it for a while and awoke nauseous every morning. Sex on Saturday night and Sunday morning didn't seem worth morning sickness the rest of the week. Nor did she like the idea of having an alien piece of metal inside her to prevent conception and so rejected her gynecologist's wholehearted recommendation of the intrauterine device whose popularity, he assured her, was growing. She told him she preferred taking the matter of birth control into her own hands and insisted on being fitted with a diaphragm. Until the rape she had had no reason to regret her decision.

The examining doctor then offered some unsolicited advice: "If you're seriously involved with a man, don't mention what happened today. It'll be easier on both of you."

Lindsay told him she appreciated his frankness, and so he elaborated.

"Men are more sensitive than women realize," he smiled. "It could affect physical performance. And you wouldn't want that."

"Could I ask you something quite apart from all this?"

"As long as you're here, you might as well get your money's worth."

"What would you say if I told you I wanted to have a baby?"

"How old are you?" he asked abruptly.

"Forty-two."

He seemed amazed. "Just because you don't look your age doesn't mean you can get away with anything. You're too old to risk having a baby. Especially if it's your first."

"What would I be risking?"

"Are you prepared to raise a mongoloid?"

She knew he wanted her to face facts, but a centuries-old fury surfaced in response to this challenge.

"How dare you try to end my life in the middle! You can father children till you're a hundred if you're in the mood—and die with a clear conscience before they've learned to walk knowing you've done all that was required of you. Mother Nature indeed! No female came up with this system. I'm forty-two years old. My time's almost up. I'm not even sure I'm ready to have a child—and you're telling me it's too late. I was almost killed today. I didn't know how much I wanted to live until I came so close to losing the chance. To losing all my chances. I can't wait any longer. I want every choice left to me."

She was suddenly sobbing—and thus conforming more closely to the doctor's idea of how a rape victim should behave. When he had first examined her, she was so calm and controlled, he was profoundly uncomfortable. But now that she was hysterical, he relaxed.

"You've been through enough for one day," he said, giving her a paternal pat on the back. "Come back and see me again in a couple of weeks and we'll talk about this some more."

"I have to know before I go home," Lindsay said quietly, her sobs subsiding. "I have to know if I have a future."

"I'd be irresponsible if I didn't give you the facts," the doctor said, apparently taking her question more seriously than the attack that brought her to his attention. "The risk of Down's syndrome—that's mongolism—increases from one in fifteen hundred children born to women in their twenties to one in three hundred in the thirty-five to thirty-nine age group, then the figure jumps to one in fifty for women who give birth after forty."

"It's not fair," Lindsay cried.

"Maybe not—but it's a fact."

"And there's nothing that can be done about it?"

"We can't keep it from happening, but at least we've learned to detect it in the womb."

"And?"

"And what?"

"What do you do once you detect it?"

"Perform an abortion. What else can we do?"

"I don't know what else. I'm not a doctor. But it seems to me that modern science with all its advances should have something better to offer a woman who finally decides in her prime that she is willing to risk reproduction than the possibility of an abortion if things don't work out the way she hoped."

The doctor was clearly not used to examining women who talked back and much as he would have liked to make his escape, he was challenged by Lindsay's question. And her passion.

"Besides the risk of giving birth to an abnormal child, there are risks for the woman too."

"What risks?"

"Toxemia, high blood pressure, kidney disorders—to name just a few."

"But what if having a child were the only reason I had for staying alive? Would you accept me as a patient?"

"It is possible, if you were willing to take precautions, to have a normal pregnancy and deliver a healthy child—even at your age—but I pity the child who provides a parent with her only reason to go on living."

"Not the child. The act of having a child."

"Don't let what happened today make you do anything stupid and foolish."

"I won't," she lied.

He extended his hand to help her from the examining table and said as an afterthought, "You'd make a good mother."

To Lindsay it had the ring of a benediction. She squeezed his hand as she relinquished it. But then she had to ask, "What makes you say that?"

"You're obviously very good in a crisis. And that's what children are—crisis after crisis."

"Isn't there anything in between?" she asked in amusement.

"Of course, but in between crises they manage fine on their own. They don't need mothers for in between."

His logic seemed unassailable, and Lindsay, despite the nightmare that had shattered her day, began to feel better about herself than she had in a long time. She was convinced she was pregnant —and determined to go through with it, whatever the consequences. The thought of a new life to protect kept her from being afraid for her own.

She put on the clothes she had stuffed in a tote bag and brought with her to the hospital. She knew better from the articles she'd read on rape (including one she'd written herself for the magazine), than to change clothes or wash away potential evidence. But once the examination was over and the police had finished questioning her, she gave them the nightgown she'd been wearing and said they could keep it. When she had washed herself all over and put on her street clothes, she felt calm. She thought she was going to be all right until the taxi stopped outside her building. She paid the driver but began to feel faint as she approached the front door.

The superintendent, seeing her stumble, quickly crossed to her and led her into his apartment to recover. While his wife made tea, he showed her the basket that had been delivered an hour earlier.

It was an elegant wicker hamper from the Maison Glass overflowing with wine and delicacies. Through the cellophane Lindsay could see smoked oysters, brandied cherries, English tea biscuits.

She was frightened. Who could be sending her such an extravagant present? And why? She knew from window shopping that it had cost at least a hundred dollars. She tore through the cellophane searching for a card, but there was nothing to identify the sender. She asked the superintendent if she could use his phone. The Maison Glass had a record of the delivery but the sender had paid cash and not given a name.

Lindsay insisted the superintendent and his wife keep the gift as a token of her gratitude for their kindness. Then she asked to use the phone once more. This time she called Todd and asked him to come as soon as he could. She would tell him why when he got there. She said she would be waiting for him in the lobby.

She didn't hear what he said on the other end of the phone. Her head was swimming. The superintendent's wife saw what was happening and helped her to a chair before she fainted. The superintendent picked up the phone to explain but it was already silent. Todd was on his way.

CHAPTER
Four

Lindsay was seated on a couch in the lobby when Todd arrived. He rushed to her, relieved that she appeared unharmed. She hid her face against his shoulder and begged him to hold her before he asked any questions. They stood there for a moment in full view of the doorman who, instead of averting his eyes in the time-honored tradition of his calling, smiled at them benignly.

Inside her apartment Lindsay's public face crumpled and she began to sob. She leaned against the front door as she closed it, her hands behind her, holding tightly to the doorknob.

Todd put his hands on her shoulders, but she continued to grasp the doorknob as if it were the only way to ground the electric current of fear running through her.

"Lindsay, what happened?"

His closeness, so warm and reassuring, began to act on Lindsay like a sedative. Finally she let go of the doorknob and moved to the couch.

"I was attacked," she said, not looking at him.

"Attacked? You mean raped?"

"No," Lindsay answered quickly. "Mugged."

"Oh. Where?" The relief in his voice was so evident that Lindsay quickly began to invent details to support her story.

"A couple of blocks from here. I was on my way to work. I guess I should have gone on to the office, but I didn't want to talk about it. Only when I got back here, I was afraid to be alone. So I called you." She turned to face him for the first time. "I've never been afraid before and now I don't know if I'll ever feel safe again."

He took her in his arms. Much as he regretted the circumstances that had led to her call, he could not help rejoicing in her surrender. When he kissed her, the desperation of her response —she pressed her mouth against his as if she were drowning and he were the only source of breath—aroused him faster than any enticement she could have attempted.

"Are you all right?" he asked softly. "You weren't hurt physically?"

"A few bruises," she said. "It doesn't matter. They won't show by morning."

"Have you seen a doctor?"

"I'm fine, Todd. Really. Let's not talk about it any more."

"What about the police? Have you reported it?"

"I tried, but they weren't very interested. I didn't lose anything. I never let go of my purse."

"Christ, Lindsay. Don't ever do anything so stupid again. You could've been killed."

"There were other people on the street. He couldn't risk a struggle."

"You were a fool. Promise me, if it ever happens again, you'll do exactly what you're told."

He had no idea how reassuring his anger was to her. Until she invented the purse-snatching attempt, she had not allowed herself to admit any doubts about the way she'd behaved. Without knowing what he'd done, Todd had freed her of any guilt about her acquiescence. She had not risked her life by trying to defend herself. She had done exactly as she was told—just what Todd was asking her to promise to do in the future.

With his arm around her, he urged her into the bedroom. But the passion of the present moment was not enough to obliterate memory. As Todd pushed aside the sheets still wrinkled from the morning's violence, Lindsay again felt the knife at her throat.

"I can't," she suddenly cried. "Not here." She struggled to her feet, stripping the sheets from the bed in the same motion.

"What are you doing?" he asked, caught off-balance by her unexpected action.

"We can't stay here. This room is a mess."

"Lindsay, you're not telling me the truth. What happened today? You weren't mugged, were you?"

"No," she said dully. "I was raped. On this bed."

"Oh, Christ," Todd said with a sharp intake of breath. He sat on the edge of the naked mattress and kicked at the covers piled on the floor. "How did he get in?"

Lindsay moved to the bed and sat beside him. She thought she heard him say it didn't matter, it didn't change anything. She took his hand gratefully, but then she saw that he was staring at her, waiting.

"What?" she asked. "What did you say?"

"I asked if you opened the door to him?"

"Of course not."

"Then how did he get in?"

"Probably the doorman was helping someone find a taxi."

"That's not what I'm asking. How did he get in here, Lindsay?"

Lindsay found his interrogation more painful than the police's.

"I'm not sure. Maybe when I took trash to the incinerator."

"You left your door unlocked?"

"Why are you so angry?"

"I'm so angry because you're so careless."

"I'm not careless. He had a knife, Todd. If the door had been locked, he would've attacked me in the hall and forced me to open it."

As long as she had been able to keep the experience to herself —to talk about it only with strangers, people she would never see again—Lindsay could almost believe the rape had happened to someone else. And with such distance she was outraged by the unprovoked violence of the attack and filled with sympathy for the victim, even admiring the calm manner in which she had dealt with her assailant. However, at the core she had remained inviolate. Until she had to tell Todd.

"Get your coat," he said abruptly. "I'll come back later for the rest of your things."

"What?"

"I'm taking you to my apartment."

"Todd, if I don't stay here tonight, it'll be that much harder to come back tomorrow."

"Why do you have to come back? Ever? I wanted to marry you the day I met you. I've never stopped wanting to marry you. I've just stopped asking."

Lindsay's eyes filled with tears. "I knew when I called you to come what you'd say when you got here. I wanted to hear it, to know in spite of everything that happened today you still loved me, still wanted to marry me. I had to know I still had a choice."

Todd was unmoved by her tears. "No, Lindsay, you don't. Not anymore. Not after this. I can't leave you alone again. Now come on, let's get out of here."

He rose and moved to the bedroom door, but she did not follow. Instead she picked up the pile of used sheets and carried them into the bathroom. She stuffed them into the laundry hamper, then took a clean set of sheets from the shelf and returned to the bedroom. As she started making the bed, Todd crossed to her.

"You're coming with me, damn it!"

"No. If I go with you, you'll feel responsible for everything that happens to me."

He put his arms around her. "I already do. That's what love is. What happened today happened to both of us—don't you know that? And now we both have to forget it. We have to make each other forget it." He began to kiss her shoulders, her neck, but Lindsay could not respond. Her body resisted his attention as stubbornly as her will refused his ultimatum. She would not move in with him—even if it meant ending the relationship. She couldn't allow herself to be possessed again. Not physically, not emotionally.

When he started to unbutton her blouse, she pushed him away. She was determined not to cry, much as she wanted to be comforted. And she hated herself for having to hurt him. But she had to say it.

"I have a husband, Todd."

CHAPTER

Five

For the rest of her life Lindsay was to wonder what would have happened if she and Meg had said good-bye after college. But they had not. Lindsay had never met John Henry Hawkins, but she knew he was waiting for Meg in Amarillo. And had been since high school. Lindsay had come to suspect that being engaged —and the status it gave her in the eyes of her classmates—meant more to Meg than John Henry himself.

So their senior year she talked Meg into spending the Thanksgiving holiday in New York City, hoping to convince her to share an apartment after they graduated. Lindsay was headed for a career in journalism. Didn't Meg want to do more with her life than just go home to Texas and marry her high school sweetheart?

Meg confessed shyly that she had always wanted to be a lawyer like her father. However, when she told him, he said a woman had no business taking a place in law school away from a man who would have to support a family.

"Why shouldn't a woman be prepared to support a family too?" challenged Lindsay. But she could see that his remark had withered Meg's ambition.

Lindsay could still remember the afternoon she proposed the summer trip. It was the week before graduation. They were in their dorm basement packing the huge trunks they had brought with them as freshmen. Suddenly Meg burst into tears. "I don't want to leave—I don't want all this to be over." Impulsively Lindsay suggested that they spend the summer driving across the country. It wouldn't cost much—they had a hundred classmates along the way who would put them up for the night. And at the end of the summer, if Meg still wanted to go home and get married, Lindsay promised to be her maid of honor. And never say another word.

When Meg agreed to go so quickly—and in her enthusiasm even offered to pay for the gas since they would be using Lindsay's car—Lindsay felt sure she would not have to keep her promise.

By Labor Day they had attended twenty-three bridal showers and fourteen weddings, and Meg had agreed to share an apartment in New York with Lindsay that fall.

Everything was working out just as Lindsay had hoped until they returned to her home in Larchmont and Meg recognized the pickup parked in the driveway.

"It's John Henry," she whispered. "He's come to take me home to Amarillo."

But he hadn't. He greeted Meg with a hug and told her he was willing to live anywhere she wanted. Everything he owned was in the back of his pickup. The next move was up to her.

Late that night Meg woke Lindsay to say good-bye. She said she was not ready to share John Henry's life—or anyone's. She was going home alone. "Please don't let him come after me," she whispered as Lindsay hugged her good-bye.

Meg had been gone a week when Lindsay discovered that John Henry was still in town. Her father, Grant Howard, who had built a successful career synchronizing other people's needs with his own, had given John Henry a job on his current construction project—a community on the shores of a man-made lake. And Lindsay, without knowing it, had given him a reason to stay.

John Henry showed her the site of a cabin he planned to build beside the lake. Within a year the lake would be surrounded by luxury homes. But for the moment it was a wilderness, with only unpaved roads and power lines to indicate its future. Mr. Howard had agreed to let John Henry live there through the winter, rent free. In return he would keep an eye on the work in progress.

As a child Lindsay had loved going with her father to inspect construction sites and by the time she was a teen-ager had learned to look at a blueprint and accurately visualize a finished building. Walking beside John Henry as he marked the boundaries of his one-room cabin, Lindsay could imagine not only the finished room but herself inside it and John Henry beside her. She knew then that, whatever else she did with her life, she wanted to end each day in his arms. But all she said to him was that she had changed her mind about moving to New York.

That night she called Meg in Amarillo but before she could confess that she was in love with John Henry, Meg announced she was going to law school in Texas.

Challenged by Lindsay's enthusiasm for the ambition she'd been afraid to admit—and without telling anyone—Meg had taken an entrance exam when she was home for spring vacation. She had never intended to go, she just wanted to know the choice was hers. But now, thanks to Lindsay, she finally had the courage to make it. She hoped Lindsay would not allow anything to stand in the way of what she wanted. Lindsay wished Meg well—and decided not to say that what she wanted was John Henry.

Lindsay got a job on the local paper in what was still being called "Women's News," and wrote wedding announcements for three months until December when she wrote her own.

She refused the formal wedding her parents had always planned for their only child, and she and John Henry were married in a simple morning ceremony at the Howard home. However, sensing John Henry's pleasure at the gift, she accepted the down payment on one of the spacious, all-electric homes under construction as a wedding present.

But she couldn't bear the thought of moving into it and living like everybody else, part of a suburban community. She was happy the house would not be finished till summer, and she and John Henry could live alone in their cabin at the edge of the lake through the winter and spring.

Instead of the Caribbean honeymoon her parents offered, Lindsay asked them to buy the boat John Henry had dreamed of owning as a boy in landlocked West Texas. The two of them took it out on the lake whenever the weather permitted, never returning until the sun had set.

When summer came and the house was finished, Lindsay didn't want to move into it. She wasn't sure the intimacy they shared in an isolated one-room cabin could survive in a three-bedroom home surrounded by friendly neighbors.

The day before the development was due to be opened to the public and their cabin transformed into a real estate office, Lindsay and John Henry moved their few possessions and one piece of furniture—a king-sized mattress resting on an oak frame John Henry had built himself—to their new house. But Lindsay refused to spend the night there.

"This is the last night we'll have the lake to ourselves. Let's take the boat out and be alone," she pleaded.

They lay locked in each other's arms watching the sun go down, feeling inextricably linked to each other and to everything around them. Even their breathing seemed to continue the motion of the water.

When they awoke, it was dark and the boundaries of the lake had disappeared from view. John Henry stood up and stretched. Lindsay was lost for a moment in the contemplation of his lean, muscled body. If he had caught her gazing at him naked with such unashamed pride and pleasure, he would have pulled her into an embrace to divert her appraising eyes. But while Lindsay was admiring him for what he was alone—apart from the feelings he awakened in her—John Henry was searching the misty horizon for a familiar landmark.

"We've drifted away from shore."

But Lindsay wasn't ready to go back. "Let's sleep till the sun rises. It will never be this perfect again."

"No. I'm going for a swim to wake up—then we're finding our way back."

He dived off the side of the boat, and Lindsay continued to hold the image of his body entering the water after he disappeared from sight. She waited for him to reappear. Her arms ached to hold him again. Then his absence began to frighten her. He seemed to have been out of her sight forever. She stood in the boat searching the water. His name burst from her lips in an agony of fear and she knelt down with an oar toward the place where he had disappeared. Only when the oar met resistance did she understand what had happened. In the darkness they had drifted back to shore. She hurled her body overboard and went flailing through the water until she found the unconscious body of her husband.

It was daylight before an ambulance arrived. And almost dark before a team of doctors confirmed what Lindsay feared. John Henry had broken his neck and irreparably damaged his spinal cord. He was still alive but all voluntary muscular activity had ceased. Inside the prison of his helpless body, however, his heart continued to beat, his lungs to breathe, and his brain to understand.

CHAPTER

Six

"Is he still alive?" Todd asked, staring at Lindsay as if she were a stranger he was meeting for the first time.

"I'm with him every night of the week," she said.

"Does he know about me?"

"No." Lindsay turned away from him and crossed to the closet. She took down a suitcase from the top shelf and silently began to pack.

"Where are you going?"

"I have to get away. I have a friend in California."

"How can you leave him?"

"I'm leaving you, aren't I? That's just as hard."

"Will you write me?"

"And say what? Wait for me?"

"What if he died tonight? Would you marry me?"

She hesitated for a long moment. Then: "I'll never marry again."

"If you just want to be alone for a while, you can have my apartment," Todd offered as Lindsay continued to pack. "I mean until you decide what to do. I can stay somewhere else. I can even stay here till you're ready to come back."

"I don't think we should see each other again," Lindsay said, closing her suitcase. "It's not fair to you. I don't want anyone to feel responsible for what happened . . . for what happens to me."

"And you don't want to feel responsible for anyone else—ever again. Isn't that what you're really saying?"

"I suppose I am."

Todd held Lindsay's suitcase as the elevator took them silently down to the front entrance.

As the doorman hailed a cab, he asked Lindsay how she was feeling.

"I'm fine now, thank you," she said, handing him a ten-dollar tip. She told him she was leaving town and asked him to hold her mail until further notice.

Todd bent over and kissed her good-bye through the window of the cab. Then he handed her a key. "The key to my apartment," he explained. "In case you change your mind." He walked quickly away without looking back.

"Take me to Grand Central," Lindsay told the driver. There was only one place in the world where she still felt safe—where no questions would be asked.

On the train to New Rochelle, Lindsay thought, as she had many times since the accident, how grateful she was that John Henry had amazed all his doctors by remaining alive. What if she had been married to Todd when she was raped? He would never have felt she was safe out of his sight again. She would not have wanted him to love her less, and yet in the end his love would have violated her more than the rape. She wondered if it was ever truly possible for two people to share their lives.

At the hospital she knelt beside John Henry's bed, laying her head against his chest. Like an unborn infant in the womb, she took comfort in the sound of his heart beating against her ear.

She was grateful that he knew nothing of what had happened to her. Closing her eyes to avoid his, she remembered the night she learned that he was not going to die.

A week after the accident the doctors told Lindsay that her husband's condition had stabilized—in other words, though he could still die at any time, it was possible he might live for several more months. Even years. They said it as if in apology for prolonging her agony.

"I think we better face the fact that this could be a life sentence," her mother said that night at dinner.

"I figured out today what it will cost—by the year," Grant Howard added. "Quite a bit more, I'm afraid, than he would have earned working for me."

"I'm going back to work," Lindsay replied. "And I'll be living at home so I won't have any expenses."

"What about his father?" Katherine Howard asked. "Can't he help?"

"I don't even know how to reach him. John Henry left home when his mother died. His father remarried and moved away. The wedding invitation was returned without a forwarding address."

"Then we're the only family he has," her father said. "What would he have done if he hadn't met you?"

"If he hadn't met me, the accident would never have happened," Lindsay said softly.

"If it had happened on the job, he'd be covered," Mr. Howard continued.

"You don't have to help," Lindsay insisted. "A lot of people can't pay their hospital bills on time. I'll do the best I can—they'll have to understand."

"Lindsay," Mr. Howard replied firmly, "you're our only child —and he's the man you married. We're going to take care of you. That's what families are for. It's easy to be independent when everything is going your way, but there are times when everybody needs help. I'm not going to make it easy for you by telling you it will be easy for us. It won't be—but we'll manage."

"When I said this was a life sentence, I wasn't referring to cost," said her mother. "At least not in dollars and cents."

"That's because you never have to worry about dollars and cents," her father replied.

"Lindsay is still young. It's not fair," she hesitated, waiting for someone else to say what had to be said next. But no one did. And so, staring directly at her daughter, she continued. "We think you should have your marriage annulled."

Lindsay looked from her mother to her father. "Do you agree?"

"We discussed it last night," Mrs. Howard answered for him.

"It wouldn't have anything to do with how you feel about John Henry," Mr. Howard explained. "We all loved him and we'll always take care of him."

"In fact," said her mother, "he wouldn't even have to know. You could still visit him, talk to him, hold his hand. From his point of view, nothing would change. But for you—even if you never married again—everything would be possible."

"I'm pregnant," said Lindsay—and left the room.

She had rinsed all the dinner dishes and arranged them in the dishwasher before her mother joined her.

"I'll do everything I can to help," her mother began.

"It's done," Lindsay answered, locking the dishwasher.

"I mean with the baby."

"I don't want a baby. I can't have another life depending on me as long as John Henry is alive. He could die tomorrow but there's a chance he could live for several more years. I can't risk it."

"What are you going to do?"

"An abortion. Are you still willing to do everything you can to help?"

"No," said her mother firmly. "I don't think it's right."

"But you do think it's right for me to annul my marriage— even though John Henry understands everything that's happening. I promised to love him all my life. I don't want to break that promise. But I can't make another one. Not now. Maybe not ever."

"It's so dangerous. You'll be risking your life."

"I'll be risking my life if I don't." Lindsay walked across the driveway to the garage apartment that had been her private residence since high school. She had moved back into it the night of the accident. Her wedding presents were still stored there. She had not wanted any of them, in fact had threatened the week after the wedding to return them to the stores, but her mother had begged her to save them for the next generation. But tonight Lindsay knew there would not be another generation. It was all coming to an end.

She had no sense of future—and felt equally disconnected from her past. The annual alumnae bulletin lying with her mail seemed like an artifact from some ancient civilization. Her life had been altered irrevocably in the year since graduation, and she no longer felt any sense of identity with her classmates.

Cissy MASON Clark, the class correspondent, had married a young IBM executive and moved immediately after her honeymoon to Canton, Ohio. But, she informed her classmates cheerfully, for the rest of her life—or until her husband retired—they would be changing cities every three years. This was the way young executives worked their way up through the ranks of IBM —proving their adaptability by starting over at regular intervals in positions of ever-increasing prestige and salary. "So you see," Cissy said in her concluding paragraph, "I'll never live in one place long enough to plant trees—or to make better friends than I made in college. Please try to write me, all of you, at least once a year—and not just the news you want published. You're the best friends I'll ever have."

When Lindsay read the brief paragraph Meg had submitted, announcing that she had finished her first year of law school in the top quarter of her class, she smiled in approval and wished desperately she could see her again. If only Meg would come stay with her—just long enough to see her through the abortion. She dialed Meg's home in Amarillo. They had not talked since the morning after John Henry's accident. Now Meg's first question was, "How is he?"

"He's going to live," Lindsay replied. Hearing Meg's gentle voice on the other end of the line, Lindsay had to fight to keep tears from prejudicing her request. "Oh, Meg, I want to see you," she began. Suddenly she heard the word "wedding." "What about law school?" she asked, forgetting the request she had been about to make.

"That's where we met," Meg explained, "so my year wasn't wasted." Lindsay thought she also heard Meg say she was moving to Long Beach. Replacing the receiver, she hoped she had remembered to wish Meg every happiness.

She walked slowly to her car, drove to the hospital, and asked the nurse if she could be alone with her husband. He was in the oscillating bed that compensated for his inability to move by redistributing his weight continually to prevent bedsores.

"John Henry," she said, calling him by name for the first time since the accident, challenging him to reclaim his manhood. "I'm pregnant."

His eyes stared at her.

"But I'm not going through it without you. I can't. And I won't."

Desperate to provoke a response from him—even anger would have been preferable to the impassive expression that greeted her announcement—she leaned down and kissed him fully on the mouth. Though his lips did not respond, his breath warmed her face. "I haven't been honest with you, John Henry," she continued, "I've tried to pretend that everything was going to be all right—finally—for both of us. But it's not. It's not ever going to get any better than it is right now. My parents asked me tonight to have our marriage annulled—without telling you. You would still think I was your wife, but I wouldn't be. I can't do that. If I'm to continue seeing you every day, I have to tell you everything I'm thinking and feeling. It's the only kind of intimacy we can have. I may tell you things you don't want to hear, but if I'm going to accept you as you are—to live with the fact that you can never speak to me or touch me again—then you have to accept me as I am. You owe me that—if we're going to stay married."

She was ashamed of the anger surfacing in what had started out to be a statement of lifelong commitment, but she couldn't help it. At first she wouldn't face him but when she finally looked into his eyes, she dared to believe she saw forgiveness there—not for what she had done but for what she was about to do.

"I don't want to have this baby. Not without you. I can't tell my parents how frightened I am. In front of them I have to pretend I know what I'm doing. But I don't know. I wish I didn't have to do anything. I wish it had never happened. But it did happen. So I have to do something. My mother wants the baby. She thinks I'm wrong. I called Meg for help but she's getting married. To a lawyer. So you see, you're the only one I can count on. The only one who won't judge me. Help me, John Henry."

She knelt sobbing beside the oscillating bed, its inexorable movement confirming the fact that life was continuing in all directions without her consent.

"I'll help you," said a voice, and Lindsay felt a strong arm under her elbow, lifting her to her feet. She stared into the eyes of Craig Sanborn, the doctor in charge of John Henry's case.

"I asked to be alone with my husband," she answered angrily.

"The nurse was afraid to leave the room without telling me what she'd done. I came to check but when I heard you talking, I hesitated to interrupt."

"Isn't it enough he can't talk to me," Lindsay cried. "Now I'll never feel free to talk to him again."

"Forgive me," said the doctor. And he told Lindsay if he were a woman in her position, he would do exactly as she was planning to do.

"Does that mean you'll help me?" she whispered, afraid to say the words aloud.

He nodded and wrote a name and a phone number on a card. "Tell him you're a friend of mine. You won't have to give your name. He'll tell you what to do."

That night when Lindsay left the hospital, she stopped at a phone booth in a deserted shopping center and made the arrangements.

When she pulled into the driveway of her parents' house, she saw a light still on in the living room. They were usually asleep by the time she came home from the hospital. She wondered if something was wrong.

Then she realized that her father was standing in the kitchen door. When he saw her car in the driveway, he crossed to her.

"Daddy, has anything happened?"

"I wanted to talk to you before you went to sleep. Let's go up to your apartment."

Lindsay couldn't ever remember being alone with her father in the garage apartment. Her mother had been the one to suggest she move into it the summer she graduated from high school. Though her father had paid the bills without complaining, it was her mother who insisted on having it painted and carpeted before it became her daughter's official residence.

Lindsay offered to make coffee for them. Her mother never served coffee after dark. She said just being around it kept her awake—it didn't matter if it was decaffeinated and it didn't matter if she actually drank it—the sight and smell set her on edge. She needed the tension to get her started in the morning but she had to begin unwinding after dinner or she would never fall asleep. Neither Lindsay nor her father ever asked her mother what it was about her life that kept her nerves so taut. Her father set the example that Lindsay learned to emulate as she grew older of acquiescing to his wife's authority inside the home. But whenever he had to work late and ate alone, he ordered coffee. And Lindsay, from the time she moved into the garage apartment, made a pot every night and usually fell asleep with a half-filled mug on her bedside table.

"Your mother told me what you're planning. She asked me to talk to you before you do something you'll regret later."

"When I told you I wanted to get married, neither of you tried to stop me. Did it never occur to you I might have reason to regret *that* later?"

"Sweetheart, no one could have foreseen . . ." her father began gently.

"No one can foresee anything," she cried, then paused as if in apology and continued more calmly, "there are always consequences."

Her father was looking at her with an expression she had never seen before. She realized she was seeing him vulnerable—open to attack, capable of suffering—for the first time in her life.

"I want to help you," he began, and she saw that he was suffering for her. He had been able to construct the defenses necessary in his own life to allow him to feel invulnerable—by making money and suppressing emotions, he had learned to move through the world without letting it hurt him, never stopping to consider that the price he had paid for peace of mind might have been too high. But he had failed in the most basic function of a man: to protect his child from harm.

"It's too late," Lindsay said, ignoring the pain his helplessness was causing him. "I've already made the arrangements."

"Then I'll go with you," he said. His offer was so unexpected Lindsay had no answer. "When is it?"

Tomorrow night, she told him. But she refused to say where. To her knowledge he had never broken a law. She could not allow him to become an accomplice in her crime.

"How does any man have the right to call abortion a crime?" he declared with unexpected passion, holding out his arms to her. She hid her tears against his shoulder just as she had when she was a little girl trying to be brave. "You're not going through it alone," he said. "That's final."

The next night when they returned, he came upstairs with her and insisted she get into bed. "I'll make the coffee tonight," he said. "Just don't tell your mother I know how."

He brought it on a tray with two mugs and sat at the foot of her bed while they drank it.

They had never had the kind of relationship fathers and daughters had in books she read. He never called her "princess" or bought her presents on impulse. She had learned early in life to look to her mother for both affection and authority. In the home her father's only function was to second the motion.

That was why Lindsay had loved going to work with him. On a job site talking to his foreman he was both more at ease and at the same time more in command than he ever was at home with her mother.

But the summer she was thirteen he stopped taking her with him. He said he didn't like leaving her with the construction crew while he was in the office. This decision marked Lindsay's entry into womanhood more irrevocably than the menstrual cycle she had accepted matter of factly. Her casual attitude toward coming of age had amazed her mother, who was waiting on her return from school that day with a hot water bottle and the new *Ladies' Home Journal,* which she generously contributed to the occasion despite the fact that she had only read the wife's side of "Can This Marriage Be Saved?"

Lindsay never experienced physical pain from the fact of being female and declined her mother's monthly suggestion that she spend the day in bed as due compensation for all the inconveniences that accompanied the ability to reproduce. The only pain adolescence caused her was the loss of her father as a friend.

Lindsay remembered reading some of the letters Scott Fitzgerald wrote his daughter, Scottie, while she was at Vassar and he was struggling to earn her tuition in Hollywood. The letters were long and filled with advice on every subject: the clothes she wore, the boys she dated, the books she read. Of course, Lindsay tried to remind herself, his letters had to compensate for his absence—and Zelda's—from so much of his daughter's life, and yet she was sure that Scottie felt closer to her father than Lindsay did to the benign presence at the dinner table each night who never seemed to have any opinions about what she was doing with her life.

But tonight he reclaimed her. "When you began to grow up, I turned you over to your mother," he admitted. "If you'd been a boy, I wouldn't have let her take charge the way she did. But I thought a woman knew what was best for another woman. Now I'm not so sure."

"Thank you for being with me tonight," Lindsay said, touching his hand. To her surprise he held it instead—and continued to hold it without a word. "It may have been your only chance for grandchildren," she said impulsively. "Did you think of that?"

"Even before your mother reminded me," he smiled.

"Don't you want grandchildren?"

"I want what I have—a daughter."

Then he gave her the advice he said he would have given a son if he'd had one: to look for work that would test her abilities and fill her life. He said a father wants better for his son than he had, but he wasn't sure a mother wants better for her daughter.

"And what does a father want for his daughter?"

"Better than he wanted for his wife," he smiled.

It was the first time Lindsay could remember her father intervening directly in her life, and she was frightened by what he suddenly seemed to expect of her.

She didn't know where to begin—but he did. She would follow the dream she had when she graduated from college and wanted Meg to share an apartment. She would move into the city and study journalism at Columbia.

"But what about John Henry?" she asked.

"It's forty minutes by train. You can still visit him every day." Before Lindsay could offer any further objection, he said firmly,

"I'm not going to allow you to argue with me. Now get a good night's sleep and I'll see you at breakfast."

As she listened to his footsteps going down the stairs, Lindsay thought that it was not through the act of sexual intercourse that men and women became parents. It was when they assumed direct responsibility for the course of their children's lives. Lindsay's mother—for better or worse—had understood this from the moment of conception. But her husband had not become the father of their child until tonight.

This thought absolved Lindsay of any residual guilt about the abortion. I'm not like my mother, she thought, never doubting that I know what's best for a child. I'm more like my father, waiting twenty-three years to offer advice. I can't have a child and not know what to say to it.

She repeated this to John Henry the next day—in front of her father—when they came to tell him she was moving into the city. Almost twenty years passed before the subject of children was mentioned in his presence again.

Seven

When Lindsay first moved into New York, work had filled her life. At graduate school, the gold wedding band she wore protected her from any invitations that might have interfered with her studies. At first she was overwhelmed by guilt to realize that the tragedy which had made her husband a prisoner for life inside his own body was working to her advantage. Like the other married students in her class, she was free from the pressure of having to go out with any man who asked in order to prove her womanhood. And yet she did not have to pay the price for this emotional security by a constant balancing act of the conflicting demands of housework, husband, and homework.

The day she enrolled—as excited as she was about classes starting the next morning—she went to New Rochelle to spend the evening with John Henry and returned to the city on the last train, establishing a pattern to which she adhered faithfully until her thirtieth birthday. No matter how busy she was during the day, she spent every evening at his side. On weekends she would stay with her parents in nearby Larchmont and drive their car to the hospital, returning to the city on Monday morning with the first commuters. She used the time on the train to study, but when she was with him, she felt she had to talk.

At first it was an enormous effort for her to assume the whole burden of a conversation. As an only child, she had grown up in silence, never acquiring the habit of sharing her thoughts with another person. Until she and Meg became roommates, she had never confided her private convictions to anyone. The intimacy she and John Henry shared before the accident was more physical than verbal. They seemed to be able to absorb each other's feelings through the skin, only having to resort to words in the presence of other people. But seated at his bedside, Lindsay discovered that by putting her thoughts into words for him to hear she understood them better herself. It was an arduous process in the beginning—conducting a monologue—until she learned to include him. Keeping her eyes firmly fixed on his face, she began to imagine the comments he might make, the objections he could offer. When she started putting his imagined point of view into words too, the monologue became a dialogue. Lindsay never cheated by allowing him to say only what she wanted to hear. On the contrary, in the guise of speaking for him, she became her own most devastating critic, cutting through any pretense of polite exchange, saying things he would never have said aloud and might not even have permitted to take shape in his own mind. He became her conscience, and she allowed none of her actions to escape unexamined for hidden motives.

As a girl, she had often envied her Catholic friends the regular absolution their religion granted them. Compared to individual confession, the public contrition of an Episcopal service seemed like a pallid statement of fallibility offered more as a pharisee for show than as a genuine admission of guilt. In John Henry's presence, for the first time in her life, Lindsay could admit everything and be forgiven.

Thus he was the first to know—just as she was discovering it for herself—when her work was no longer enough to fill her life. She had gone from graduate school to a job in the circulation department of the magazine she had most admired as a student. On the advice of her favorite professor, she had turned down a more impressive title on a less influential publication to be part of an organization she respected. Though her ambitions were literary, she was grateful to get the job in circulation, and the insights she acquired into the tastes of the existing readership were a valuable asset when there was an opening in the editorial department a few months later.

She submitted a proposal for a monthly feature to be called "Give and Take" in which she would profile a married couple who by joining forces reached goals they could never have attained alone. She made six copies of the proposal and submitted them simultaneously to the six editors who guided the editorial policy of the magazine. One ignored it, two filed it under "future projects," one expressed interest and passed it on to the editor in chief for an opinion, one reworded it and presented it at the weekly staff meeting as an original proposal; and the sixth, the male public affairs editor, hired Lindsay on the spot.

He called her into his office and asked for case histories to support her thesis: that marriage can actually enlarge and extend individual ability. She had to admit there weren't any—yet. Her thesis was conceived in the abstract but she was convinced she could find concrete examples to prove it. Noticing her wedding ring, he asked if perhaps she had some personal basis for her conclusion. She said she had not studied journalism to write about her own life; the subject of marriage was interesting to her purely as a reporter.

He confided that his own marriage had been an obstacle course, but he'd built crucial muscles learning to clear hurdles he wouldn't have faced if he'd stayed single. So perhaps he proved her point.

"I'd have to meet your wife to know if I agree with you," Lindsay replied. "What have you done for her?"

"Kept her innocent. That woman actually believes she could walk out the front door any day of her life and earn a living. She has no idea how hard it is just to break even, let alone come out ahead. Life is a treadmill—you have to keep running just to stay in place. I've not only supported her and the kids, I've supported all her illusions. But because of her, I have something nobody else on this magazine does—one of our readers sitting across the dinner table every night telling me exactly what she thinks about everything going on in the world. That's why I hired you. She'll love this feature. Because she'd like to believe it as much as you would. And anything she likes you can bet the rest of our readership will buy."

Lindsay liked her boss. She always knew where she stood with him and could count on his unqualified support for any idea he approved. As he had predicted, "Give and Take" soon became one of the most popular series the magazine had ever offered. Readers wrote in by the thousands to propose candidates, though in the beginning Lindsay found very few of the suggestions usable as an example of give _and_ take. She often wrote back personally to explain that a wife who supported her husband through graduate school then retired from the working force to stay home and raise children was _not_ an example of a mutually profitable partnership.

It was not until she told John Henry about the series that Lindsay understood how and why the idea had come to her.

"Don't you see," she said, "it gets us all off the hook. As long as there is the possibility that marriage can make us into better people than we would be alone, it doesn't seem like a compromise —or just an escape from solitude. Even though that's all it usually turns out to be."

Then examining her motives through John Henry's all-seeing eyes, Lindsay admitted, "Of course the idea came from us. After the accident I had to wonder where I'd be if I hadn't gotten married. How much all this had cost me. If marriage had done anything for me I couldn't have done on my own. But it was asking myself those questions that gave me the idea for the series. And the series has secured my place on the magazine. If I had known this was ahead of us, I can't imagine that I would have found the courage to marry you. And yet, in spite of everything, my dearest love," she said, holding his passive hand against her cheek, "I have continued to take as much from you as I've given."

The doctors were amazed as the years passed that John Henry continued to stay alive—and that Lindsay continued to visit him every night. Except for the people she saw at work she had no friends in the city. Everyone on the magazine knew she was married and gradually, after she had repeatedly refused invitations to after-hours parties, the circumstances became known and Lindsay was left alone.

On her thirtieth birthday she was made an editor. Both events seemed to her less a cause for celebration than an acknowledgment of the inexorable passage of time. Her progress toward a position of prominence on the magazine seemed as steady and unfaltering as the movement of the hands on a clock.

She had surmounted—if only by accepting it and assigning it a place in her life—the overwhelming tragedy that had ended any chance of a conventionally happy marriage. And she felt entirely responsible for what remained of her life.

That night she went to her parents' house in Larchmont for dinner before driving the short distance to New Rochelle to visit John Henry in the hospital. Her mother had, as usual, overridden her objections and prepared a birthday dinner, complete with cake and candles. Lindsay's place at the table was marked by a small, beautifully wrapped package.

"I know you don't like jewelry," her mother said as Lindsay opened the package, "but we wanted you to have something permanent to mark the end of another decade."

Lindsay smiled, remembering the gold ring they had given her when she was ten and the gold bracelet when she was twenty. And now she lifted from the jewelry box a delicate gold chain. Ever-widening circles of gold, marking the decades like the age rings of a tree (which, Lindsay thought ironically, can never be measured while the tree is still alive and rooted in the earth; the concentric rings are only visible when the tree has been felled and its trunk bisected). She placed the chain around her neck, feeling it cling to the contours of her chest.

"Of course your promotion is a better birthday present than anything we could give you," her father said proudly.

"And you certainly deserve it," said her mother, then added without realizing she was being unkind, "after all, you've made your work into your whole life."

Her mother's words were still ringing in her ears when Lindsay took her nightly position by John Henry's bed.

"I am thirty years old tonight, John Henry," she sighed, taking his hand in hers in the way that had become a habit. She felt young as long as she was at the office seeing people older than herself getting paid to do what she did—but that would only last a few more years. Alone at night her body seemed to be growing old without her.

She continued to weave her fingers into his until she could feel her wedding ring cutting into her flesh. With her right hand she slowly unbuttoned her blouse, then placed his unresponsive fingers against her breast. His touch sent ripples of remembered pleasure through her body.

"Will you give me your consent, John Henry," she whispered, "to do whatever I have to do to stay alive?" She guided his hand into the hollow of her chest and with both her hands pressing it in place, allowed it to rest between her breasts, hoping by some miracle that he would respond. But his hand could not take part in what was happening to her. The weight of it against her chest seemed like an attempt to restrain her rising desire. In despair Lindsay stood up and returned his hand to the bed.

"I don't want to fall in love with anyone, but I can't go on alone." With that she removed her wedding ring from her left hand and slipped it onto the gold chain her parents had just given her. The largest circle of gold, celebrating her ever-widening circle of experience, now contained the smallest circle of gold (and experience?)—her wedding band.

"I haven't lived inside my body since that night on the boat," she said to him. That night there had seemed to be just one body between them, its nerve cells so interconnected that one touch set in motion four arms, four legs. But for the past seven years, Lindsay had felt as alienated from her body as John Henry had been from his. She had read somewhere that the cells of the body replace themselves every seven years. She wouldn't look it up to verify the fact, she would believe it. She was no longer the woman John Henry had married.

"I thought if you couldn't feel anything, it wasn't fair for me to feel anything," she said, kneeling beside him. "But now I have to be alive for both of us. I will wear your ring around my neck. I will feel it like a seal of ownership against my breasts. But whenever I undress, I will remove it. Naked, I will belong to no one but myself."

Then she stood and buttoned her blouse so the ring was no longer visible. When she bent to kiss him good night, his eyes were closed. It was the first time he had ever fallen asleep during one of her visits.

Eight

The next weekend Lindsay decided to stay in the city. On Friday night she told her parents she needed some time to herself. She would not see them or John Henry until Monday. When she awoke at noon on Saturday, it was raining. There seemed to be no reason to get out of bed. In fact there seemed to be no reason to be awake. So she closed her eyes again and the next time she looked at the clock it was three in the afternoon.

When she spent the weekends at home with her parents, she had always brought work. It filled the hours between meals and visits with John Henry—reminding her that she had another life back in the city and a professional identity that had nothing to do with her personal life.

But she didn't need to be reminded of that fact when she was alone in her apartment. And she had already reasoned that if she worked hard during the week and took any required reading with her on the train each night when she went to see John Henry, she could keep her weekends free.

"Free for what?" Lindsay thought, reluctantly climbing out of bed and crossing to the window. The rain had stopped, which seemed like an invitation. She dressed hurriedly and left her apartment. There was no one in particular she wanted to see. She had made a point, from the day she began work on the magazine, of keeping office friendships confined to office hours. She had no intention of changing this rule now that she had decided to spend her weekends in the city. She had another life—one that had nothing to do with her work or her family. The fact that she didn't know what it was or where it would lead her was not important. But as she crossed streets filled with people carrying folded umbrellas, exhilarated by the unexpected emergence of clear skies at the end of a day defined by rain, she began to anticipate the act of discovering her other life.

She realized as she moved with the crowd that this was the first time since she had moved into the city that she had left her apartment without a destination. She had never been a random shopper who took pleasure in buying something she hadn't even known she wanted just because the price was right. She couldn't remember the last time she'd been inside a department store alone. Shopping was one of the few diversions she and her mother could share, so her wardrobe was always replenished in advance of need on Saturday shopping excursions through suburban centers.

But on this Saturday, Lindsay seemed to be drawn by magnetic force through revolving doors, up escalators, past counters of merchandise. She didn't stop anywhere long enough to buy anything—there was nothing she wanted—it was enough just to be carried along in the current of lives driven by needs and desires she did not seem to possess.

When the stores closed, Lindsay made her way along Fifth Avenue to a bookstore that stayed open until ten. Book browsing had always been as alien to her temperament as window shopping. She read reviews and planned her purchases in advance. But tonight she wanted something she couldn't name.

She was glancing through a stack of remaindered books—the cut price creating previously unsuspected interest in obscure authors and subjects—when she felt a hand on her shoulder.

"Are you really going to spend Saturday night reading the diary of a Russian serf?" a friendly, somehow familiar male voice asked.

Lindsay turned and connected the voice with a face she had last seen on the cover of the magazine. Her first cover story— Alan and Marietta Compton—the Iowa couple who had launched the "Give and Take" series.

Marietta had been an undergraduate when Alan arrived at her college to teach English. He was just out of graduate school, with a new Ph.D. under his belt, and he entered the classroom with an overwhelming sense of mission. For him, teaching was not a means to an end—the end having something to do with making a name for himself—it was his whole purpose in life. "Passing the torch" was how he put it. It had never occurred to him to try to start a fire of his own.

As a student, eagerly embracing every idea he had to share, Marietta provided the perfect objective for all his aspirations. By the end of her senior year she had accepted both his proposal of marriage and his challenge to continue her studies in graduate school. He set free the poet imprisoned within the more conventional personality she had adopted to pass unnoticed in her home state and made her pregnant three times before she had completed her first book-length collection of poetry. When the book was published and subsequently awarded a Pulitzer prize, she abandoned her dissertation on Anne Bradstreet, the Puritan poet, and accepted a position as poet-in-residence at the state university. She was not required to perform any teaching duties in return for her stipend—she was being paid simply to live on campus with her family and provide the example of a working writer.

Her salary freed Alan for the first time since he had reached adulthood of the necessity of earning a living, so Marietta persuaded him to take a leave of absence from the teaching post he had always enjoyed to write the novel she was sure he had in him. He wrote a book about a man who impregnates his wife with ambition, then watches her career eclipse his. But resisting the obvious temptation to re-create Dr. Frankenstein and his monster in man-woman terms, he resolved his saga in an optimistic vision with the husband retiring to the country to raise the children they shared and the horses he had dreamed of having as a boy, and the wife traveling the world but returning to the farm every Sunday in time to cook dinner. The book—though sufficiently well-reviewed to add an impressive credential when he returned to his chosen profession, teaching—was never considered a commercial prospect by his publisher. It had been acquired for the literary cachet it provided the company. The book was out of print and the publisher amazed (though no more amazed than the author, who had felt amply rewarded for his efforts when his book was bought and listed in the card catalogue of his local library) when, two years after its initial publication, it was discovered by the newly emerging women's liberation movement and hailed as a prophecy of the peaceful revolution to come. It was reissued in paperback and became a belated best seller.

This was the year Lindsay proposed the "Give and Take" series and, having just read the novel, decided Alan and Marietta Compton were the perfect couple to make her point. Marietta would never have attempted to write poetry if Alan hadn't encouraged and educated her in the form, and without Marietta's success, Alan would not have had a subject for his first novel. Each not only had inspired previously unimagined ambitions in the other but had helped provide the means of fulfilling those ambitions.

The lead paragraph for Lindsay's cover story had said it all: "If they had not met, Alan and Marietta Compton would be leading very different lives today. He would be an assistant professor of English in the small state college Marietta was attending when they met, and she would be the wife of an Iowa farmer, winning blue ribbons for her cherry pies at the county fair. But they did meet and marry—and dared each other to dream bigger dreams than either would have dreamed alone. As a result of this double dare, Marietta won a Pulitzer prize for her first collection of poems, *Feeding the Flames,* and Alan has just closed a major motion-picture deal for his widely discussed first novel, *Banking the Embers.*"

When Lindsay interviewed them for the cover story, for the first time in their married life neither was having to support the other. Finally both could afford to work full time at their writing. They had decided to move with their three children to an island off the coast of Oregon and try to become as self-sufficient physically as they were intellectually. Like a male and female Columbus electing to share a single ship, they seemed to be on the verge of discovering a new world uncharted on any map in existence before their voyage.

Since the interview, Lindsay had often thought of the Comptons and wondered how they were doing and what they were writing. She subscribed to *Publishers Weekly* and scanned each issue carefully, hoping for word of a new book from one or both of them, but their names were never mentioned.

"Alan, I'm so glad to see you," Lindsay said, turning to face him and impulsively leaning forward for the kiss that accompanied the most casual greeting among her friends. Alan hesitated briefly, then realizing what was expected of him, leaned toward her cheek just as she was pulling back, embarrassed, and their lips met. To cover their confusion, Lindsay reached for his hand, squeezed it warmly.

"What are you doing here? And how's Marietta?"

He answered the questions in order. "I'm teaching at N.Y.U. She's still on the island with the kids."

"Like your book—in reverse," Lindsay said.

"Not really. I left in September. I haven't been back. We're not officially separated, just physically. I still love her and the kids. I'll be going back for Thanksgiving. I just can't live on an island. Unless it happens to be overpopulated," he added with a grin.

"I know how you feel."

"Are you free for dinner?" he asked.

"As free as *you* are."

"I see you're no longer wearing a wedding ring," Alan said later that night as they left the restaurant.

"No, I'm not, but you are."

"I wasn't planning to make a pass. I happen to be in love with my wife."

"I'm glad," said Lindsay. "You know, when we met, I liked you both equally. I seldom feel that way about couples I interview."

"Until we met, I'd never looked at that magazine. Now I never miss your interview. Do you know what I've learned from it?"

"What?"

"How many women I could have been happy with. I could have had a good life with almost every one of the women you've written about."

"But would you have as much to show for it if you'd married any of those other women?"

"I might not have written a book, but I could have been happy."

"And yet you love Marietta?"

"I made a choice."

Lindsay was silent. Alan took her arm as they crossed the street and they continued to walk without any apparent destination. "Why does everybody want to believe there's only one perfect partner per lifetime?"

"Monogamy makes the world go round," said Lindsay, her fingers inadvertently seeking the wedding ring concealed beneath the folds of her blouse.

"Oh, I believe in monogamy," Alan replied. "The big decision in life is not whom you marry but simply to marry. If you love somebody enough to marry them, you should love them enough to do whatever you have to do to make it work and to keep it going. And growing."

"You've given me an idea for another series," said Lindsay. "A follow-up on all the couples in 'Give and Take.' I wonder how many are still together."

"Marietta and I will always be together," Alan assured her, "even though we may be living apart."

"A follow-up may not be such a good idea after all," Lindsay reflected. "I shouldn't push my luck."

"You haven't said anything about what you've been doing," Alan said, continuing to keep his hand on her elbow.

"If we don't talk about my life, I can see you again," Lindsay said. "And I'd like to see you again."

He took her hand and held it till they reached her building. She told him good night at the elevator. He didn't ask to stay with her, so she didn't have to say no. He did ask if they could have dinner again next week. She told him to call her at the office on Friday, explaining that she was never free on a weeknight, but if Saturday was good for him it was for her. And so it began— the pattern of separating her different lives.

Nine

It was after midnight when Lindsay left Alan but, having slept until midafternoon, she was exhilarated and wide awake. Alone in her apartment, she tried on every article of clothing she owned, discarding items she had not worn in years and until tonight had acknowledged were out of style only by her indifference to them. Then, drawer by drawer, she organized her desk, collecting unanswered letters that had been hidden out of sight behind assorted boxes of stationery and displaying them in a letter box that matched her blotter. When the sun rose, she was at work on her bookshelves, taking down the books one by one, dusting them, making a stack of the ones she'd always wanted to read but never had the time and another stack of books that, once read, had no further place in her life.

Finally, having gone over every inch of her apartment, stripping it of excess baggage in every form, she got into bed, feeling emotionally stripped as well. Her life—or at least part of it—

had been restored to her. By dividing it according to allegiances owed, she had multiplied her possibilities. The days of the week were committed to her work, and the nights to the man whose life had been joined with hers in marriage. But finally, after years of allowing this obligation to overwhelm all that remained of her life, she had dared impose limits on its claim by demanding the two days at the end of each week for her own. Not to be alone —today had proved that what she wanted was more complicated than that—but to live for just a few hours a week entirely in the present, unburdened by prior claims or future plans.

Sunday she slept. She awoke after a few hours to fix a breakfast tray and bring it back to bed. Then she reread and answered the letters she had excavated from her desk the day before—except for the annual postcard from her class secretary, Cissy MASON Clark, announcing another move, the third in a decade of marriage, and soliciting news for the alumnae bulletin.

Lindsay read the postcard again: "Thank goodness my children are at an age where their parents are part of their lives. They are the best friends I have, and the only ones I don't leave behind when we move to a new town. Through them I also meet my first new friends—the parents of their schoolmates. Sometimes I wonder what I'll do when they're too old for a car pool. I think I'd better develop some skill best practiced in private—like illuminating manuscripts." Cissy's attempt at humor only succeeded in irritating Lindsay.

Why don't any of us ever have the courage to admit we've failed, she thought. When we knew each other, we all thought we were capable of changing the world—but by means no more revolutionary than marrying more interesting men than our mothers. Maybe that's why we have to put a good face on whatever has happened to us. We can confide in next-door neighbors (though Lindsay never had) or in girlhood friends growing old alongside us (like Meg, Lindsay thought, and then remembered—her last letter to Meg had been returned marked "Not deliverable, unable to forward") but we have to put on a show for those who last saw us poised at the threshold—our hopes unblemished by hard facts, everything still possible. The class letter is our communal report card—only it's not our work but our lives being judged and the grades are not given by teacher to student, they are the verdict we invent to placate our younger, truer selves.

Lindsay thought back to the sentences that Cissy had framed about her in the seven years since graduation to keep their classmates au courant with her life.

"Lindsay HOWARD, who has been covering the wedding beat ever since she started work on *The Mamaroneck Times,* will be the lead in the biggest story of her career when she marries John Henry Hawkins of Amarillo, Texas."

"Our sympathy to Lindsay HOWARD Hawkins, whose husband of less than a year remains hospitalized as the result of a near-fatal diving accident last summer. Though the accident left him completely paralyzed (he can neither move nor speak), Lindsay says she is grateful that his mind was spared. He knows everything that's happening and always seems glad to see her."

"Grateful that his mind was spared?" thought Lindsay. How many times since the accident had she prayed for the day she would walk into his room and he would fail to recognize her.

The existence of a husband in Lindsay's life was ignored in subsequent reports—except for the addition of his name to hers.

"Lindsay HOWARD Hawkins now has a monthly byline in *Metropolitan* magazine. If you want to catch a glimpse of our classmate plying her glamorous trade, she can be seen almost any weekday lunching at one of New York City's top restaurants in the company of a name you would recognize from the morning paper."

Cissy had come to New York for what she called her annual injection of culture—a nonstop week of museums, concerts, and theaters that left her both physically and mentally winded and quite content to spend the next twelve months in Canton, Ohio, or Phoenix, Arizona, or wherever IBM had deposited her family in their most recent executive shuffle. Not being free at night, Lindsay had arranged to meet Cissy for lunch at the Four Seasons. At the last minute, Lindsay learned that a famous French woman of letters, in town to promote the American edition of a new book, had agreed to be interviewed over lunch. She invited Cissy to join them.

Cissy had spent her junior year abroad and almost married a graduate of the Ecole Polytechnique but decided against it when she realized it would mean spending her life in Algeria while her husband explored for oil in the Sahara. During lunch Cissy overheard several comments the literary lioness made in French on the subject of American men that the official translator, whom the publisher had hired to protect and defend their author from the press, neglected to make available to Lindsay. Cissy did not reveal what she had heard until they were back at the office.

Lindsay was amazed by both her alertness in hearing and retaining an offhand remark much more provocative than any-thing officially translated for publication and her discretion in waiting to share it until they were alone. Lindsay then located the great woman's former American lover, who had made their affair notorious if not immortal in a best-selling novel of his own. She read him the comment, without revealing that his name had not been mentioned in the conversation. His reaction was imme-diate, intense, eminently quotable, and became the lead for her interview.

For Cissy the experience epitomized her classmate's career. Though Lindsay assured her that much of her work was routine and often lunch was no more than an apple eaten at her desk, the interview she witnessed at the Four Seasons remained typical for Cissy of the life Lindsay led. As tragic as the circumstances of her marriage were, Lindsay suspected that there were times when Cissy envied her life and felt she had won bigger than anyone from their graduating class.

But lying in bed that Sunday afternoon, assessing her life, measuring it against what she knew of the lives of her classmates,

Lindsay felt she belonged to a generation that had failed to keep its promise. Half-lives, the lot of them. None of her contemporaries had structured a life with any real purpose. The ones who took jobs after college promptly abandoned them, if not at the altar then in the delivery room. Lindsay was the only one currently engaged in what could be called a career—and her freedom to pursue it with her whole heart had been bought at a terrible price: the complete physical incapacity of the man she married. But even the severely limited demands of her marriage created occasional conflicts at work. She refused any assignment that required travel. She had promised John Henry her presence every night. And precisely because he could not hold her to it, she never felt she had any choice but to keep it. Until this weekend, she had been with him every night since the accident. She felt justified in claiming time alone, but then what had she done but spend her first night of freedom in the company of another man?

Refusing to allow remorse to color her memories of the night before, Lindsay composed the following bulletin for Cissy: "Last night, instead of visiting my husband in the hospital where he is capable of nothing more than anticipating my arrival, I had dinner with a man who still loves his wife, even though he's not living with her. I wanted to sleep with him. I have stayed in bed all day wishing he were with me."

She looked down at what she had written, imagined Cissy reading it, then quickly crumpled the paper and threw it in the wastebasket. She couldn't do that to poor, sweet, trusting Cissy whose college classmates remained the best friends she would ever have. Two years earlier, when Cissy's five-year term as class correspondent was up and it was time to elect a successor, Lindsay had written the alumnae director to propose that Cissy be made class correspondent for life. The proposal was put to a vote and carried unanimously.

Cissy had received the news of her classmates' support simultaneously with her obstetrician's confirmation of her suspicion that she was pregnant again, despite the fact she was still breast-feeding her second child. "So much for *that* as a reliable method of birth control," Cissy wrote in the next class letter, pleased at the sophisticated tone she had found to describe a predicament that seemed anything but sophisticated at the time. Her husband had come home at lunch that day—something he never did—armed with a bottle of champagne, to find Cissy sobbing into the strained peas she was trying to feed their older son, a recalcitrant toddler who hated being made to sit still three times a day for meals and forever after associated food with a feminine conspiracy to curtail his physical freedom. Cissy, assuming the obstetrician (her husband's weekend golfing partner) had telephoned him after she left the office to share the glad tidings, started sobbing again when Charles popped the cork on the bottle of champagne.

"What's wrong with you?" Charles demanded angrily. "This is the last time I come home when I have something to celebrate."

"Bang," shouted Charles Jr., otherwise known as Chuckie, in delight, "Mommy's dead. Peas all gone." And he threw the plate on the floor to celebrate his liberation.

Charles went to the kitchen cabinet where the two champagne glasses Cissy had stolen from room service on their wedding night were gathering dust behind plastic tumblers. He held them to the light and grimaced silently. Then, by way of apology, he refrained from criticizing her out loud and carefully washed and dried the glasses. He poured the champagne and put Cissy's glass on the table near the floor where she was kneeling, sponging up the strained peas. When she continued to ignore him and the champagne, he called loudly to his son, who, having disposed of the hated green stuff that kept him confined in his feeding chair, was happily building block towers behind the television set in the living room.

"Come here, Chuckie," he called seductively. "Want some of Daddy's bubbly?"

Chuckie came running. "Bubbly," he said happily. "Want bubbly." He had no idea what the word meant but the sound promised new and exciting adventures. He imagined the two of them—his father and him—enclosed in a giant bubble floating in the sky. "Bubbly go bye-bye," he said, scrambling excitedly onto his father's knee.

"That's right, son. How did you know? The bubbly's because we're going bye-bye."

Looking up in disbelief and realizing for the first time that the champagne had nothing to do with her, Cissy said sharply, "Don't give him champagne. He's just a baby. You'll make him sick."

"He's acting more like an adult than you are," Charles answered. "He's even guessed why we're celebrating."

"Good for him. Now explain it to me," Cissy said slowly.

"Bubbly go bye-bye," said the heir apparent, bouncing up and down, trying to set in motion the hidden mechanism that would bring the magic bubble into being and carry him and his fun-loving father far away from his food-fixated mother and the next meal, which he knew was as inevitable as the soft mound he felt collecting in his pants. He wrinkled his nose in disgust. "Mommy make poo-poo," he said quickly, hoping to shift the blame before it was too late. And in his mind somehow she really was responsible. Not that he understood the intricacies of the digestive system —or any intrinsic connection between what he took into his body and the waste that inconvenienced him at regular intervals. All he knew was that both irritated his mother and required him to remain immobile and get either his bottom or his mouth wiped before he was allowed to run free again.

Wearily Cissy got to her feet and took her firstborn into the bedroom to change his pants, warning him not to wake his little brother, who, with luck, would sleep another hour.

With the arrival of a second child six months earlier, Cissy had started getting up at five in the morning so she could make coffee and read the morning paper in peace before the baby began clamoring for her breast at six. For that hour Cissy felt part of the world around her—she had attitudes toward current events, political convictions, and sufficient background to laugh out loud at Art Buchwald (who had been living in Paris when she was a student there and writing about it in the Paris edition of the *New York Herald Tribune*—now that they were both back home, Cissy felt they shared a special point of view that less traveled Americans could not truly appreciate; she often clipped out his columns and enclosed them in letters home to her parents with the comment, "My feelings exactly").

By the time the baby began to cry for her, Cissy would feel like a citizen of the world, and that sense of being connected to the center of life did not disappear when she sat down in the rocking chair in the children's bedroom, unzipped her quilted housecoat, reached inside her V-necked nightgown, and gently guided her nipple to her baby's waiting mouth.

Rocking with her eyes closed, feeling the baby sucking contentedly, hearing her firstborn son breathing peacefully, uncomplaining for once about being still, Cissy felt whole and complete, as if the secret of life had just been whispered in her ear. It was enough—children, home, husband. It was enough for anybody. Sometimes she would even fall asleep rocking, not noticing when the baby, warm and satisfied, let the nipple fall from his mouth and slept again too, lulled by his mother's heartbeat into imagining he was once again enclosed in a timeless womb.

One morning when she had fallen asleep in the rocking chair with the baby in her arms, Cissy felt a hand suddenly covering her exposed breast. She opened her eyes and looked up to see Charles standing behind her. He bent down to kiss her neck, continuing to caress her breast until the milk began to flow again.

"Honey, you're a fountain," he said hungrily. "Put the baby in his crib and come back to bed."

Cissy did as he instructed and took care of his needs as quickly and efficiently as she quieted her children's cries. Though she would never have admitted it to anyone and indeed avoided making any connection in her own mind, there was a very thin line between the physical sense of satisfaction she got from nursing her child and from having sex with her husband. She was aroused by the unashamed needs of both. The big difference was that with the baby the afterglow lasted longer. And she was usually the one who severed the connection.

Ten minutes after he had come into the children's bedroom to claim her, Charles was out of bed again, ready to begin his day. Cissy continued to revel in the luxury of lying naked between the sheets, something she had taken for granted as a young bride. But motherhood now required her to be warmly clothed and ready to provide instant attention. Charles, usually more modest about his body than she was but now armored by postcoital pride, walked naked into the bathroom, leaving the door ajar. Cissy watched his reflection in the full-length mirror opposite the bed as he stood urinating with obvious relief.

She had never watched him in the act of performing this simple function before and marveled at how comfortable the male is with his body. It had never occurred to her what an advantage it was for a man to be on such familiar terms with his sexual organs. He held that part of himself every day in an act unrelated to sex. It was a natural next step to realize that sexual pleasure was also within his control. Whereas for women it too often remained a mystery.

Cissy's father had bluntly furnished her with the facts of life while her mother was fumbling for the words. "Babies come from between the legs—it's just like going to the bathroom." For years afterward Cissy always checked the toilet before she flushed to make sure a baby wasn't floating around in it. No wonder women were so much more furtive about their bodies, thought Cissy, since they were never sure of what mysteries they contained and might produce without warning.

These thoughts occurred to Cissy again on the day Charles brought home the champagne to celebrate what she now realized was another move. Even though it represented a promotion to him, all it meant to her was that in seven months an obstetrician she had yet to meet in a city where she'd never been was going to be delivering a baby she didn't want. It was her fate to have each of the children delivered by different hands in different hospitals in different cities. The only continuity in her life since college was contained in the person of her husband. Quite a burden for one individual, she thought, to have to answer for the destiny of another. The reverse was not true. She was not the sole source of continuity in his life. He was securely locked into a corporate structure. Though each time they moved he had to meet new people, their roles and methods were already familiar to him. Wherever they went, he quickly found his place within a well-ordered universe.

"It's not fair," thought Cissy, smacking Chuckie lightly but firmly on the thigh to stop him from squirming while she changed his pants. He immediately began to howl, a grandstand play to attract his father's attention and bring him into the bedroom. "I don't want another baby," she cried, which of course woke the one she already had, who was napping in the crib.

The baby diverted Cissy's attention just long enough for Chuckie to crawl down from the bed, smearing his unwiped bottom on the brand-new comforter Cissy had bought him the week before.

"Me no baby," he said in angry rebuttal, interpreting Cissy's anguished outburst as a personal accusation. "Me pee-pee like Daddy," he announced, standing proudly at the toilet. At that moment Charles entered the bedroom. Chuckie turned around to demonstrate his accomplishment, dousing his father's tweed-covered leg with a stream of urine.

"Christ, I must have been crazy to come home in the middle of the day," said the master of the house, furiously sponging off his pants leg with a mildewed washcloth that had been left in a wad on the edge of the bathtub. "This house is a zoo!" He then saw the trail Chuckie had left between bed and bathroom. "And this room smells like a cage!"

He crossed to Cissy, who was bending over the baby. "Try to have the animals fed by the time I get home tonight—okay?"

She turned to face him. "I'm pregnant," she said quietly.

His reaction was total and spontaneous: equal parts joy and pride. He hugged her as she held the baby. "Honey, that's great. Now we both have something to celebrate. And I'm going to make you a promise. When we move to Great Falls, we're going to buy a house big enough to keep each kid in a separate room."

"Great Falls?" asked Cissy. "Where's that?"

"Great Falls, Montana," he answered expansively, "land of the new frontier. All they've got out there is space."

"I'm not surprised," said Cissy.

"And that's the only thing missing in our lives."

"Space?"

"Sure. Room to get away from each other. So Chuckie won't wake the baby and the baby won't wake me."

Cissy imagined a huge house with herself stretched over it, pulled taut in every direction as she struggled desperately to provide some connection between the separate rooms housing the separate lives. She felt herself stretched so perilously thin she was in danger of ripping apart and yet she knew if she did, the individual destinies she was keeping in conjunction by sheer force of will would scatter, never again to inhabit the same universe.

Sometimes she wondered why it was so important to her that this not happen—why the family unit seemed worth preserving even at her own expense. She wasn't at all convinced that any of its individual members were better off together than they would have been apart. Specialists trained in psychology and the principles of sound nutrition could undoubtedly do a much better job of child raising than harassed parents. With professional guidance a child could develop his full potential without interference from jealous siblings or parents not even sure of their relationship to each other, much less to their children. Men and women would meet by mutual desire in the course of full individual lives, lives whose purpose was never simply to please other people. Any relationship between children and adults would again be a matter of choice—not merely the result of sexual activity. People who wanted clothes laundered or letters typed or homes cleaned or bills paid or meals cooked would pay to have these services performed. Those who enjoyed doing their own work would perform at their own pace and for others only by choice.

Her wandering thoughts restored a tranquillity to Cissy that eluded her whenever she was confronting the reality of her own life. She was smiling when Charles kissed her good-bye.

"I knew it would lift your spirits to think of the big house we're going to buy," he said. "We may even get one with an extra bedroom—and see if we can fill it before I get promoted again. Cork that champagne and put it in the refrigerator. We'll finish it when I get home tonight. I hope I've made you as happy as you've made me," he said, taking her silence as assent.

The afternoon mail brought the news that her classmates had unanimously voted Cissy their correspondent for life. "What does it matter where I live?" she thought. "As long as there are letters, I can take my friends with me anywhere."

She composed an enthusiastic paragraph for the next alumnae bulletin describing their prospective move. "I feel like a modern pioneer woman," she wrote. "I wouldn't know what to do with myself if I had to live in the same place longer than three years at a time." She undercut her enthusiasm with the news that she was pregnant for the third time. Then she sat down with the letters that had arrived over the last few months in answer to her postcards soliciting news. She worked through them quickly, priding herself on finding a positive angle for each item.

She saved Lindsay's letter for last. Her tragic marriage overshadowed any good news she could report. As hard as she tried, Cissy could not put herself in her friend's place. She could not imagine how Lindsay found the courage to go on living, let alone try for a career. "The popularity of Lindsay HOWARD Hawkins' series on successful marriages, 'Give and Take,' has earned her a promotion from editorial assistant to assistant editor," Cissy wrote, marveling to herself that Lindsay could still believe in marriage after what she had been through. "If she can, I can," thought Cissy, feeling suddenly blessed to have a handsome husband who came home to her with champagne when he had something to celebrate.

Impulsively she made dinner reservations for two at a downtown restaurant, then called the office and left word with his secretary that Charles was to meet her there for dinner. She arranged for a baby-sitter and told Chuckie he could scrub her back while she shampooed her hair. She did not dare leave the children alone long enough to bathe in private. Instead she moved the playpen to the bathroom door so her infant son could watch her splashing with Chuckie in the tub. Of course, she had no sooner lathered her hair for the first time than the baby was crying to get in with them. Quickly rinsing her hair under the faucet (which required contortions that gave her a catch in the chest—but sharing a shower with a wiggly two-year-old was out of the question), forgoing a second lather and a creme rinse, Cissy stood dripping on the bathmat and did a little dance to make the baby laugh. She let Chuckie continue to splash in the tub while she dried her hair, amusing the baby by turning the hair dryer in his direction occasionally and letting the hot air hit his face.

When the baby-sitter arrived at six, the children were clean and fed and ready for a bedtime story. Cissy felt young and pretty in a cocktail dress she had bought for the obligatory dinner at the home of her husband's boss when they first moved to town. The boss's wife had promised to take Cissy under her wing but the next week when she called to invite her to a planning session for a charity bazaar, Chuckie was running a temperature, so Cissy apologetically declined. She had not seen either the boss or his wife since, nor had she had an occasion to wear the dress.

Her heart was pounding when she got to the restaurant. She had never in their entire marriage attempted to surprise Charles or to initiate any kind of private occasion. But when he joined her at the table, where she was already seated sipping a whiskey sour, she knew she had done the right thing.

"I'd forgotten how beautiful you look when you're pregnant," he said as he kissed her.

"And I'd forgotten how lucky I am to have you for a husband," she said. And she meant every word.

Early the next morning, instead of reading Art Buchwald, Cissy wrote Lindsay to tell her that the vote of confidence from her classmates, arriving in the middle of a hectic afternoon, had restored her sanity and saved her marriage. Again, she meant every word.

Lindsay remembered Cissy's comment now as she struggled to compose a few hope-sustaining sentences to capsule the changes the last year had made in her life. "I got the best birthday present imaginable this year when I turned thirty—I was made an editor on the magazine and didn't have to replace anyone to do it. A title was created for me: editor in charge of domestic relations." She did not add that she had formally marked the end of her third decade by removing her wedding ring from her finger and hiding it on a chain around her neck.

Finally—shelves cleaned, closets straightened, letters answered —Lindsay got dressed and took her letters to the corner mailbox. With her annual report off to Cissy, she felt she had closed the door on the past for another year.

She walked toward Central Park. The sun was setting and pedestrian traffic was flowing against her as exhausted parents corralled their still-exuberant offspring and tried to persuade them—with decreasingly civilized tactics—that it was time to go home. The children seemed to take pride in doing everything within their power to prolong the outing, knowing instinctively that once home, each would return to the lonely responsibility of leading his own life.

The children's zoo was preparing to close as Lindsay reached the turnstile but when she told the attendant that she only wanted to use a phone, he grudgingly allowed her to go through the gate without paying.

Alan Compton answered his phone on the first ring. "I thought you were Marietta," he said quickly, as if it were necessary to explain his promptness. "I just talked to her and she always calls right back with something she forgot to say."

"Should I call again later? So your line won't be busy?"

"No—don't hang up," he said with unexpected urgency. "I've thought of you all day. I planned to call you next Saturday but it was beginning to look like a long week. Can we meet for dinner tonight?"

On the Monday night after she met Alan, Lindsay told John Henry, "I'm seeing a man I used to know." She had asked the nurse on duty to teach her massage techniques that could be practiced despite the machinery to which he was married more irrevocably than he had ever been to her. She wondered later if she sought a more active physical relationship with him in order to focus her attention on a useless limb and thus avoid his all-knowing eyes.

"He's married and he still loves his wife—even though they're not living together. I wanted to sleep with him the night I met him. But I didn't. And I haven't. And I won't," she promised, standing behind him, the top of his head touching her womb as her hands, liquid with lotion and unreturned love, met at his forehead then slowly parted and moved down his cheeks to encircle his face, coming to rest in an attitude of prayer beneath his chin.

But finally she had to face him. "Not because I'm married," she admitted. "Because he is."

And she began to cry. She cried for John Henry—sentenced to a life more painful than the most agonizing death. She cried for Alan, overwhelmed by the demands of loving and being loved. And finally she cried for herself.

Ten

Six weeks after they met and began to share their weekends, Alan returned to his family for Thanksgiving. Lindsay felt obligated to spend the long holiday weekend at home with her parents.

Seated at the dining table, she watched her father carve the turkey and her mother pass the pumpkin bread with the comment that had become a Thanksgiving tradition: "For those who don't like their pumpkin in a pie." Lindsay had grown up with her parents' prejudice against pumpkin pie ingrained in her thinking. Not until college, when she spent her first Thanksgiving away from home, did she discover that there was nothing wrong with pumpkin pie. Nor, for that matter, with people who had voted for Truman.

Lindsay was dutifully struggling to keep up her end of a conversation that did not recognize the existence of Alan Compton when her mother set dessert on the table—a brandied plum pudding accompanied by brochures for a Caribbean cruise.

"Christmas at sea," said her mother. "Wouldn't that be a nice change for us?"

It was only then Lindsay realized that the holidays were as hard for her parents as they were for her. The sense of obligation she felt as an indulged and overprivileged only child, reinforced by her guilt at having denied her parents a grandchild, always brought Lindsay home for the holidays. Only now did it occur to her that they might feel as obligated to create an occasion as she did to attend it.

"What a terrific idea," she said, leafing through the brochure. "A different port every day, dancing under the stars every night."

"You will go with us?" her father hastened to add. "That's the point. You need to get away more than we do."

"Actually, I'd rather enjoy staying in the city this year," Lindsay answered quickly. "There's a lot happening over the holidays—I've made some new friends . . ." she hesitated, not wanting to supply details if she could avoid them. It was one thing to tell John Henry about Alan Compton—all he could do was listen—but she preferred to keep that part of her life private from her parents. However, she didn't have to worry. The mention of friends seemed to fill her mother with relief.

"Of course it would be more fun to be with people your own age," her mother said with such enthusiasm Lindsay knew she was imagining a round of parties in penthouse apartments, with a piano player providing unsentimental renditions of Christmas standards in the background.

In fact Lindsay had only one real friend. And though he was returning on Monday and they would spend the next three weekends together, he was expected back in Oregon for Christmas. But Lindsay knew if her parents realized she'd be spending Christmas Day at the hospital with John Henry, they would never leave her. There was no way to explain to them that on a holiday traditionally reserved for family gatherings she would feel less alone if she were left alone.

The day after Thanksgiving Lindsay helped her mother shop

for cruise clothes and enjoyed her pleasure at the prospect of the trip. Though Katherine Howard had spent a lifetime sharing water sports with her husband, this was her first ocean cruise, and her excitement had erased ten years from her appearance. Lindsay realized with a twinge of guilt that on shared shopping expeditions in the past she was always the one being outfitted—for college, for marriage, for a career—with her mother content merely to advise and consent. Now that their roles were reversed, Lindsay understood for the first time the vicarious pleasure a parent takes in a child's adventures.

"I haven't had a new wardrobe from the inside out since I was a bride," her mother confided, trying on a set of coordinated lingerie, "but a ship's cabin is close quarters. I want everything to pass inspection. I mean, when I hang them on the shower rod to dry," she added, blushing, which made Lindsay suddenly aware that that was not what she meant at all. As she watched her mother stepping into a lacy beige slip, adjusting the shoulder straps, Lindsay had an image of her father pulling the straps down from her mother's shoulders.

The image jolted her thought patterns, though she had always been pleasantly aware of how physically comfortable her parents were with each other—a finger against an eyelid to urge rest, a hand on a cheek to reinforce a farewell kiss, an arm around a shoulder to share a joke.

Her mother used to put a stack of Eddie Duchin records on the Magnavox every afternoon around five. She would change out of the slacks or skirts and blouses with spectator pumps she wore during the day into the kind of long dresses department stores advertised as "hostess gowns." She wore them at the end of every day, even though the only guest she was expecting was her husband. She loved the freedom of a long gown and welcomed the escape it provided from the girdle that every well-bred woman of her generation considered necessary for street wear, to conceal the mechanism of the female body in motion.

When Lindsay was a baby, her mother would hold her in her

arms and dance to the music. When she learned to walk, her mother would bend down and take her hands and twirl her around. When she was ten, her mother taught her the proper position for ballroom dancing, and it was only then, with her head resting against her mother's bosom and her arm around her waist, that Lindsay realized that underneath her hostess gown her mother was not wearing any underwear at all.

Katherine Howard was usually still dancing when her husband came home from work, but, responding to his mood, would quickly turn down the volume and fix him a drink, then sit beside him on the couch while Eddie Duchin continued to make keyboard magic softly in the background. Lindsay never wanted to stop, though, and, with her parents smiling their approval, twirled and dipped till the maid announced dinner.

One day Lindsay was dancing with her mother when her father came home elated with a piece of property he had just acquired. When Mrs. Howard crossed to the Magnavox to turn down the music so that they could talk, he followed her and took her in his arms. "No," he said, "we'll talk later. Let's dance." They moved together in a fluid rhythm that made Lindsay, dipping and twirling alone, suddenly feel awkward and exposed. Without a word, she slipped out of the room and ran up the stairs to her bedroom, where she stayed till dinner. When she came to the table, her parents smiled at her warmly, but failed to ask why she had left the living room. They hadn't even noticed, Lindsay realized.

After dinner her mother whispered that her father wasn't feeling well and she was going to be taking care of him, so would Lindsay please kiss them good night now and not disturb them in their bedroom. After that night Lindsay never danced with her mother again. She pleaded homework and remained in her room till dinnertime.

Watching her mother unselfconsciously remove the brassiere she was buying and turn barebreasted to smile at her as if they were college roommates accustomed to seeing each other in all stages of undress, Lindsay realized with a pang of jealousy that her mother still considered her body a source of pride and pleasure. Lindsay felt old and unused by comparison.

"We're going to have such a good time," Mrs. Howard said, pulling on a sheer nightgown that served to emphasize the fullness of her breasts.

"You really are a beautiful woman, Mother," Lindsay said softly.

"Why, darling," Mrs. Howard cried out in surprise. "You haven't said anything about the way I look since you were a little girl. You used to tell me how pretty I was when I'd get dressed up for a party."

"I'm sorry. I'm afraid I stopped looking at you."

"You've had so much to face in the last few years. How could you be expected to look at anyone?" Suddenly she pulled Lindsay to her and held her, as if she were ten years old again, against her bountiful breasts. "Oh, darling, if only you'd come with us. You need this trip more than we do."

"Even if I came, I wouldn't be getting away. Not really. But the two of you can. You have each other. You can escape. And after dinner you can dance all night or go straight to bed— without having to pretend to anyone that you're not feeling well."

Her mother took her arms away from Lindsay and looked at her sharply. "When did you figure out what we were doing?"

"Not until right now," laughed Lindsay.

Eleven

The cruise sailed from New York City on December twenty-third, due to return January third. Ten days at sea with calls in Antigua, Martinique, Barbados. On New Year's Day her parents cabled Lindsay from Puerto Rico: "Don't meet ship. Delaying return. Peter Duchin playing here. Flying home on weekend."

As she took her seat on the train returning from her evening visit with John Henry, Lindsay saw the headline. The man seated across from her was reading a late edition of the Friday paper. The plane crash was a banner headline.

"Is there a passenger list?" Lindsay finally found the courage to ask after staring at the headline in silence for several minutes.

"What?" the man asked, annoyed at the interruption.

"The plane crash. Is there a passenger list?" she repeated.

The man had to turn again to the front page to see where Lindsay was pointing before he understood her question. "I don't know. I didn't read about it," he said, turning to the inside page where the article was continued. "I hate disaster stories."

"So do I," said Lindsay, then answered his question before he could ask it, something she tried never to do with strangers, "but my parents were . . . are in Puerto Rico. I can't help worrying."

"There's no list," said the man, suddenly solicitous. "When did you expect them?"

"I don't know. They said this weekend. I'm not even sure which airline."

"It's Friday," he reassured her. "The weekend begins tomorrow."

"I hope so," said Lindsay, sitting back with a sigh.

The man continued reading his paper but when the train stopped in Grand Central, he handed her his business card: "Todd Newman. Life Insurance." As if that were possible, mused Lindsay. At the bottom of the card he'd written his home number in ink.

"I'm sure everything's all right," he smiled, "but here's my number in case you need anything."

Lindsay put the card in her purse. "Thank you," she said, feeling sure she would never see him again.

When she got back to her apartment, she found the telegram from the airline under her door, notifying her officially of what she already knew. She entered her apartment, pulled a chair to the window without turning on any lights, and sat waiting for Saturday. Saturday—the day she had reserved for herself, the day she had been determined to keep free from family and husband —today it found her more alone than she had ever been in her life or ever imagined she would be. She didn't even know whom to call to share the burden of the news she found impossible to absorb. By tomorrow her parents' many friends would have heard and she would be overwhelmed with calls of condolence. Then she would have an official role to play: bereaved only child. And a function: she would have to put her parents' house on the market and dispose of their possessions. But for now she was a woman alone: no brothers and sisters to comfort and support her, no close friends who knew anything about her personal life.

As the sun began to rise she was still seated in the chair by the window. She decided it was time to tell Alan everything. It had been a foolish conceit on her part to think two people could exist purely in the present tense without attempting to understand the forces—people, places, events—that had shaped their attitudes and ambitions.

She checked her engagement book. He was due back from Christmas vacation on Sunday. Classes started again Monday. Maybe he had changed his mind and returned early. Hopefully, she tried his number but there was no answer. She held the receiver numbly in her lap while the phone continued to ring in his empty apartment.

Finally she broke the connection, dialed the operator, and placed a person-to-person call to Alan Compton in Oregon. The phone had rung several times before Lindsay thought to ask the operator what time it was in Oregon. "Four A.M.," she replied.

"Oh, my God, I'll call later."

But then Marietta answered the phone. She said Alan was asleep. Was this an emergency? Should she wake him?

"I'm so sorry," Lindsay interrupted the operator who was asking if she wanted to leave a message. "I forgot about the time change."

"Lindsay, is that you?" Marietta asked warmly. "Are you all right?"

"Yes, of course," Lindsay lied. "What about you?" She was surprised to realize she wasn't just being polite—she really wanted to know.

"Happier than I've ever been," Marietta answered quietly, without a hint of arrogance. "I made an extraordinary discovery this fall. I can live without Alan. I can even write without him."

"How wonderful," answered Lindsay. "When is he coming back?"

"Oh, he's not," said Marietta. "He's happier than he's ever been too. Both of us are happier than we've ever been—separately and together. We're moving to Seattle so he can teach in the winter, but we'll come back to the island for the summer. That way we can be here when the baby's born."

"Baby?"

"Oh, dear, I forgot—Alan wanted to be the one to tell you. Don't say anything about it when you talk to him, would you mind?"

"I don't need to talk to him," said Lindsay quietly, swallowing the news she had been about to share. "I just called to say Happy New Year—to you both."

"I think it really will be a happy new year. We've learned to live apart, which means when we're together it's because we want to be."

"Was it the baby?" Lindsay had to ask.

"Was what the baby?"

"That made you decide to live together again?"

"Of course not," replied Marietta, refusing to take advantage of her right to be indignant at the question. "The night he came home, he said he wasn't going to leave again. I didn't find out I was pregnant till yesterday. It must have happened while he was home for Thanksgiving."

"What would you have done if he *had* been planning to leave?"

"Done about what?"

"The baby."

"I would've had it, of course."

"Without telling him?"

"Oh, I would've told him eventually. But not right away. I wouldn't have used it to lure him back home, if that's what you're asking."

"I couldn't do that," Lindsay said.

"What?"

"Have a baby alone."

"But I'm not alone," answered Marietta. "I have my children and my work. Alan's been more alone than I have while we were apart."

"Yes, I know."

"If it hadn't been for you, I don't know how he would've gotten through the fall," Marietta continued. "I'm very grateful to you, Lindsay—and so is he."

Lindsay knew when she began to sob that she should put the receiver back on its hook but everything in her rebelled at breaking the connection—however tenuous it had become.

"I'm sorry, Lindsay," Marietta said softly. "You love him, don't you?"

"No," Lindsay sobbed, "I loved my parents and now they're dead."

And then, in a burst of anguish, she told Marietta about the plane crash. If she'd just gone with them, they would have all come home safely by ship—as scheduled. And yet, even now, the image that stayed with her was of the two of them alone, their arms around each other, dancing.

"I'm sorry you had to listen to all that," Lindsay said, dry-eyed and calm again, like an island after a storm. "It has nothing to do with you, with either of you."

"I know Alan will want to talk to you," Marietta said. "Give me your number."

"He has it, but please tell him not to call. It was better to talk to you—better for both of us. In fact, I'd rather he didn't even know. Just tell him I called to wish him, to wish you both, a happy new year."

After she replaced the receiver, Lindsay dressed and left her apartment, so she never knew how many times the phone rang that weekend.

Twelve

When Lindsay reached her parents' house in Larchmont, she stopped at the front door, unable to go inside. Not yet. She moved quickly to the garage door and opened it then reached for the set of keys to her parents' house and car that she always carried in her purse. The car was difficult to start in the icy weather but finally the motor began to hum and she backed out of the driveway. She wondered if John Henry would be surprised to see her so early on a Saturday morning.

As she walked past the nurses' station to his room, a nurse called out, "Good morning, Mrs. Howard. You're early today." Lindsay turned around, surprised, and the nurse realized her mistake.

"I'm sorry. I thought you were someone else."

"My mother?"

"Yes," said the nurse. "I always look for her on Saturday. She comes regular as clockwork, brings a radio so she can listen to the opera. She's even got me interested. Now sometimes I take the intermission quiz with her. She almost never misses an answer." It was only then that Lindsay realized her mother had quietly replaced her at John Henry's bedside when she started spending her weekends in the city.

"I come every weeknight," Lindsay found herself volunteering defensively.

"I always work the day shift. I guess that's how I've missed you," the nurse explained.

As Lindsay started toward John Henry's room, the nurse walked beside her, continuing to talk. "She always brings a big bag of needlepoint with her. She was working on a beautiful purse when she left on her trip."

"Yes—she sent it to me for Christmas."

"I've missed her. Is she back yet?"

"No," said Lindsay. "She's not." And she hurried into John Henry's room.

At first she found the sameness of his response reassuring. There was no apparent surprise at seeing her so early on a Saturday morning, no shock on hearing that he would never see her parents again. John Henry seemed to embody the indifference of the world to individual tragedy. His oscillating bed continued to turn as inexorably as the earth continued to orbit. It was easier to announce her loss to his impassive face than it would have been to Alan, who had never even met her parents. Yet finally everything in her demanded a response.

"They're dead, John Henry, and you can't even cry. You're the only family I have left and it's not enough." She had never let him see her this angry before. Suddenly she was ashamed to face him.

"I'm going home for a while," she said at the door, looking away from him. "I'll be back this afternoon."

As she drove home, she decided that John Henry came close to providing a human face for God—seeing everything, responding to nothing.

Baskets of flowers and potted plants were already piling up on the doorstep at her parents' house and the phone was ringing inside. She dealt with one call after another but was grateful for the unexpected appearance of a next-door neighbor whom her mother had asked to bring in the mail while they were away.

"I'd forgotten how many friends my parents had," Lindsay said, hanging up the phone and accepting the neighbor's awkward embrace.

"That helps, I'm sure—knowing how many people loved them," the woman smiled.

Lindsay answered with a smile that was noncommittal, then asked the neighbor if she would mind staying at the house while Lindsay went back to the hospital.

"Of course not, I'll take care of everything," she replied, grateful for the opportunity to translate her grief into action.

Finding an unexpected sense of purpose in what she was about to do, Lindsay loaded all the floral arrangements into the backseat of her parents' car and took them to John Henry. Placing the flowers within range of his restricted vision and then putting her face against his and her arms around him, she whispered, "I love you, John Henry. Thank God you're still alive."

As she sat beside him through the afternoon, she wondered why it had taken her so long to realize that what mattered was being able to love. Being loved in return was beside the point. John Henry had taught her that. Her parents had fed her, clothed her, called the doctor when she ran a temperature, shared the early joy of her marriage and the ensuing sorrow, but nothing they did for her as devoted parents equipped her to deal with their loss as much as John Henry's failure to share or even acknowledge it. His lack of response taught her that she carried the life force within herself. By actively continuing to love people, she could keep them alive—at least for herself—though to the rest of the world they were dead or permanently disabled.

Watching the winter day disappear in an early sunset, Lindsay even came to the conclusion that the existence of God could be proved by the love contained in a single human heart. It doesn't matter whether or not God loves us, she thought, as long as there is one person alive who loves God.

Turning the universe into a one-man show was a comforting illusion. It allowed Lindsay to put her parents' death into perspective, at least for the afternoon. However, driving home in the darkness, she found she was no longer able to sustain it.

Inside her parents' house their friends had begun to gather— drinking, talking, laughing, sharing memories. There were flowers everywhere, and the dining room table had been set with a variety of foods brought to express the sympathy words could not. Lindsay felt as awkward and unwanted as a child who gets caught sneaking uninvited into an adult party.

"I hope you don't mind," said her neighbor. "People were asking about you, wanting to see you. I said it would be all right to come over. It helps to be with other people at a time like this."

"Of course," Lindsay smiled—though she didn't feel a part of anything happening in the room. She spoke politely to the people who interrupted their conversation to greet her then excused herself and went upstairs to her bedroom.

She had to talk to someone who could root her to reality. Since reading the telegram the night before, she had felt suspended in some ambiguous time zone, connected to neither past nor future. She was floating in a dream world of confused images, familiar faces expressing unfamiliar sentiments. She had to find someone who could make her feel awake again—and part of a world that was not of her own making, where the existence of other people was not wholly dependent on her perception of them.

She wanted Meg. But she no longer even knew where her former roommate was living. She recalled again how it had hurt her the year before when her Christmas card had been returned, marked "Unable to forward."

Though they hadn't seen each other in almost a decade, they had at least made contact every year at Christmas. Until last year.

Lindsay had thought all year that Meg would get in touch, at least let her know where she was living, but now another Christmas had come and gone and still no word. What had happened? Did their friendship mean nothing to Meg?

Lindsay began to feel she was losing everybody who mattered in her life—her parents, Alan, now Meg. In an old address book dating back to her college years, she found an Amarillo number and dialed Meg's parents. There was no answer.

In frustration and despair, Lindsay buried her face in her pillow. The pillowcase still smelled faintly of rose petals from the handmade sachets her mother kept tucked in the linen closet. When she failed to respond to a knock at her bedroom door, the neighbor who apparently had organized everyone else's grief opened the door hesitantly and crossed to the bed.

"How hard being an only child," she said, taking Lindsay's hand.

"Forgive me," said Lindsay, wiping her eyes and sitting up in bed. "I hate people who feel sorry for themselves."

"You have a right."

"No, I should be downstairs."

Later that night when the last caller had left, her neighbor cleared the dining table and put away the food offerings. Lindsay couldn't help remembering how crowded her parents' kitchen usually was after the holidays—the remains of Christmas turkey and New Year's ham occupying an entire shelf of the refrigerator, along with half-eaten jars of homemade chutney and spiced fruit, extra loaves of nutbread in the freezer, brandied fruitcake and bourbon candy continuing to age in their tin containers—always enough food to extend the holiday spirit into the early drab weeks of the new year.

But this year, in preparation for their absence, the refrigerator had been stripped of everything but essentials. Her mother, organized and efficient to the end, had left the makings of a single meal in the freezer—so she could fix a simple dinner the night they returned.

Lindsay herself had never really cared about cooking. But now she was sad, thinking of all the things her mother could have taught her if she had only been willing to learn. Not just the mechanics of putting a meal together but the whole art of enriching life.

Most of her childhood memories were sense memories: the fragrance of freshly cut flowers, the polished look of the living room right after it had been swept and dusted, the touch of a thick terrycloth bath sheet against wet skin, the sound of her mother singing as she cooked, the taste of hot batter bread just out of the oven.

Her life since she left her mother's house had been sensually deprived compared to her childhood—in a way that had nothing to do with the absence of sex. She wondered if her contemporaries felt the contrast she did between the quality of life as she lived it and as her mother had.

Katherine Howard had created a career out of making life more enjoyable for everyone around her—and continued to take pride in her profession despite the condescending label of "housewife" society placed on it. Lindsay had decided early in life to avoid that label at all costs and for a time judged her mother as harshly as society for her choice. Only now did she realize how much her naive contempt had cost her. Her own life and the lives of many women of her generation would be the poorer, not because they failed to follow in their mothers' footsteps—there were too many exciting, unexplored paths opening to women—but because they failed to appreciate their mothers' accomplishments.

Looking at the food offerings her mother's friends had taken such time and pains to prepare, Lindsay wondered what a woman like herself was equipped to offer in time of grief as a tangible expression of sympathy. Not that sympathy had to take the form of food but, comparing her friends to her mother's, Lindsay realized that what had been lost, more than the specific skills of cooking and keeping house, was a whole tradition of selfless giving. A generation of women raised to believe the feminine mystique had devoted themselves to making life as pleasant as possible for the people around them—not a frivolous goal, as Lindsay had once thought, but one born out of the knowledge, sometimes instinctive, sometimes earned through bitter experience, that life at its core is raw and brutal and filled with pain. Now even volunteer work was considered a betrayal by women who demanded that all their efforts be rewarded with salary.

Lindsay had never envied her mother's life, but she realized—too late—that in her own way her mother had made a rich and rewarding difference in the lives of people around her. Lindsay wondered if her own accomplishments would amount to as much at the end of her life. She considered with new respect the network of friends her parents had built over the years—and felt even lonelier by comparison.

She didn't even know how to reach her college roommate. Maybe Cissy could help. She got out her current address book —Cissy (Mrs. Charles Clark) occupied most of the page under "C," one obliterated address after another. The current one was Great Falls, Montana. Quickly Lindsay calculated the time change—she didn't want to wake anyone again—then realized gratefully that it was still early evening in Montana.

Cissy answered on the fifth ring, clearly irritated and out of breath, and Lindsay realized too late that the dinner hour was no time to disturb the mother of young children.

"Actually all I wanted was Meg's address," she explained apologetically, then quickly surmised from Cissy's hurt silence that stating her reason for calling was more tactless than her bad timing. "I'll call back later when the children are in bed," she continued hurriedly. "When you have time to talk. We have a lot of catching up to do." She paused and waited for Cissy to say something but the silence continued. Then in the background she heard Cissy bribing her children with an offer of dessert before dinner—in return for silence.

"Can you hold on for one more minute—I'll find her address," Cissy said. "They've moved, you know. It was on her Christmas card. Just a second."

Lindsay was grateful that she could get the necessary information without revealing her reason for wanting it. She had accepted all the condolences she could handle for one night. Waiting for Cissy to return with the address, she suddenly heard an eager voice on the other end of the phone.

"My mother had to go to the bathroom, but she'll be right back."

"Who's this?" asked Lindsay.

"Chuckie. Who's this?"

"Lindsay. I'm a friend of your mother's."

"No, you're not."

Lindsay couldn't help laughing. "Yes, I am, Chuckie. We've been friends a long time. Since college."

"I have three friends," declared Chuckie proudly. "The day after Christmas they came to my house—all three at the same time—we played with my new toys. I wanted them to come over again today but my mother said three friends was too many. My daddy said she was a lazy mother. Then my mother cried and said she didn't have *any* friends. So I don't know who you are. And I'm not supposed to talk to strangers." And he hung up.

Lindsay decided against calling back right away. She would try again in a couple of hours—when the children were in bed.

But half an hour later Cissy phoned her.

"I would have called back right away," she apologized wearily, "but after I spanked Chuckie for hanging up, he said he was going to tell everybody—his father, his teachers, even his friends' mothers—that I always make him eat dessert first. So I spanked him again."

"Sounds as if he deserved it."

Cissy began to sob on the other end of the phone. "I'm so ashamed."

"Ashamed?"

"I sat outside my supermarket for two hours this morning collecting signatures on a petition to make capital punishment unconstitutional and I can't keep my hands off my own child."

"It's hardly the same thing, Cissy."

"Of course it is. Corporal punishment begins with a spanking and ends with the electric chair. You know what Chuckie said when I put him to bed just now? He said he likes his father better than he does me. He wouldn't even kiss me good night—just hid his little face in the pillow. I had to kiss his hair." Cissy broke into fresh sobs. "If my children don't love me, what have I done with my life?"

Suddenly Lindsay found herself telling Cissy about her parents. Cissy's response was immediate and total. "Oh, Lindsay, how could you have let me go on about my own problem? I'm so sorry. Is there anything I can do?"

Lindsay assured her there was nothing she needed—except Meg's address.

"Oh, of course. I forgot why you called. I have it right here." She gave the address and once again extended her sympathy. Then she had a final question.

"If you'd been able to reach Meg, would you have called me, too?"

Lindsay tried to explain, "It was just that Meg knew my parents. She came home with me the summer after graduation."

"I understand," said Cissy. "It really doesn't matter why you called. I feel so much better for having talked to you anyway." She stopped abruptly. "I'm sorry, that sounds terrible. I didn't mean it wasn't heartbreaking to hear about your parents. It's just that sometimes I miss you so much."

Lindsay hesitated. She had never once since graduation missed Cissy and she couldn't bring herself to say she had.

"I'll try to call more often. My college friends are really all the family I have now—not counting John Henry."

"How is he?" Cissy asked hesitantly. It was clear she wouldn't have mentioned his name if Lindsay hadn't brought it up first.

"The same. But today I was grateful even for that. Good night, Cissy."

When Lindsay replaced the receiver and allowed herself to surrender completely to the sobs she had suppressed all day, she realized she was grieving as much for Cissy and herself, each alone in her own way, as she was for her parents who, even in death, had each other.

Thirteen

Now that she knew how to reach Meg, Lindsay was suddenly hesitant to call. How had they grown so far apart in the years since college? During those four years their friendship had been so intense, Lindsay was sure they would be part of each other's lives forever, no matter how far apart they lived or how often they saw each other. When Meg first married and moved to California, Lindsay would frequently call long distance. But Meg was not at ease on the phone; her answers sounded strained and uncertain, as if Lindsay were putting her to a test for which she was unprepared. At first Lindsay assumed it was because Mark was in the room, overhearing her answers, so she tried calling during the day when he was at work. But Meg seemed equally ill at ease when she was alone, invariably making excuses to get off the phone, promising to write. But except for a vague assurance of well-being on her annual Christmas card, she never did. And so Lindsay finally grew to accept the fact that their friendship had never meant as much to Meg as it had to her.

Tonight, lying fully dressed in the darkness, Meg's new number in Los Angeles on a pad beside her bed, Lindsay felt as bereaved by the loss of her best friend as by the death of her parents. But at least Meg was still within her power to reclaim. She turned on a light and dialed the number.

Mark answered. He and Lindsay had never met or even spoken, so she asked to speak to Meg. He said brusquely that Meg was away for a few days and asked who was calling. Lindsay gave him her name and when he didn't react, reminded him that she and Meg had been college roommates. He asked if there was any message. Lindsay said no, just to tell Meg she had called. He said he would. But Lindsay never knew whether Meg actually got her message—she never returned the call.

Lindsay put her parents' house on the market, had the few pieces of furniture her apartment could accommodate shipped to New York, and sold the rest.

She packed in her briefcase two scrapbooks she had discovered beside her mother's bed—one devoted to her father's awards and accomplishments, the other filled with Lindsay's "Give and Take" columns. There was nothing in print to indicate that her mother had ever lived.

Her parents' lawyer called her to his office to explain the terms of their will. He said she wouldn't be inheriting very much immediately; most of the money had been put in a trust fund to cover John Henry's hospital costs. Lindsay had never known how much money her parents had. She just knew that her father had graduated from college owing ten thousand dollars for the education his father considered unnecessary. He built a prosperous business but continued to account for every cent. The lawyer showed Lindsay the ledgers her father kept. The pages devoted to Lindsay began with the obstetrician's bill when she was born, continued through pediatricians, private schools, orthodontists, the wedding, and the boat. Their wedding present, the down payment on the house, was listed then crossed through when the house was sold after the accident. But the sum total of what Lindsay had cost her parents was a fraction of what they had paid to sustain the life of the man she married. And would continue paying.

The lawyer assured Lindsay that John Henry's expenses would be covered as long as he lived—even though he had already outlived everyone's expectations, including his doctors'. When he died, the money would go to her or, if he outlived her, to her heirs. It had never before occurred to Lindsay that she might die before John Henry. It was impossible for her to imagine. Even less conceivable was the idea that she would have an heir. How could she have an heir when she felt no connection to any living thing except John Henry?

Returning by train to New York, Lindsay felt like a displaced person, forced to flee the familiar country of childhood. She had to hold tightly to the arm of the upholstered chair in which she was riding to keep her hands from trembling. Her left arm was pressed against her stomach and locked in place underneath her right elbow like the safety bar on a roller coaster car. And in fact the vehicle that was hurtling her through time and space seemed closer to a roller coaster than to a commuter train. She felt it was only the pressure of her arm against her stomach that kept her insides from spilling onto the floor, leaving her physical form drained of content. Who was she and what kind of choices was she going to have to make to prove that she existed? She could never remember being so terrified. Even at the accident, when she feared she had lost John Henry, her own center had remained inviolate. But now the loss of her parents had forced her from the protective womb in which she had continued to live as an adult.

All these years Lindsay had fooled herself into thinking she was doing her parents a favor, having dinner with them most week-nights before driving to the hospital to see John Henry. Now she realized that in fact it was the reverse. The role of dutiful daughter had provided an emotional structure for her private universe. Without it, even though she appeared to the outside world as an independent, self-reliant adult who lived alone and paid her own way, she was just another homeless orphan.

Back in her apartment, facing an unscheduled weekend in the city, Lindsay thought of all the people who were going to miss her parents. Who would miss her if she died? There were half a dozen eager young editorial assistants on the magazine, already convinced they could do everything she was doing given the opportunity. And as for John Henry, Lindsay often wondered if her visits didn't cause more pain than they assuaged, reminding him of past happiness, offering nothing to replace it. Perhaps the kindest thing she could do for him now was to spare him her presence.

She reached into her purse for the sleeping pills she had requested from her family doctor in lieu of flowers. She would try to sleep through the weekend.

Her fingers encountered a card. "Todd Newman. Life Insurance." She had felt certain when he handed her his card that she would never refer to it again. And yet she had kept it. It was not often in her experience that one stranger reached out to another, offering an unreciprocated identity in the form of name and telephone number.

She reached Todd at his home number. When he heard her news, he offered to come to her apartment immediately. She looked at her watch before replying. It was after midnight.

"No, you mustn't. It's much too late," she said quickly. "I just need to talk to someone. Perhaps in the morning?"

He said he would call her. She left the card by the phone and shut her purse, the sleeping pills still undisturbed inside. She was asleep as soon as she closed her eyes.

The promise Todd's voice contained when he woke Lindsay the next morning to invite her to lunch was far more than just a physical connection with another person. He offered her access to his whole life, complicated with enough emotion to allow her to forget her own.

"I was an only child," he said over lunch, "so when I married, I'm afraid I wanted children even more than I wanted a wife. And ended up with neither."

Her relationship with Alan Compton had been confined exclusively to the present tense. He only mentioned Marietta and the children when he had to tell her he was going home for the holidays. She never referred to John Henry—or admitted that she was married. Each of them deliberately withheld their past, with its precious cargo of experience, from the friendship they shared, unwilling, or perhaps unable, to reconcile past and present emotions.

Todd, in contrast, wanted Lindsay to know everything about him. At an earlier time in her life, she would have resented the emotional burden he placed on her by revealing so early in their relationship the tragedy of his aborted marriage. But now, with her parents dead, her childhood home about to be occupied by new owners, and John Henry an impassive witness to her everwidening sense of isolation, Lindsay embraced his need as eagerly as his body. Like two interlocking pieces of a puzzle, whose awkward protrusions and gaping hollows disappear when they are joined, they recognized in each other everything that was missing from their lives when they were alone.

Fourteen

Until the night of the rape Lindsay never stopped to think how much of herself she had withheld from Todd during the twelve years of their friendship—how one-sided their intimacy had been. He had spared her none of the details of his life and assumed, because she had shared the pain of her parents' death so openly, that she had made her life equally accessible to him. Everything she had told him about her background was true— she had simply excised John Henry. Sometimes she thought that what Todd knew of her life was what it might have been if Meg had gone straight home from college, and Lindsay and John Henry had never met.

Once she began seeing Todd, Lindsay had ceased using John Henry as a confessor. She continued to visit him every week-night, but she no longer talked about her life outside his room. She felt instinctively that she owed Todd her silence. As long as he was unaware of John Henry's existence, she felt it would be wrong for John Henry to know of him.

But the rape had cut through to her most private core, allowing the secrets she had hidden from Todd to come spilling out of the open wound. He had been as injured by the assault as she—how could she ever forget the pain on his face as he put her in the taxi? She would not allow John Henry to suffer as Todd had by telling him things it was better for him not to know. And she was grateful he no longer expected anything but silence from her. If only she could stop thinking about the rape herself. Then perhaps she could stop trembling. But as visiting hours drew to a close, she knew she couldn't return that night to her apartment.

When the nurse made her midnight rounds, Lindsay explained that she had missed the last train back into the city and asked if she could stay with her husband till morning. The nurse replied that it was against the rules but who could invoke rules in front of John Henry? She brought Lindsay a pillow and blanket and promised no one would disturb her for the rest of the night.

It was the first time since the accident that Lindsay had spent an entire night with her husband. She was grateful for the darkness that allowed her to escape his eyes. Also after being with Todd, who wanted to know everything, it was a relief to be with John Henry, who asked nothing.

She leaned over and kissed his sleeping face, as if to seal her vow of silence. "I love you, John Henry," she said. Then she settled down in her chair with the pillow and blanket and finally fell asleep, lulled by the sound of his oscillating bed.

As she slept she dreamed that she was being raped, entered again and again against her will. This time, however, her hands were not tied—they rested unrestrained at her side. She lay paralyzed like John Henry, unable to speak or move, submitting passively, neither resisting nor encouraging her assailant, who wore a mask to hide his face. His naked body was lean and muscled. As he came to a triumphant climax astride her unresponsive frame, he removed his mask to reveal the smiling face of the man she had married. "I knew it was you," she cried out.

And so six weeks later when the doctor confirmed that she was pregnant, Lindsay wrote John Henry Hawkins as the name of the father—and it did not seem like a lie. However, she was determined to hide her condition from him until she could invent an explanation that involved neither love nor rape.

There were daily letters from Todd, always marked "Please forward." The words differed from day to day but the message was invariably the same: He wanted to be with her. Lindsay knew he was trying to give her time and distance to recover—but she could not imagine ever wanting to make love again. She realized now why it had been so essential for her to believe that even as she was being violated, she was conceiving a child. Pregnancy was a legitimate excuse for lack of sexual desire, and she prayed it would protect her against the possibility of further violation. She was beginning to feel safe for the first time since the attack. Then one evening after work the superintendent greeted her with a huge bouquet of flowers that had been delivered earlier in the day.

"What's the occasion?" he asked as Lindsay searched frantically for the card she knew she was not going to find.

"There is no occasion," she replied tersely, refusing to believe the flowers had anything to do with the fact that she was now officially pregnant.

"All the better," he smiled, carrying the bouquet to the elevator.

"You're sure there wasn't a card?"

He shook his head. "They must be from your secret admirer —the one who sent the food. My wife and I really enjoyed that basket. We ate everything but the smoked oysters. You can have them back if you want."

"No, thank you. And I don't want these flowers either. Do whatever you like with them."

"Better hold on to me. You look like you're about to faint," he said, helping her into the elevator.

Once inside the apartment, the door safely locked behind her, Lindsay's knees buckled and she collapsed into a chair. She wanted desperately to believe the flowers had come from Todd, but she knew the superintendent was right. The flowers—like the basket of food—had been sent by the father of her child.

She was overcome by a wave of nausea but when she tried to stand, her head kept circling above her shoulders like an airplane waiting to land. She crawled to the bathroom on her hands and knees and vomited. Wishing she could escape from consciousness, she stretched out on the floor, pressing her cheek against the cold tiles. But there was no escape.

Finally she gave up and got slowly to her feet. She splashed her face with cold water but then felt what remained of her insides turning to liquid. Bolting the bathroom door, she sat on the toilet, placing her head between her knees to keep it from falling off her body, and sobbed. Even here in this most private space, with no window, the door locked, and no one else in the apartment, Lindsay felt she was being watched.

The basket of flowers waiting in her building had dispelled forever the brief illusion of safety her unborn child had given her. Since the rape Lindsay had tried to come to terms with what had happened. She could accept the fact that her body had been violated—that was a single act of unprovoked violence, limited in time and space, no different really from a robbery. What she was not sure she could handle was the feeling that her life had somehow become public property.

She had not answered the telephone since the attack. It was ringing again now, as it did every night just before she tried to fall asleep. She was not sure how much longer she could continue living alone. She thought of Todd and wondered what he would say if he knew she was having a child. If she had not been pregnant, nothing could have stopped her from calling him.

The next morning the flowers Lindsay had refused to accept

were on the lobby table. She hurried to the office, avoiding the eyes of everyone she passed on the street. Now, instead of making her feel safer, the knowledge that she was not alone, that there was a new life beginning inside her, made her feel more vulnerable.

She began to take a different route to work every day, cutting through any hotel whose crowded lobby could provide a temporary refuge from the street. One night on the train, a man bumped into her as he hurried to get a seat. He apologized and reached toward her. "Don't touch me," she said and walked to the other end of the coach. Whenever a man walked behind her for more than a block, she imagined he was following her, trying to talk to her—as a man had done the first time she came into the city alone.

It was the weekend before she began her sophomore year. Meg had come to New York with her parents, and Lindsay was to meet them at the Plaza for lunch. Leaving Grand Central, she thought she heard a man behind her whisper, "You have beautiful legs."

She kept on walking without looking back. As she passed the window of a shoe store, she glanced quickly at her reflection and saw a soldier in uniform just behind her. He was smiling.

"Has anyone ever kissed your legs?" he asked.

She turned abruptly into the store and, passing racks of shoes, took a seat at the back. Just beyond the entrance, the soldier stood waiting, looking in the store window at the shoes on display.

When the salesman asked what he could do for her, Lindsay wanted to tell him just to keep talking. The soldier walked past the entrance to look in the window on the other side. Lindsay pointed to him. She said there were some black suede pumps in the window right by that soldier. She'd like to try them on.

The soldier saw the salesman coming toward him and moved quickly out of sight.

Returning with the shoes, the salesman pulled his stool close to Lindsay, brushing her knee, and cradled her stockinged foot in his hand. "These are going to look great on you. You have great legs."

Lindsay stood up abruptly, sliding her foot back into her own shoe. "How dare you!" she said.

At lunch she talked Meg into coming back to Larchmont for the weekend so she wouldn't have to take the train alone.

If only Meg were walking beside her now. Lindsay had picked up the phone to call her a dozen times since the attack—just to hear her voice, her outrage at what had happened. But she never dialed the number because she had not been able to imagine the rest of the conversation. What did she and Meg have to say to each other after twenty years?

But she had to do something to combat her fears—or at least to identify them. She decided to buy a telephone answering machine. She read the directions carefully, then connected the phone to it and turned up the volume so she could hear the caller leaving a message. Her fears were reinforced every time a silent caller hung up at the sound of her recorded request to leave name and number—even though she realized it might just be someone who disliked talking to machines. However, the machine did allow her to make one reassuring discovery. The call that came late every night was from Todd. He knew she was back in her apartment—if indeed he ever believed she had left it. But he asked no questions, made no demands in the message he left each night on her machine: "I'm here if you need me. Good night, Lindsay." Often Lindsay would rewind the tape and play the message again before she turned off the light and tried to sleep.

Fifteen

On the train each night Lindsay was able to forget her fear of being followed. In the room with John Henry there was no past or future—only the present was possible. Since the rape, she had come to take increasing comfort in the restricted nature of their relationship. To be accepted exactly as she was, no questions asked, no demands made—was that only possible between a man and a woman at the cost of physical incapacity?

Sometimes, sitting beside John Henry, she wished she could move into the room with him and wait there for the baby to be born—life would be so simple and safe. In his silence she dared imagine acceptance of anything she might tell him, and yet she continued to withhold everything for fear of destroying the only part of him that was still intact as far as she could tell—his love for her.

Soon she would have to tell him she was pregnant. How could she explain without hurting him? Or had her silence on the subject of her life in the years since Todd became part of it caused him more anguish than anything she could tell him now?

Her thoughts were interrupted by Craig Sanborn, the doctor who had helped her the last time she was pregnant. He asked if he could speak to her in his office. Lindsay was startled. Though he was officially in charge of John Henry's case, she had only seen him a few times in recent years. John Henry's condition got neither better nor worse, so there was little to discuss. Following him down the corridor, Lindsay thought how out of step she was with her times. When abortion was illegal, she had been convinced it was the only way she could save her life. Now it was legal, and she was just as convinced that her life depended on having the baby. But she didn't want to discuss her decision with anyone. However, the life Dr. Sanborn wanted to discuss was Lindsay's own.

"I just want you to know we're all aware of what you've accomplished," he began. "I never imagined he would live longer than a year. There's no medical explanation. It's clearly you."

"Why do I have the feeling you're not thanking me?" Lindsay asked, trying to hold back angry tears. She hated to cry in front of a man who believed her to be so much stronger than she was, but she couldn't help it.

Putting an arm around her, he said no one had the right to expect the devotion she had shown John Henry.

Lindsay remained silent, allowing him to comfort her, but her mind instinctively challenged him. What she was doing was the least John Henry—or any man she might have married—had a right to expect. He was not in a coma: his mind continued to function. It was not in her power to pull a plug. As long as he was alive, she owed him part of her life. That was the promise they had made each other when they married. But it was not a promise she would ever make again or allow anyone to make to her. She would never want Todd to feel he owed her what she felt she owed John Henry.

"I wouldn't allow you to give blood every day—even if it

meant your husband would die without it," the doctor continued. "I've been married twice myself. Neither wife thought I spent enough time with her. You seem to keep giving without asking anything in return."

"Why are you saying all this? Why now?"

"We had a visitor today."

"A visitor?"

"John Henry's brother. At least that's what he said."

What brother? John Henry had no brother. No family beyond a father whose whereabouts were unknown, if indeed he was still alive. For a moment Lindsay dared imagine that it was true, that a brother did exist, that she was not the only person in the world responsible for the man she had married.

When they met, it was John Henry's independence as much as anything about him that had excited and attracted her. When they married, she had thought what a blessing to be spared ritual visits to in-laws whose company she would never have chosen, how fortunate to escape the net of familial obligation in which so many marriages are trapped. Even after the accident, she was relieved that, except for her parents, there were no relatives to notify. She didn't want to share her grief with people who couldn't possibly love him as much as she did.

But now, just hearing the word "brother," she sensed how her burden would be eased if there were someone else to share it. The fiction was so comforting she allowed herself to cling to it.

"When was he here?"

"This morning. He said he's just moved east from Texas."

"You let him in the room?"

"No. I'd never do that without talking to you. He said he came because he was worried about you."

Then she knew. Todd. Of course.

"He mustn't see John Henry," she said quickly, wishing the doctor would put his arm around her again. She wanted desperately to be held by someone who didn't want to own her. Why had Todd come to the hospital? Was it out of curiosity—to stare like a driver who slows at the scene of a wreck to assess the damage? Whatever his motive, he had no right to violate her marriage.

Until the rape Lindsay had been able to lead separate lives—at work during the day, at night with John Henry, and on the weekends with Todd. Now she felt them colliding, and pieces of herself scattering in all directions. She had to protect what mattered most to her—her marriage and her unborn child.

"What do you want me to tell him when he comes tomorrow?" Dr. Sanborn asked.

"He won't be coming," Lindsay replied firmly—and returned to John Henry's room alone to tell him good night. She resolved that before she saw him again she would end her relationship with Todd. Forever. Then she would tell John Henry she was having a baby. She would stay with him until he understood that it belonged only to the two of them, that in spite of everything she was still his wife and he was the only husband she would ever have. She had no way of knowing when she kissed him good night how many hours and events would unfold before she saw him again.

Sixteen

When she got back to the city that night, Lindsay took a taxi to Todd's building. For the first time since the rape she was not afraid of being followed. The doorman rang his apartment, but there was no answer. He seemed surprised when Lindsay took a seat by the elevator and said she would wait. Though she had Todd's key in her purse, she had no intention of using it. She knew she wouldn't have long to wait because she knew where Todd had been. All the pieces finally fit.

As he entered the building, Todd saw Lindsay waiting and hurried to her. "Are you all right?" he asked, trying to put his arms around her, but she pulled away and entered the elevator.

"You know exactly how I am. You've been following me everywhere, haven't you? Even to the hospital. How could you?"

"How else could I make sure you were safe?"

"Safe? I was terrified. I knew someone was following me, but I didn't know who. Or why."

"I love you, Lindsay, and I'm not going to let you live alone. Not after what happened. You wouldn't live with me—so I did the only thing I could."

"I can never live with you. I have a husband. How dare you try to see him!"

"I had to know."

"What? That he can't move, can't speak, can't do anything but wait for me to come?"

"I had to know what it was like for you. What you were going through."

"Why don't you want to know what it's like for him—what he's going through? I can take care of myself."

"I stood in the doorway, saw the bed moving. I couldn't have gone inside even if the doctor hadn't stopped me. The doctor said you were keeping him alive—and he wasn't sure it was an act of mercy."

Tears stinging her eyes, Lindsay slapped Todd as hard as she could across the face. Then she began to beat on his chest with her fists. He grabbed her roughly by the shoulders.

"Let him go, damn it," he shouted. "Love somebody who can love you back."

"I love *him*. I'll always love him," Lindsay sobbed. "He gave me everything I ever wanted from a man. Just the memory of what I had with him is better than anything I can ever have with you."

She turned away and said something in a voice so low Todd couldn't hear the words. "What? Say that again," he demanded.

"How dare you love me when he can't?" she shouted defiantly.

"I can dare to love you *because* he can't," he answered. "*Because* I can make love to you and make you love me back. Don't be afraid to love me back, Lindsay." He turned her to face him again and his lips stopped her tears.

"Why did you say you were his brother?"

"Now that I know, how can I ever be anything less?" he answered, leading Lindsay to his bed as if she were a traveler at the end of a long and solitary voyage.

"No," she protested as he tried to put his arms around her. "I won't let you care like that. Not about me. Not about him. None of this has anything to do with you. It's my life. Stay out of it."

"Damn it, Lindsay, I don't have a life without you." He took her in his arms and pressed his mouth to hers. Again she felt the knife at her throat. She was as powerless to prevent him from loving her as she had been to prevent a stranger from taking her by force. And again she was convinced that her life depended on allowing it to happen.

Unbuttoning her blouse, Todd sought her breasts as desperately as an infant who knew he would die unless she nourished him. Gradually he reawakened in her sensations suppressed so completely since the rape she thought they no longer existed. His mouth seemed to be forcing the breath of life back into her body. She never wanted him to leave. She would learn to breathe through him, to live through him if only he would stay, covering and filling her wherever she was vulnerable and open to attack alone. The more he gave, the more she asked—as if he only had one night to compensate for his long absence from her bed and to make her forget the reason he had left.

Neither of them felt in control of what was happening. Though they had always given and taken pleasure from each other, tonight their two selves seemed to construct a bridge of bone and blood and sinew that would never allow them to separate again.

She was asleep in his arms when the nightmare began. Blood. Blood between her legs. Blood everywhere. Everywhere she turned life was ending.

She woke Todd with a scream. "Call an ambulance," she cried. "I'm bleeding to death."

Todd sat in the back of the ambulance beside her, holding her hand, promising she would not die. Only Lindsay knew it was not her own life she was losing.

Seventeen

Todd was standing at the door when the doctor emerged from the examining room where Lindsay had been taken from the ambulance.

"How is she?" he asked anxiously.

"She's all right," the doctor replied, "but you're going to have to take very good care of her for the next few months. She almost lost the baby tonight."

Todd's face went pale. Lindsay pregnant? Why hadn't she told him? He stared at the doctor blankly.

"I don't want to scare you, but your wife can't afford to take any more chances. Just being pregnant at her age is risky enough." The doctor outlined the regime Lindsay would have to follow for the next seven months to carry the baby safely to term. "Complete bed rest. It's going to be hard on both of you, but you've got to keep her in a time capsule—no emotional or physical disturbances. That means no visitors, no newspapers, no television. And, of course," he added, giving Todd a sympathetic pat on the shoulder, "sexual contact is out of the question."

Todd followed the doctor to the door. "Can I see her?"

"She needs to rest—and so do you. You can take her home in the morning."

It was six A.M. when Lindsay awoke. Todd was seated beside her bed.

"Why are you here?" she whispered. Hadn't the doctor told him she was having a baby? Didn't he realize he had no part in what was happening to her?

"I'm taking you home. I'm going to take care of you—and the baby." Then, as he kissed her gently on the forehead, he repeated the doctor's injunction that they had to be extremely careful. But everything was going to be fine, he assured her. He would move into the apartment with her, sleep in the room she now used as her study.

"Just get me home, Todd. I'll do the rest. This has nothing to do with you."

"Nothing to do with me?" He took her hand, unconsciously stroking the finger on which John Henry had once placed a ring. "Darling, you're having my baby."

Lindsay closed her eyes to keep him from seeing the tears. His baby! Well, of course. What else would he think? He probably even thought that was why she had been avoiding him—to keep him from feeling obligated. How could she tell him the truth? And yet how could she not?

"I'm so tired," she murmured, not wanting to think about any of it. "Please just take me home."

Once Lindsay was resting comfortably in her apartment, Todd called the employment agency that had provided him with a cleaning woman when he first moved into the city after his divorce. He now said that his wife was expecting their first child and the doctor had ordered her to stay in bed. Someone needed to be with her while he was at work. No special training was necessary, he just wanted a quiet, sympathetic woman who would respond when needed and stay out of sight otherwise. The woman on the other end of the phone sounded dubious. "Who wouldn't want someone like that? But I'm afraid she may be a bit hard to find. All our applicants are somewhat overqualified for what you have in mind." However, she promised to come up with at least a couple of candidates for him to interview the next day.

That night as Todd cleared the remains of a delicatessen dinner from a table beside Lindsay's bed, she tried to explain that she had never planned to get pregnant.

He embraced her gently and assured her that he was delighted —and he wanted the baby as much as she did. Even if she couldn't be his wife, she would be the mother of his child—and that was more than he had hoped.

"Todd, it's not yours," she said finally.

"What do you mean? Who? Is there someone else?"

"You know better. You've been following me for the past two months, haven't you? There's been no one but you. Until the rape." She stopped abruptly. Todd stared at her, refusing to comprehend.

"Are you saying he's the father? The man who raped you?" Lindsay nodded.

"What makes you think that? That was one time only. Of course it's my child."

Patiently, painfully, Lindsay explained. With Todd she always made sure she was protected. On the day of the rape she wasn't expecting to be with anyone. Then she revealed the promise she had made her assailant—to have his baby. She still believed the promise had saved her life.

"Why do you have to make it so goddamned hard to love you?" Todd asked.

Lindsay had no answer. All she knew was that she had tried to make it easy for him in the beginning by not allowing him to feel bound to her as she felt bound to John Henry. But the day of the rape she saw that he was as vulnerable as any husband to what she had been through. She had spared him nothing—and had cost him the chance to have a family with someone else. No limited commitment was possible between them. It never had been. So she had to do what she had not been strong enough to do in the beginning, or even last night: set him free forever before he became permanently entangled in lives that had no moral or legal connection with his.

But all she said was that she needed to be alone. The doctor had told her to avoid emotional as well as physical exertion. She wanted Todd to go home—to his own apartment. In fact she felt it would be better if they didn't see each other again.

"Is that what you really want? To do it all alone? To have sole responsibility for an invalid husband and a child whose father was capable of killing you?"

"It's not what I want—it's what I've been given," she replied quietly. "Please go now, Todd. I'm very tired, I need to sleep."

He left the employment agency's number by her bedside telephone and told her to call them in the morning. He was sure they would be able to find someone to look after her, and he knew Lindsay would be more comfortable if she were allowed to pay for services rendered. He promised he would not call her again. If she needed him, she knew where to reach him. But a week later when Lindsay called his apartment after midnight, there was no answer.

Eighteen

Todd decided to walk back to his apartment through Central Park, even though it had been dark for several hours and he knew it was dangerous. But tonight a physical attack would be an act of mercy, punishing him for leaving Lindsay and obliterating from his mind at least momentarily the cruel joke life had played on him. He had always wanted a child—and now the woman he loved was pregnant but he had no part in it.

He walked slowly, purposelessly, along the dark path, prepared to offer himself as a willing accomplice to the first assailant. However, the only violence he encountered were the dark thoughts stirring ominously inside his head. He reached his apartment unharmed—but uncertain of the value of his life if Lindsay were not part of it. And yet he also wondered if he would ever be capable of accepting a child conceived in terror—especially knowing it had usurped the place of one he would so eagerly have fathered out of love.

For a second night he found himself unable to sleep. Only twenty-four hours earlier Lindsay had surrendered to him with a passion he had never known. It was the only time he had ever felt he possessed her completely—and yet within hours he had lost her, perhaps forever. Even if she were to become part of his life again, she would never belong to him as she had the night before. Now there would always be another life between them.

The memory of the previous night awoke in him such longing as he lay in the darkness that he finally responded with angry defiance, furious at what Lindsay had denied him—fertile ground for the seed he was forced to waste now on sheets still blood-stained from the aborted passion of the previous evening. He felt like a confused adolescent again—his body ravaged by an uncontrollable urge that had no place or function in his waking life. Spent and despairing, he climbed out of the bed that without Lindsay could offer no comfort or refuge and slowly dressed. He walked the fifty blocks to Penn Station and still had to wait several hours in the predawn darkness for the first train to Long Island.

He walked from the suburban station at Pond Crossing to the tree-lined park whose flat stone markers lay unnoticed in the short, cropped grass glistening with early morning frost. Todd was beginning to succumb to a fatigue so pervasive it seemed to be rooted in the marrow of his bones like an incurable cancer. He leaned against a tree for support while he stared at the three small markers that represented his failure to perpetuate himself —still in his mind the principal attainment to which any man could aspire. Finally he knelt and, his eyes blinded with tears, traced with his fingertips names and dates engraved on each marker.

The first had only the family name—Newman—and a single date. For Todd's first child, an unnamed daughter stillborn at six months, birth and death had arrived together. In an awesome illustration of divine omnipotence, God had given and taken away in a solitary gesture. The other two markers each bore a full name and two dates showing the brief life-spans they com-memorated—William White Newman, who lived twenty-four hours, and Mary Anderson Newman, dead at the age of two months.

Todd had bought the plot the day his first child was born dead, while his wife was still recovering in her hospital room.

"Claire," he thought now, touching the family name on the marker. That was what he had wanted to name her. Claire. In memory of his grandmother, whose luminous presence had so enlivened and enriched his lonely childhood. But his wife had refused to name a child who had never been alive in her presence. It would make everything so much harder to bear, she had said, and Todd, anxious to comfort her in any way within his power, had quickly agreed. But now he knew he had been wrong. A person had existed, however briefly, and in the overwhelming context of eternity her life was as important as that of her most aged neighbor in the cemetery.

Two years later, when their first son's heart failed after only twenty-four hours, Todd did not consult his wife before ordering the marker engraved with the name they had chosen; she did not accompany him to the service and so did not see the two small graves until she and Todd brought their two-month-old daughter to join her brother and sister. Trying to comfort his wife that day, Todd revealed that he had bought two adjoining plots for the two of them, so that their children would not be alone. "I'm never coming back here again," she said, and sat alone in the limousine while Todd stood helplessly beside the minister, listen-ing to him pray.

This was the first time Todd had been back since that day so many years ago. Now he looked at the two adjoining plots and wondered who would occupy them. At that moment he felt no ties with anyone, dead or alive. He leaned against the tree and closed his eyes.

When he awoke, it was afternoon. He was stretched out on the grass, and the caretaker was shaking his shoulder, asking if he was all right. He got slowly to his feet. The sun was shining brightly but the air was cold and his clothes were damp from the morning dew. He began to shiver as he asked the caretaker if he could use his phone to call a taxi.

When the driver asked where he wanted to go, he had no answer. He couldn't face the train ride back into the city. He couldn't sleep in his apartment without thinking of Lindsay. Finally, after the meter had been ticking for several minutes, he managed to reply, "Los Angeles. I mean the airport—Kennedy."

Nineteen

Mrs. Blayne sat at the counter of the coffee shop, staring at the apartment building across the street. She counted up to the eighth floor, trying to see if anybody was looking out a window, waiting for her. She glanced at her watch. Still another fifteen minutes before her appointment.

She paid her bill and went to the restroom. When she emerged, she resolutely pulled on her white gloves and headed for the door. She stood for a moment outside the building and looked at her watch again. Ten minutes to go. She thought of her friend Georgia and laughed. The last time Georgia had taken her shopping, twelve minutes were left on the parking meter when they returned to her car with their packages. Georgia sat at the wheel of the car with her hands folded, saying she'd paid for another twelve minutes of parking and the city wasn't going to cheat her out of a minute of it.

But Mrs. Blayne had never been one for wasting time. If she

lost the job because she was early, then it wasn't the right job for her anyway.

She started to remove her gloves to open the door of the building. She hadn't worn them since the funeral. She wondered if women still wore gloves to church—or anywhere. No one she'd passed on the street since she left the bus terminal had been wearing gloves. Or a hat. Maybe she should remove her hat, too. But what would she do with it?

Suddenly the doorman was opening the door for her. When she explained why she was there, he nodded and showed her to the elevator. As the elevator door opened, she turned to thank him, but to her surprise he got in with her.

She and her husband used to come into the city on special occasions but she had never known anyone who actually lived there. The inside of an East Side apartment building was as alien to her as it would have been to someone raised in the Midwest. All she knew was what she'd seen in the movies. But she'd never seen a doorman go up an elevator and unlock the front door of an apartment.

"She's expecting you," he said. "Straight down the hall and into the bedroom."

"You're early," Lindsay smiled, indicating a chair opposite the bed. "I like that." She looked appraisingly at Mrs. Blayne. What she saw was a middle-aged woman. (Funny, Lindsay thought, she would never have used that phrase to describe herself and yet in terms of chronological age, she and the tired-looking woman nervously rolling her white gloves into a ball were probably contemporaries.)

Lindsay really didn't know what kind of questions to ask. She had never had to hire someone whose only function was to make her comfortable, to do anything she asked and even be expected to anticipate her needs. So she asked Mrs. Blayne what it was about the job that interested her.

For Mrs. Blayne the answer was simple. She had used up the money from the insurance policy her husband left and would not be eligible to collect his social security benefits until she was sixty-five. She had tried to find a job in Nutley, New Jersey, where she had lived all her married life but, apparently unqualified for anything that paid a decent salary, decided on the advice of a friend to see if she'd have better luck in the city. After all, she shrugged, a lot of women in poor countries have to leave home to make a living, often turning over their young children to relatives to raise, not seeing them for years at a time. Mrs. Blayne considered herself fortunate. Her children were grown with families of their own; they no longer needed her and she prided herself on not yet needing them. All she would be leaving behind was a house—and it was just across the river.

"Did the agency tell you how much this job pays?" Lindsay asked.

"Two hundred dollars a week."

"But that's to be on call twenty-four hours a day. Seven days a week. No time off guaranteed—just an hour or two whenever I can spare you. You'll have to do all the cleaning, all the cooking, all the errands, anything else that needs doing. I don't think two hundred a week is enough—but it's all I can afford."

"I don't know anything about salaries," Mrs. Blayne admitted. "I've never had a job. All I know is what you're asking me to do is what I did when I was married and I never earned anything."

"Make it two hundred and fifty a week," Lindsay said. "And of course room and board. When can you start?"

"I'll have to go home and pack a suitcase, but I can be back in time to fix dinner," Mrs. Blayne said, looking at her watch and calculating quickly.

Lindsay extended her hand. Instead of shaking it, Mrs. Blayne held it for a moment. "I never had a daughter," she said. "It grieved me when the boys were young. I wanted a little girl so bad. But now that they're grown, I don't mind anymore. It breaks my heart to see little girls grow up."

CHAPTER

Twenty

Todd had never been to Los Angeles, but the wedding invitation had said the Bel-Air Hotel, so when he landed at Los Angeles International he told the taxi driver that was where he wanted to go. (Los Angeles International Airport—LAX—Todd laughed at the pun and wondered how many out-of-towners had enjoyed it before he had.) As they drove along Sunset Boulevard, he marveled at the passing landscape. Everything he had read or heard about southern California had reinforced the image of an arid desert land with cities built on shifting sands.

He had always imagined Los Angeles as a flat horizon broken only by an occasional palm tree rising to chastise a smog-filled sky, but this image had no relation to the luxuriant reality the city was presenting to his astonished eyes. There was nothing flat about the landscape. It was as varied in its contours as the reclining body of a woman whose endless curves confirm her appetite for life. Sunset Boulevard never insisted on its right to traverse the shortest distance between two points but curved in a leisurely caress around the base of the foothills that gave such variety to the setting. No two homes along their route were alike. Tree-guarded Spanish haciendas adjoined Tudor mansions fronted by formal English gardens. If God wanted to hold the whole world in his hands, Todd thought to himself, all he would have to do is reach for Los Angeles.

When he left New York, the sky had been cold and gray, the air icy with rain threatening to turn into sleet by dark. But the sun was shining in Los Angeles and the air so fragrant Todd had the impression he had moved ahead his calendar while turning back his watch.

The excuse Todd had seized for his trip was a family wedding involving the daughter of one of the cousins who had crowded his childhood Sundays. He had sent an expensive present along with his regrets in response to the invitation, but standing alone in the cemetery that morning, he had been overwhelmed by the need to renew family ties—and at the same time flee further thought of Lindsay.

By the time the taxi turned into the West Gate of Bel-Air, the landscape that had at first delighted Todd had begun to repel him with its unrestrained abundance. Everywhere he looked, the world seemed to be reproducing. The life force to which he had lost Lindsay reappeared in new and exuberant forms. Stone walls, wooden fences, clipped hedges here and there, suggested a civilizing semblance of control over nature's reckless and profligate pace, but Todd had the feeling that the first time a gardener failed to make his scheduled rounds, these great estates would be reclaimed by the primeval forest from which they had been forcibly delivered. Like wild animals raised in captivity who carry within them the savage instincts of their untamed ancestors, these verdant acres of land contained forces of nature capable at any moment of breaking through the restraining bonds their owners only imagined they had erected. It seemed to Todd that nature was imposing her will everywhere he turned—from the seed implanted by an act of violence inside the womb of the woman he loved to the ivy thrusting its way so tenaciously through a stone wall that several stones had been forcibly displaced and now lay in defeat along the side of the road.

"Where are we?" Todd asked, wondering if the taxi driver had forgotten his destination. Surely no commercial hostelry could be hidden in this towering forest.

"The Bel-Air Hotel," announced the driver, pulling to a stop in front of a bridge that appeared to disbelieving New York eyes to lead directly into the Garden of Eden. Todd only regretted that he had not brought with him the innocence necessary to enjoy it. His flight into exile, undertaken in despair and confusion in the face of knowledge he never sought, seemed to be leading him back into the garden from which Adam had been banished. As he crossed the bridge to the hotel, two swans gliding under it turned back to stare. Todd felt naked—and abandoned not only by God but by the woman with whom he had hoped to share the joys and sorrows of Eden.

However, once inside the lobby he began to relax. A couch and chairs were comfortably grouped around a woodburning fire. Except for a front desk that blended unobtrusively into the setting, it could have been a living room on Long Island.

Todd explained that he had arrived early—and unexpectedly— for a wedding scheduled to take place that weekend. No, he was not a member of the wedding party and it was not necessary for his room to be located near them. In fact, he would prefer privacy.

It was not until the desk clerk rang for a bellhop that Todd realized he had arrived conspicuously unencumbered. He had called his office from the airport to say there had been a death in the family, and he would be out of town for the rest of the week, but until now he had not concerned himself with luggage. Except for the raincoat he was carrying over his arm, he had nothing to hand the bellhop.

"There was a mix-up at the airport," he suddenly heard himself explaining. "My suitcase is arriving on a later flight. I hope," he added with a laugh. The bellhop responded with an understanding grin—in gratitude for which Todd decided to give him a five-dollar tip.

He led Todd through a garden and up a flight of stairs to a small corner room that could be quaintly described as a garret. It reminded Todd of guest rooms he had occupied on the weekends following his divorce when he would take refuge with married friends until he could escape again to his office on Monday morning.

Suddenly the sleep that had eluded him until that morning on the grass seemed within his reach again. All he wanted was oblivion. He took off his shoes, loosened his belt and tie, and fell immediately and soundly asleep.

It was dark and quiet when he awoke and the scent of night-blooming jasmine filled his room. He felt rested and at peace for the first time in months—since the day Lindsay told him she had been raped. He was also, to his surprise, hungry. He washed quickly and went to the dining room, reacting with pleasure to the blossom-proud garden he had to cross to get there.

A waiter was serving escargots to a woman seated alone. Todd savored the aroma of garlic, enjoying his dinner in advance. But the maître d' approached and told him regretfully that the dining room was closed. Then an elderly couple rose to leave and he realized that the solitary diner at the booth just to the right of where he stood was the only customer left in the room. However, she clearly had several courses to go.

"I don't have to have a complete dinner," Todd explained, glancing at the woman then looking away, embarrassed, as she met his gaze with an open smile. "Soup or a salad would be fine," he continued, waiting for the maître d' to react. "I just got in from New York, and I don't have a car. If I can't get something to eat here, I don't know how I'll make it through the night."

He realized in midsentence that the maître d' was neither moved by nor even interested in his plight, but the woman was giving him her full attention.

"I'm sorry, sir," the maître d' began—but was interrupted by a smiling invitation from the next table.

"Would you like to join me?" the solitary diner asked.

"I'm sorry, madame, we can take no more orders," the maître d' interrupted.

"I understand. I'm offering to share," she explained quickly. "I've ordered more than I can possibly eat."

At another time in his life Todd might not have responded to such a spontaneous invitation, but now he accepted gratefully and slid into the booth beside her, oblivious to a blatant look of disapproval from the maître d' as he turned his back on them.

Briskly the woman—who suggested that they wait until after dinner for introductions or explanations—summoned a waiter and requested a second place setting, including another small fork for the escargots, only two of which had been touched.

"I hope you like steak au poivre," she said as Todd took a shell from her plate.

"It's what I would have ordered—if I'd been allowed to order," he replied.

"My husband thinks it's a criminal offense to ruin a good steak with all that pepper. So I never order it when I'm with him."

Todd realized that her injunction against introductions and explanations, designed to keep him at an impersonal distance, apparently did not apply to her. Whether she was doing it consciously or not, his new dinner partner had already established her husband, a man of strong if restricted tastes, as a silent third at their table.

Todd was grateful for the intrusion and the boundaries it established. They allowed him to concentrate completely on the moment and the meal at hand. He could not remember when he had been so hungry—for food or companionship—and now he was being offered both in abundance.

He ate all of the remaining escargots and when the steak was brought to the table and flamed in cognac, his hostess insisted it be placed in front of her guest. He asked the waiter to bring another plate so the steak could be divided, but she rescinded the order with a smile, insisting that her appetite was fully assuaged by the pleasure of watching him enjoy what she had ordered.

When salad was served after the main course, a refinement he would not have expected to encounter west of the Hudson River, he asked his new friend where she was from.

"I've lived in Los Angeles all my life," she laughed.

"Then you're not a guest at the hotel?" he asked in some confusion.

"Oh yes. I arrived yesterday." She hesitated for a beat before continuing. "I thought once our children were grown my husband would start taking me with him when he traveled. But he didn't, so I decided to travel on my own. However, this is as far from home as I've had the courage to go. Last night I ordered room service—but tonight I decided to see if I could handle eating alone in public."

"From the way you took charge, I assumed you'd been doing it all your life," Todd smiled.

"It turns out I'm very good at it," she laughed, signaling the waiter. "Could we order dessert?" she asked, ignoring the fact that he had already totaled the bill in anticipation of their imminent departure. "What would you like?" She turned to Todd with a smile as the waiter reluctantly handed them menus open to the dessert selection.

"You decide. I like your taste," he smiled agreeably, not wanting to inject his personality or opinion into an evening that was proceeding so pleasantly without his guidance.

"I think we can both order dessert, don't you," she said cheerfully to the waiter, "since we accommodated the chef by sharing our main course." It was a statement, not a question, to which the waiter assented by taking their orders without comment.

While she was finishing her flan, Todd excused himself and arranged with the maître d' to have the dinner check billed to his room, at the same time pressing a twenty-dollar bill against his palm. In return the maître d' seemed happy to provide the name and room number of his dinner partner. Then Todd crossed quickly to the front desk and ordered a dozen red roses to be delivered to her room the next day. He returned to the dining room as the waiter was explaining that the bill had already been paid. When she protested, Todd suggested she buy him a night-cap.

"But you're on New York time. You must be tired."

"Not at all," he insisted then introduced himself.

"I'm Laura Scott," she smiled, placing her hand on his arm as they left the dining room. Walking arm in arm through the garden, Todd sensed for the first time the generous corporeality of his dinner companion. Seated in the booth beside her, he had thought her attractive and unusually open, but no different in appearance from any other well-tended woman of her station in life. Her clothes were elegant mainly by virtue of being under-stated. She wore a silk blouse open at the neck and restrained at the waist by a crushed leather belt. A hip-length embroidered vest made everything it covered a matter of conjecture. To the casual observer she would not have appeared any more substantial in a physical sense than an average customer browsing through the boutiques of Beverly Hills. Any excess pounds or inches were cleverly disguised by the high-priced garments designed for that purpose. But a woman is naked to the touch, and when Todd slid his arm around her waist, a more fully fleshed form was transmit-ted to his imagination.

"I hope you don't think I make a habit of picking up men in restaurants," she said, lightly stroking the hand at her waist with her fingertips.

"I'm sure you do nothing out of habit," he answered.

"I used to go to Tecate with my women friends every time my husband left town," she confided as they settled in a booth at the hotel bar.

"Tecate?"

"That's Californian for losing weight," she confessed. "He thinks I'm there this week, in fact."

"But you checked in here instead?"

"I was married in the garden here—to my first husband," she explained, slowly sipping her brandy. "We spent our first night here—and came back every year on our anniversary." She paused, signaling the waiter to bring another round of drinks. "Are you married?" she asked suddenly.

"Divorced."

"I'm sorry," Laura responded, silently grateful that she had lost Brad through death, not divorce. At least she was allowed to go on loving him. It was good to be able to mention him to someone. Paul refused to discuss the past. She wondered if Todd hated his ex-wife as much as Paul hated Anne. But when she attempted to question Todd about his life, he said he had come to California to get away from it.

"Do you think that's possible?" she wondered aloud.

"Only if you find someone generous enough to let you into their life," he replied, kissing her gently. "Thank you for dinner."

They had reached her room. He took her key and turned it in the lock.

"Don't leave me," she whispered, suddenly putting her arms around his neck.

Her need aroused him more than the abandon with which she took him into her bed. She welcomed and encouraged and insisted until at last the solitude in which all his emotions had been imprisoned since leaving Lindsay was eased.

"Stay with me," she said sleepily when he started to get out of bed. He lay beside her again, brushing a lock of hair from her face. He had not realized until now how angry he was at Lindsay for withholding so much of her life from him.

And yet when he finally closed his eyes and fell asleep, it was Lindsay's voice he heard inside his head continuing to plead, "Stay with me, stay with me, stay with me." When he awoke the next morning, his arms were encircling the pliant form nestled contentedly against his chest, preventing her escape.

Twenty-one

"If we want room service, we have to order now," Laura murmured sleepily as Todd got out of bed.

"I'll get dressed so I can answer the door," he said, looking for his tie.

"No," Laura insisted. "The whole point of room service is that you don't have to get dressed."

"Then you can answer the door," Todd replied. "I'll be in the shower."

She smiled and sent a kiss in his direction, then rolled over and reached for her reading glasses to give serious study to the breakfast menu.

She surprised him in the shower. "I ordered enough to keep them busy for at least half an hour," she said, reaching for a tube he thought was shampoo and lathering his back.

"What is that?" he asked curiously as an herbal fragrance filled the room.

"Shower gel. I haven't used soap in years," she said, moving around to face him and placing his hands on her waist so they would not interfere with what she was doing.

They were just stepping out of the shower when there was a knock at the door. Laura wrinkled her nose in a playful show of disgust at the unexpected promptness with which room service had responded to her order, then quickly grabbed a terrycloth robe hanging on the bathroom door. "Stay here," she cautioned. "I'll call you as soon as they've gone. Just don't make the mistake of getting dressed."

Over a lavish breakfast—a mixed grill, fresh fruit platter, blueberry muffins—Laura described in laughing detail the limited menus she would be facing if she were where her husband thought she was.

Later, after they had rolled the breakfast table into the corridor and put the "Do not disturb" sign back on the door, she described a typical day at Tecate—the jogging, the exercises, the saunas. "But the worst time is at night," she said, sitting comfortably astride his buttocks while she massaged his shoulders with a sweet-scented lotion. "There is absolutely *nothing* to look forward to after dinner." She rolled over and lay beside him. His eyes were closed and only the faint smile on his lips suggested he might be listening.

"All those women spending all those days depriving themselves of food and sex just to stay attractive for husbands who remain comfortably behind at home cheating on them," she sighed, immediately regretting the edge of bitterness creeping into her voice. She glanced quickly at Todd and was relieved to see that he was asleep. She continued to watch him, caressing him with her eyes, as if that were occupation enough for a morning. It had been a long time since she had lain in bed beside a man who seemed to have no place to go. Her husband got up earlier on weekends to play tennis than he did during the week to go to work. He would come home to find her still asleep, shed his sweaty tennis clothes, and take her quickly in an athletic afterglow on his way to the shower. He was usually out of the house again before she was fully awake.

She stroked Todd's long, lean body and admired its uniform whiteness. Paul looked faintly ridiculous naked, with clearly outlined areas of white skin calling attention to the absence of shorts and socks. Todd by contrast appeared completely comfortable in his unmuscled, untanned body. He rolled over with a sigh that seemed to release the last of the tension he had brought with him in place of luggage and lay sprawled on his back, as vulnerable and trusting as a still-innocent Adam.

Laura looked at him lovingly, longing to touch him but grateful that at last he seemed able to sleep. The previous night he had kept her awake with an insistence that seemed more a way of resisting surrender to the tyranny of a dream than a desire to possess or even pleasure her. She covered his hand with hers and closed her eyes.

They were awakened by a persistent knocking. Laura hurried to the door, angry at the sudden guilt the sound provoked in her.

"Who is it?" she demanded.

"Housekeeper," a peremptory voice replied. "Do you want your room made up or don't you?"

By this time Todd was out of bed and into his trousers. He nodded hastily to indicate acquiescence.

Laura sighed. Whatever spell leisure and anonymity had been able to cast in that room from the previous midnight until now had been broken. She looked at her watch, determined to rally a tone of authority to equal that of the paid employee standing on the other side of the door, and ordered crisply, "Come back in half an hour."

When Todd emerged from the bathroom fully dressed in his business suit, she braced herself for the good-bye she knew was inevitable. Until now her life had always proceeded on course, with clearly established conventions of behavior at every turn— daughter, student, wife, young widow, sophisticated matron with grown children and frequently absent husband. This was the first interlude she had ever had, and though she knew brevity was inherent in the nature of an interlude, she was not ready for it to end. It was as if she were taking time out from a game she had no choice but to keep playing—and yet the clock continued to tick. If only she could stop it.

"Well, good-bye," she said, extending her hand.

"Are you going home today?" he asked, clasping it in both of his.

"Oh, no," she answered quickly. "My husband won't be back till Sunday night. I'm staying till then." She hesitated briefly before asking what she hoped sounded like a casual afterthought, "What about you?"

"Actually I'm here for a wedding Sunday morning." He paused, then smiled in answer to her unasked question. "Would you go with me?"

"This is the only place in the world for a wedding," she said, though not really to him. "But I don't have anything to wear, I mean not with me. And I don't want to go home."

"I didn't even bring a suitcase," Todd replied. He then suggested that Laura take him shopping—to buy clothes for the wedding and any other occasions likely to occur before Sunday. He suspected from the ease with which she had ordered dinner and then breakfast that she was more comfortable with clerks than he. She admitted she loved to shop and he looked forward to watching her in action. Lindsay never wanted to waste any of their weekend hours together shopping nor did she display any enthusiasm for things he tried to buy her, so except for the places he took her and the necessities he bought for himself, he had neither the incentive nor the occasion to spend the money he earned.

At a Beverly Hills men's store Laura encouraged him to buy a suede jacket that cost more than the monthly rent on his New York apartment, then found cord pants to go with it and a long-sleeved Italian knit shirt. She insisted he let the sales clerk wrap the dark business suit, white shirt, and tie he had been wearing since he arrived and change into what he had just bought.

When it came time for her to buy an outfit to wear to the wedding, Laura bypassed the fashionable boutiques that served wine to customers in the hope of relaxing inhibitions and standards of judgment. She told Todd she would never be thin enough or rich enough to feel comfortable in those places and took him down the street to Neiman-Marcus, where the clerks were too busy to hover appraisingly over potential customers. Relaxing in the atmosphere of inattention, Laura found three outfits that she liked on the rack—one on sale for half price. If she had been shopping alone, which was her habit (friends distracted her and her husband didn't care what she wore as long as she didn't look different from other people), she would have bought the sale dress simply for the value it represented and returned the other two outfits to the rack. But when she tried them on for Todd, he liked all three and paid for them while she was getting dressed—so she couldn't change her mind and return them, he said over lunch.

Laura and Todd were together until the morning of the wedding. Then, even though they stood side by side through the ceremony, the words they heard reclaimed them for their absent partners. Though they had never exchanged vows of any kind, Todd knew he had to return to Lindsay—on whatever terms she would allow him to live with her.

Laura insisted on driving Todd to the airport. The sun had shone for the outdoor wedding but as they drove west toward the ocean, the sky seemed to be mustering sinister gray clouds to prevent any possible invasion of the air. By the time they reached the airport the fog was so thick that Laura knew from past experience what Todd did not learn until he reached the check-in counter. The airport was fogged in until morning.

"If you can't get out, my husband won't be able to get in," Laura said. "So it seems pointless to say good-bye."

She asked if he had urgent reasons for returning to New York.

"Urgent? No."

"Good."

"Where are we going?" he asked as Laura moved her car into the flowing stream of traffic. "Back to the hotel?"

She shook her head. "I think," she said, heading north on the San Diego Freeway, "we should go somewhere neither of us has ever been before."

CHAPTER

Twenty-two

At first Lindsay was not sure how she would react to the constant presence of another person in her life. It had been so long since she had lived with anyone—a husband or even a roommate.

She thought of a "Give and Take" she had done a few years back: on a couple whose careers required them to live in separate states and take turns commuting to be together. Lindsay's angle, of course, was the strain physical separation imposed on their marriage. To her surprise each of them privately—and on the condition that she not reveal the conversation to the other—confessed that they were not sure the marriage would survive if they had to share a roof. "My married women friends ask me how I learned to live alone," the wife said. "And I want to ask them how they learned to live with someone. Living alone is elementary. It's other people who complicate your life." Lindsay couldn't help agreeing but when she showed Todd the article, he refused to read it, saying it sounded too much like their own arrangement and hardly met his definition of marriage.

But after Mrs. Blayne had been with her a week, Lindsay began to depend on her unquestioning compliance and to understand why so many men continued to cherish the time-honored concept of marriage—and to feel threatened by anyone who wanted to change it. It was wonderful having someone around whose only purpose was to please her, someone who expected nothing in return except money.

The day she hired Mrs. Blayne, Lindsay had called the office and requested a year's leave of absence, saying an opportunity had arisen unexpectedly to research a book she had long been interested in writing. There was a lot of travel involved, so they should not expect to hear from her or try to contact her for the next twelve months; however, she promised to send a detailed memo before she left outlining the work necessary to complete her current projects. She refused to give any details when pressed to reveal the subject of the book, thus offering irrefutable proof of its commercial potential if not its literary importance. Lindsay made it clear that if there was any objection to the unpaid leave, she was prepared to resign permanently from the magazine. To this her former boss, now editor in chief, replied that his only concession to her absence would be to change her title to "contributing editor" on the masthead. He said her salary would continue—to consider it an option on first serial rights to the book.

"But you don't even know what the book's about," she protested.

"Doesn't matter. You have an instinct for writing what people want to read. My opinion is irrelevant."

"Not to me," she said. "I'm going to miss you."

However, she did not miss leaving her apartment every day, knowing the father of her child was out there somewhere watching her. She welcomed the emotional and physical isolation to which she had been sentenced as gratefully as an aging courtesan retreats to a cloister—and surrendered completely to the experience at hand.

The rape had tested to the extreme her ability to separate what the body was experiencing from what the mind could acknowledge. "This is not happening to me—not to the me that matters," she remembered thinking to herself over and over that morning. But what was happening to her now as a result of that violation was affecting every cell of her being.

All the thoughts she could no longer speak aloud to another person she could communicate without words to her unborn child. Flesh and spirit—split asunder in an act of violence—were joyfully reunited in a shared purpose that seemed reason enough to awake each morning.

Even the simplest act—washing her face, eating breakfast, reading a book—seemed fraught with significance, and Lindsay understood finally what her mother had been trying to tell her when she was thirteen and her father had refused to take her with him to a construction site. "Men are doers. They have to have a product to prove their right to exist. Women are content just to be part of the process."

Lindsay had cried that it wasn't true—and accused her mother of being afraid of life, afraid of testing her abilities, of taking chances. "You never did anything with your life but have me," she had screamed. "You never even risked getting pregnant again. I had to grow up alone—an only child. Daddy was my only friend in this house. You were jealous when he took me with him to work. It's your fault he left me at home today, isn't it?"

Her mother had stared at her and said finally, "I love you, Lindsay, more than you'll ever know." She held out her arms, but Lindsay had turned her back and run into her room, pushing her bed against the door so that her mother couldn't enter. She lay there sobbing, waiting for her mother to come and discover that the door was blocked. But her mother never came, and Lindsay fell asleep waiting.

She awoke to the sensation of her bed being pushed across the room as the door slammed against it and her father entered. He appeared so burdened with grief when he sat on the bed beside her that Lindsay's first instinct was to console him. But something in his manner—like an unexploded bomb embedded in the facade of a familiar landmark—prevented her from touching him.

Then he said in a voice that sounded as if it were coming from someone she had never met, "Your mother says you're too old to spank, but this is between you and me. Turn over."

His voice was cold and unemotional. Lindsay had never been so frightened in her life. She was too terrified to cry. Besides, her heart was pounding so loudly she was convinced it would have obliterated any noise coming out of her throat.

"Pull down your underpants," he ordered, taking off his belt. "I want this to hurt. Your mother is right. You are too old to spank. I'm not going to touch you. That's why I'm using a belt. I want you to remember this for the rest of your life."

Lindsay bit her lips until they bled. She was determined not to cry, not to let him see or hear how much he was hurting her. Strangely enough, she had stopped being frightened once she felt the belt across her buttocks. Once she realized that this was it, this was the worst that could happen to her, anger replaced fear, making her strong and defiant.

"You're not getting to me, you can't touch the real me," she remembered thinking then, and it was only now, lying in bed to save the life of her unborn child, that she realized she had reacted exactly the same way to the rape—terror followed by defiance and determination to guard her essential self intact and finally, at last, acceptance.

She continued to lie facedown on her bed, her buttocks exposed in reproach, as her father buckled his belt. She pressed her pillow against her mouth to prevent any sound from escaping and kept her eyes shut, waiting for the sound of the door closing to indicate that her father had left the room and it was safe to release her emotions. But there was only silence.

Suddenly she felt a hand on her back gently pulling down her

skirt to cover her bare buttocks and thighs. Trembling uncontrol-
lably at the touch, she tried to force the pillow down her throat
to stop the tidal wave of sobs rising from her chest. Then she was
choking and her father was holding her against his chest, her head
resting on his shoulder, as if she were a baby beset by anxieties
too enormous for one tiny body to contain.

Her sobs gradually subsided as he stroked her back. Then, still
not facing her, his head lightly touching hers as it rested against
his shoulder, he described the agony her mother had gone
through to have her.

Her doctor had told her in the first year of their marriage that
she would be risking her life if she tried to have a child—her pelvis
was too small—but she was determined and ignored her husband's
pleas that they adopt instead. By the time she was five months
pregnant, her physical discomfort was so intense she could only
find relief on her hands and knees. For the next four months she
moved around the house like a clumsy, four-legged creature,
sleeping on the rug with a pillow under her head and another
supporting her swollen stomach, waking every half hour to move
around in an attempt to keep her muscles from cramping.

When Lindsay was two years old, her mother wanted to have
another baby, but her father forbade it by the only means within
his power—a vasectomy.

Still stroking Lindsay's back as she lay weeping silent tears
against his shoulder, he told her in a voice whose tenderness
compelled obedience more readily than the corporal punishment
which had preceded it that she would answer to him if she ever
again accused her mother of having done nothing with her life.

"All I do is change the landscape," he said. "Nothing I've done
with my life seems very significant compared to what your
mother has accomplished. She willed into being a life that no one
else, including me, thought had the right to exist. You owe your
life to her, Lindsay."

"Why didn't she ever tell me?" Lindsay cried, looking at her
father for the first time since he had come into her room.

"She didn't want you to be afraid . . ." he hesitated briefly as if summoning up the courage to continue.

"Afraid?"

"Of being a woman. Promise me you'll never tell her that you know."

In response Lindsay had solemnly taken her father's hand and guided his finger in an X across her heart. Trying to show him without words that she understood and forgave him everything, she continued to hold his hand against her heart. After a moment, he withdrew it uncomfortably and hurried from the room.

At the time Lindsay had thought he was embarrassed by the violence of the emotions he had displayed, for he prided himself on being a rational man and had always abided by what he considered a cardinal rule of childraising, "Never discipline a child in anger." This was the first and only time Lindsay could remember feeling any passion in the punishment he was administering and also the first and only time she forgave him before he left the room.

But suddenly now, her stomach churning in an upheaval that had no physical connection with the fetus taking shape inside her, Lindsay understood why her father had exited so abruptly that day. It wasn't his emotions that had embarrassed him as she pressed his hand against her beating heart in a pledge never to share or openly acknowledge the perils of being a woman, it was the awareness of her budding breasts beneath his hand. Did he find himself responding to her as a woman, Lindsay wondered? Slowly she began to caress her now ripening breasts and tried to imagine what life was going to be like for her baby without a father.

She had a husband in name and had paid dearly for the right to pass that name on to her child. She carried inside her like a sharp instrument swallowed by accident the accusation Todd had attributed to Craig Sanborn: "You have kept him alive but what makes you think that has been an act of mercy?"

She lay in her bed brooding. For the first time in almost twenty years of marriage, she had allowed over a week to pass without seeing or speaking to John Henry. The doctor's order confining her to bed until the baby was born had given her a valid excuse for not going to visit him. Thus she could no longer be held accountable for the fact that he was still alive. She would never have been capable of doing what his doctor had advised—forgetting him, or at least making him a less important part of her life —without a larger cause to claim her.

Sometimes she wondered why this child, conceived in violence, seemed to have such an inalienable claim to life when she had been so determined to deny the same right to the legitimate issue of her marriage. In the years since the abortion, she had never had reason to regret her decision. At the time John Henry was not expected to live longer than a few months, and she did not want to raise their child alone. Now what gave her the strength to go through with the sentence life had imposed on her was the knowledge that no man could claim her child. It would belong to her alone.

She remembered thinking all those years ago that she could not risk having a daughter because she would have nothing to bequeath a child of her own sex except her own confusion. Now she prayed for a daughter. Not that she was any more sure of what to say to her—with each passing year she grew more ambivalent about what she owed in return for the unsolicited privilege of being alive—but she hoped a daughter might provide the chance to learn from the objective vantage point of age just what was expected of her. And neither husband nor father, however well-intentioned, could help in achieving that goal.

Still, her thoughts returned to John Henry many times in the course of each day as she lay in her bed and imagined him in his. His ordeal became even more horrible to her as she began to share his vantage point. However, the comparison made her feel less helpless and left her grateful for all the abilities she still possessed. She could still talk, though since there was only Mrs. Blayne to answer, she seldom did. However, she kept the telephone connected to the answering machine beside her bed and rested secure in the knowledge that there were at least a dozen lives immediately accessible to her. The fact that she chose not to make contact for the moment was irrelevant. What mattered was that for her, unlike John Henry, other lives existed.

A few of her closest friends on the magazine had called to wish her well with the book, urging her to keep in touch during the coming year with an occasional postcard. Todd, however, had not called—and Lindsay was grateful. For his sake she prayed he wouldn't try to make contact again.

When Lindsay told her boss she was taking a leave of absence to write a book, there was a part of her that wanted to believe it was not a lie. She kept a spiral notebook beside her bed and one night when she couldn't sleep opened it to the first blank page and wrote, "When I was forty-two, I was given what appeared to be my last chance at life—and I took it."

But after that sentence she stopped. Just whom did she think she was addressing? And what audacity to imagine anyone outside herself cared what she was going through—or why. Anyone, that is, except John Henry. She had no proof that he even listened, yet she dared to believe he not only heard, he cared. When she talked to him, she exposed her emotional underbelly as she had once offered her body, allowing him to see her naked thoughts as proof of the intimacy that still existed between them. She became convinced that she shared with him thoughts and fears that she would have kept hidden had their marriage continued in a conventional course. She knew this because after she met Todd, sometimes late on Sunday night falling asleep alone, she tried to imagine what it would be like to be married to him. But no matter how hard she tried, she could not imagine telling him the things she shared so effortlessly with John Henry. And now once again alone in her bed, not just at night but around the clock, separated from the two men who had defined her existence for so many years, it was John Henry she missed most.

She picked up the phone and dialed the hospital. She was put through immediately to his doctor, Craig Sanborn.

"How is John Henry?" she began hesitantly but he immediately deflected the focus to her and it was much later in the conversation before she realized he had not answered her question. He said he hoped her absence from the hospital meant that she was taking his advice and concentrating on her own life. He wanted her to know she had his support in whatever decisions she was having to make.

His voice was so kind and strong she found herself telling him she was pregnant. "But it's not like the last time," she was quick to assure him. "I want this baby." When he did not ask about the circumstances of its conception, she knew what he was imagining: that the man who had appeared at the hospital calling himself John Henry's brother had fathered her child. She said nothing except that she was going to have to stay in bed until the baby was born. Something in her wanted him to know exactly what she was going through to have this baby—perhaps to even the score for the one she hadn't wanted earlier.

Dr. Sanborn listened sympathetically, then asked if she had a good doctor. Lindsay said she hoped so. She had been going to him once a year for a routine exam ever since she moved into the city. He greeted her by name and, after a quick look at her file in which he jotted reminders, asked how things were going at the magazine. She used her married name and gave him no reason to suspect there was anything unusual about her life. Until now she had never had any reason to see him more often than once a year, but she was counting on his impersonal manner to continue, even though he would now be coming to her apartment once a week to check on her condition.

"I'd feel better if a friend of mine were taking care of you," Dr. Sanborn said firmly. Before Lindsay could find a discreet way to say that she did not want a continuing emotional connection with the doctor who would be bringing her baby into the world any more than she did with the man who had fathered it, she heard a name that she recognized.

"Did you say his name was Stephen Presnell?"

"I'm not surprised you've heard of him," Dr. Sanford continued. "He's one of the best obstetricians in the city. We were in medical school together."

Was it possible he didn't remember that this was the same name he had given her on that desperate night so long ago?

"Actually this will give me a good excuse to call him. His son was killed in a traffic accident last summer. I keep meaning to call or write . . . something . . . it's just so hard to know what to say."

Lindsay wondered if Dr. Presnell would remember her. She had used a false name—and doubted that he would recognize her face. Suddenly she felt she would be able to trust him, to tell him everything. She desperately needed someone in her life who was strong enough to know everything and still withhold judgment, at least in her presence.

"Do you mind if I ask him to take a look at you?" Dr. Sanborn asked for a second time.

"Please. I'd like him to come as soon as possible. I'm so frightened."

She regretted immediately acknowledging the fear she had been successful in hiding from Todd: that the man who had raped her would return to end her life and with it the life of the child he had unintentionally fathered. The promise she had made in order to save her life had connected it forever to a man who was capable of killing her.

"Frightened of what?" Dr. Sanborn was asking on the other end of the line.

"Of losing my baby," she answered quickly.

"I'll take care of everything. You have my word." Dr. Sanborn's voice was warm with reassurance.

Once again, without realizing it, he had come into her life at a critical juncture, given her a name she could trust. She could feel herself letting go, allowing him to accept the responsibility for her life as well as John Henry's.

Then with a jolt she remembered that he had not answered her question—the question that was her reason for calling.

"You have to help me," she said. "I haven't told John Henry anything. He must wonder where I am, why I haven't come."

"The first day you didn't come I told him I had ordered you to rest. I said I was afraid you had jeopardized your health by trying to lead two lives—that you had to stop coming so often. I'll tell him you're following my advice by taking a long vacation."

"Is there any difference since I stopped coming?"

"You can't live his life for him, Lindsay. You've got another life depending on you now."

She knew then that he was deliberately evading her question. "What's wrong, Craig? You mustn't lie to me. What's happened to John Henry?"

"He's been running a high temperature for the past few days. We're not sure what's causing it. We're running some tests."

"He's been sick before," Lindsay reminded him, trying to make it possible for him to reassure her.

"I know. We're just not sure what it is this time."

"He has to stay alive till our baby is born," Lindsay said with a desperation she could not hide.

"We're doing everything we can," Dr. Sanborn promised. "But you must leave it to us. And try not to worry."

"I have to leave it to you. I have no other choice," Lindsay said slowly.

But as she lay awake that night in the darkness, she knew she had to do something. She couldn't let John Henry think she had left him without a word. She had to find a way to make a human connection—something more than a phone call or a letter. If only there had been a real brother—someone besides Todd—who loved him and wanted his life, despite its limits, to continue. But Lindsay only knew one other person who had ever loved John Henry, and that was Meg.

Twenty-three

Meg was on jury duty, Mark said when he answered the phone, but he would have her call when she got home.

"Please tell her to call collect," Lindsay said, wondering if that was the reason Meg had failed to return her call the last time she had tried to make contact—the night her parents died. Were there really marriages in which nonworking wives felt less than free to return long-distance calls from old college roommates? There was a time when Lindsay would have said no, not possible, but she had come to know better. Still, she was relieved when Mark sounded cordial and said he would be happy to pay for the call.

Mrs. Blayne was bathing Lindsay when the phone rang the next morning. This was not one of the duties Lindsay had mentioned in the interview—she was not looking for a nurse, just a full-time companion. She felt entirely capable of taking care of her personal needs. But the day after Mrs. Blayne arrived Lindsay had fainted in the bathtub. Fortunately Mrs. Blayne came into the room with a breakfast tray minutes later and, hearing no response when she knocked at the bathroom door, opened it to find Lindsay underwater, unconscious. She lifted her out of the tub and gave her artificial respiration (her husband was a policeman, she told Lindsay later—the only information she had ever revealed about him beyond the fact that he was dead).

Since that day, she had insisted on bathing Lindsay in bed. Every morning after breakfast, she would set up a table with fresh towels, sponges, lotions, dusting powder, and cologne. It was a leisurely ritual and Lindsay began to look forward to it. She had never been touched by someone with whom she had no emotional connection, who neither expected nor wanted words and feelings in exchange for the warm state of well-being induced by her fingers.

Except for the night with Todd, when anger and passion and need converged in a union so intense that in retrospect its near-tragic consequences seemed inevitable, Lindsay had worn her body like a shell since the rape, an impenetrable armor whose only function was to protect the soft essential core of her being. But the impersonal reassurance of Mrs. Blayne's silent care restored her trust in strangers and wove connective threads between what the skin felt and the heart acknowledged. At such times the burden of the alien being claiming space inside her became absorbed into her own existence, and she felt at one with everyone, friend or stranger.

The feeling of oneness was shattered now by the ringing of her telephone. "Meg!" Lindsay cried eagerly, reaching for the receiver before the answering machine had a chance to intercept the call.

But a man spoke, introducing himself as Dr. Stephen Presnell and asking if he could stop by and see her at noon. She thanked him for calling so promptly—and decided not to tell him they had already met.

When Mrs. Blayne brought Dr. Presnell to her bedside, Lindsay was waiting expectantly—wearing makeup for the first time since she began staying in bed. As her housekeeper left the room, Lindsay detected in her manner an air of unmistakable relief at being able to share the responsibility for her employer's physical welfare with a professional.

Lindsay wondered if she looked as old to Stephen Presnell as he did to her. He had been a young doctor just beginning his practice when he performed the abortion; now his face was lined with years and doubts. Lindsay, on the other hand, did not feel she had aged in the twenty years of her marriage—perhaps because John Henry was her mirror, and his face was sculpted into a smooth mask of acceptance, a visible measure of the experience denied him. By contrast, Dr. Presnell looked old enough to have fathered the man to whom Lindsay remained so irrevocably married.

"Is this your first pregnancy?" he asked after completing the examination.

Lindsay felt a flash of disappointment that this man who had figured so importantly, albeit briefly, in her life did not even remember having met her.

"I had an abortion right after I was married," she said, deciding to be direct. "Does that count?"

"No," he said, continuing to make notes.

"Funny how something that changed the course of my life would have no effect on my medical history."

"It would have if it hadn't been done right," he said matter-of-factly. "Were there any unforeseen consequences?"

"None," she answered, and then watching him carefully, "and no regrets. I wasn't ready to have a child then."

"And you are now?"

"Time's running out. It's no longer my choice."

"It would have been easier then. The next few months are going to be rough—even rougher than you think. You're going to have to have someone do everything for you. I don't want you leaving this bed again—not even to go to the bathroom."

"Then you're taking the case?"

"I've already taken it. I called your doctor this morning and got your history."

"You didn't have any right to do that!" Lindsay declared indignantly. "Not without asking me."

"I had every right," he said firmly. "I owe you this baby."

"I didn't think you remembered."

"I had to be sure you wanted me to remember," he said slowly. "I'll look in on you every evening around seven—on my way home from the hospital."

"Have you had lunch?" Lindsay asked impulsively.

"Actually, this is my lunch hour," he confessed. "I'm due back in the office at one."

"I thought that might be the case," Lindsay smiled and rang a silver bell by her bed. "We'll have lunch now," she said as Mrs. Blayne appeared at the door. "Don't worry, it's all ready," she added, seeing Dr. Presnell glance at his watch. "You won't be late."

"This was very thoughtful," he said, still recovering from his surprise, as Mrs. Blayne set a table beside the bed and placed a chair for him across from Lindsay.

"It's easy to be thoughtful when all you have to do is think of it," Lindsay said, nodding toward the door through which Mrs. Blayne had just exited. "I now know how nice it is for a man, having a wife."

"It wasn't for me," he smiled ruefully. "But I don't know any men, even happily married ones, whose wives welcome them home for lunch."

Mrs. Blayne reentered with a bowl of hot potato salad in time to overhear his last remark. "I cooked lunch for my husband till the day he died," she stated flatly then left the room before anyone could comment.

They ate in silence until Lindsay asked how he had known who she was, reminding him she had used a false name the first time they met.

He said in those days he had never paid attention to the name of anyone who came to him for an abortion, assuming that the name would inevitably be false, but he knew all about Lindsay and her particular circumstances from Craig Sanborn and had kept up with her through him.

"Then you know my husband is not the father of this child?"

"I'm here to see that you stay healthy and give birth to a healthy baby—not to pass judgment. All I have to show for my life are the lives I've brought into being—none of them related to me by blood."

He got up suddenly, walked to the window, and stood staring out in silence. Finally Lindsay said softly, "I'm sorry about your son."

He began to talk without turning to face her again. He loved children and became a doctor for only one reason: to take care of them. But once he finished his training and began his practice as a pediatrician, he felt overwhelmed by what he encountered. If the children had come to him alone, he might have allowed himself to feel some small sense of accomplishment at being able to heal their visible wounds, but the parents who accompanied them, even the ones who appeared loving and intelligent, gave the doctor no assurance of being able to protect their offspring against future pain. Indeed there were times when he felt the threat of violence was implicit in the parent–child relationship. The more he saw of parents punishing their children for qualities they had come to loathe in themselves or their mates, the less committed he became to his profession.

Finally, the day he was unable to save the life of a ten-month-old baby brought to him with a fractured skull from what her mother said was a fall down the stairs, he performed his first abortion. Gradually he let it be known among his friends that he was willing to terminate the pregnancy of any woman who was unwilling, for whatever reason, to have a child.

As he began to devote more and more of his time to perform-ing illegal abortions, he decided to change his practice from pediatrics to obstetrics, reasoning that if his professional purpose was going to be the prevention of unwanted pregnancies, this could be accomplished more safely and effectively by contraception.

He found it ironic that just as medical science was making a birth control pill widely available, abortion became a legal option—though, as always, of course, only available to those who could afford it. Women ignorant of birth control techniques and unable to pay for abortions continued to have children who would ultimately pay the price for their mothers' ignorance and poverty. And so Dr. Presnell would go from his well-paying obstetrics practice in midtown Manhattan to a neighborhood clinic in Spanish Harlem and spend his evenings performing for nothing whatever services were required of him.

In the course of caring for a woman with nine children who stubbornly submitted, against his advice, to a difficult and painful pregnancy in order to hold in her arms the last child she would ever have by a beloved husband who had died of a heart attack three weeks after conception, he came to understand in a way he never had what was meant by "the right to life." It had nothing to do with any argument against abortion. The right to life meant simply that a child was entitled to at least one individual who wanted it and was willing to care for it.

"Do you want to know who fathered my child?" Lindsay asked.

"All I need to know is that you want it."

Lindsay didn't know why she felt compelled to tell him the circumstances under which the unborn life being consigned to his care had been conceived. For some reason she felt she owed him an explanation. Or maybe she just wanted to keep him beside her, listening, a little longer.

When she was finished, he took her hand and said calmly that he could not speak for all of medical science. No doctor could, no matter how erudite he happened to be. All he could tell her was what he knew from his own experience. He said he had come to believe that children were the only hope for civilization, the source of any faith he had in the future of the human race. He was firmly convinced that any child, no matter what his genetic heritage, raised in a caring, nurturing environment, could become a productive and peace-loving adult.

He hoped there would come a day when he would no longer have to perform abortions—not because they were prohibited by law but because the responsibility for every child born into the world would be shared by its present inhabitants and not require of the mother the commitment and too often the sacrifice of her own life to its care. He said that if the "right to life" forces were fighting for that goal, he would be the first to enlist in their cause. But until that enlightened day arrived, the fate of a child still rested in the hands of its natural parents and often in the hands of the mother alone. Lindsay must be sure she knew what she was doing. If she had any doubts, it was not too late to terminate the pregnancy, give her back her freedom.

Of course she had doubts, Lindsay answered. Like any woman becoming a mother for the first time, she wondered if she had the skill and patience a child deserves. And what if something were to happen to her? Would her child be turned over to the care of someone even less competent? As for giving her back her freedom, Lindsay said, in her experience, which she admitted was unique but was nevertheless all she had to draw on, freedom was only possible in the absence of love. She would merely be exchanging the loss of freedom on one front for the loss of freedom on another. Then she told him if she did what he insisted was necessary to give birth to a healthy baby and stayed safely in bed, her husband might die.

Stephen nodded—and she realized he knew a great deal more than she had told him about John Henry and probably more than Craig Sanborn had told her. "What am I going to do?" she asked helplessly.

"You have no choice," he answered firmly. "You have to think of the child—that's the only life that's truly within your power to protect." Then he looked at his watch and said he had to leave. He had patients waiting.

"Sometime this month we'll get you to the lab and do an amniocentesis—make sure everything is okay. I'll arrange for an ambulance. It takes a couple of weeks to get the results, but then I'll be able to tell whether you're going to have a daughter or a son," he smiled, taking her hand to say good-bye.

Lindsay closed her eyes as she heard Mrs. Blayne shut the door behind him, secure in the knowledge that there was someone outside her life who cared what happened to her, who knew everything about her and still believed the life she was carrying had a right to exist. Someone who, unlike Todd, would take care of her without having to sacrifice his own life in the process. If only John Henry had someone like that. There was only one person Lindsay could offer him in her place. Meg. If Meg came, it wouldn't be a lifetime commitment—just an acknowledgment that his life had touched hers once in a way that was unique and important. Oh, why didn't she call, Lindsay thought? How long does jury duty last?

By the time the phone rang that night, Lindsay had convinced herself that once she explained everything to Meg, the years and events keeping their lives apart would evaporate and Meg would respond without hesitation to old allegiances. She would do what Lindsay could no longer do—go to John Henry and tell him his life mattered to her, as well as to Lindsay. She would keep him alive until Lindsay could return.

At first Lindsay couldn't understand the voice on the other end of the phone. "Who is this?" she asked.

In a whisper, as if unsure of its identity, the voice answered, "It's Meg. Mark said for me to call you."

Why did she have to make it sound as if she were only doing it to please him, Lindsay wondered? But she knew better than to say anything except that she had missed Meg and now needed her desperately. There was no one else who could do what had to be done.

Meg listened to everything Lindsay said without comment. The rape, the baby, nothing seemed to surprise her.

"Meg, can you hear me?" Lindsay asked finally, in desperation.

"Yes," Meg answered calmly, sounding farther away than ever. "I just don't know why you called me, what I can do from here."

"I want you to come stay with me," Lindsay answered, adopting Meg's matter-of-fact tone and realizing for the first time that it was not to keep John Henry alive that she was calling Meg. She wanted Meg to stay with her till the baby was born. But Lindsay knew she couldn't say that. She couldn't ask someone she hadn't seen in twenty years to leave her husband and fly across the country to sit for over six months at the bedside of her college roommate. "You wouldn't have to stay long," she lied. "Just long enough to see John Henry, to let him know he hasn't been abandoned. I know Mark needs you, but he's not the only one who has a claim on you. Oh, Meg, I've missed you so much," Lindsay continued, desperately afraid of the silence she would face if she stopped talking.

"But didn't Mark tell you? I can't come now. I'm on jury duty. Tomorrow we're being sequestered—no one will even be able to reach me. I'll write you when it's over. I'll always love you, Lindsay, and I'm sorry. I seem to be failing everybody I ever loved." And then she hung up, before Lindsay could find false words to reassure her. She thought briefly about calling back but she didn't want to risk talking with Mark again.

She connected the phone to the answering machine, but it didn't ring, and she finally fell asleep, taking deep breaths to try to sustain all the lives depending on her.

CHAPTER

Twenty-four

John Henry was listed in critical condition when Lindsay called the hospital the next day. His temperature remained high and none of the tests could determine the cause. Meg was not coming; Lindsay knew that now and felt ridiculous for imagining that past affection gave her any claim on present loyalty. Somehow in the back of her mind all these years, she had imagined Meg waiting, wanting to help. Night after night, taking the train to see John Henry, she had drawn comfort from the knowledge that another woman had loved him first—imagining, indeed believing, that once you love someone, no matter what circumstances come between you, you will never cease to love them, if not for what they have become, at least for what they once were or were to you.

This axiom, though it apparently did not apply to Meg, remained true for Lindsay. She would never be able to abandon anyone she had once loved—not Meg, who had failed her, not Todd, whose love she could no longer accept knowing she could not return it in full, and, most of all, not John Henry, who for almost twenty years had lived only to be loved by her. She knew that now, and there was no vanity in the knowledge; it was simply that he was dying without her. And yet to keep him alive, to go to him, would risk the life she was nurturing inside her.

Why had this life, conceived in violence, provided her with a purpose that nothing she had initiated on her own ever had? She had to protect it—and yet she couldn't consciously sacrifice the life of the man she loved to it, even though it was a life he was no longer capable of living in the eyes of the outside world. She had to have help, and there was only one person left to ask. Todd. He had posed as John Henry's brother once—in an attempt to manipulate her life. Now she would ask him to play the part again, but this time without any concern for her and her connection with the case. She would ask him simply to act as if John Henry were in fact his brother.

It was after midnight when she dialed his number. No answer. This was the first time she had tried to contact him since he had learned about the baby. Even though she had begged him then to leave her alone, now that she needed him and he was not there, she felt irrationally betrayed.

The next morning she called his office. His secretary said he was out of town—a death in the family. No, there was no forwarding address or phone number. Would she care to leave a message? No, thank you.

She hung up and struggled to her feet. There was no one else she could call. She would have to go to John Henry herself. She got as far as the bathroom before she fainted.

When she regained consciousness, she was back in bed, and Mrs. Blayne was sponging the sweat from her forehead.

"How did I get here?" she asked weakly.

"I had to carry you," Mrs. Blayne responded, "but don't expect me to do it again."

She asked Lindsay what she was doing, disobeying doctor's orders, where she thought she was going.

"To my husband."

"Has he always been in a hospital?"

"There was no way I could have taken care of him at home —I mean and still had a life of my own," Lindsay replied, surprised at how defensive she suddenly felt. She had come to expect pity from anyone knowing the circumstances of her marriage for the first time. Now suddenly she sensed a challenge for which she was unprepared.

"The agency said your husband was the one who called about this job."

"No, that was someone else."

"The father?"

"No—not the father."

"It's okay. I don't like talking about my life either. It's enough having to live it."

"Thank you," Lindsay said, grateful not to have to answer any more questions. "I think I can sleep now."

"I'm not going to leave you alone unless you promise to stay put," Mrs. Blayne warned. "You're not going to do anybody any good by getting out of this bed—not your husband, not yourself, and certainly not your baby. And it's the baby that matters most, isn't it? If you have to choose, that's the life to protect—the only one that hasn't suffered, made mistakes."

Mrs. Blayne fluffed the pillow behind Lindsay's head then gently stroked her forehead as she lay back on it. "And don't worry about your husband. All those years you spent taking the train to see him every night—they have to count for something. He has to know you love him—even though you're not right there with him telling him," she said with a conviction she did not feel, her eyes filling with tears as she turned and hurried from the room.

Lindsay was asleep when the phone rang. "Meg?" she cried hopefully into the receiver.

"No, I'm sorry, Lindsay. It's Cissy."

"Oh. Cissy." Lindsay struggled to clear her head.

"Were you expecting to hear from Meg?"

"No. I don't expect anything from Meg. I don't know why I ever did."

Cissy seemed confused and uncertain of how to proceed on the other end of the phone. Lindsay finally woke up enough to feel sorry for her.

"Where are you, Cissy? Are you calling from California?"

"No. I moved back to Connecticut last year after my husband died."

"Oh, Cissy, I'm so sorry. I didn't know."

"You didn't? I wrote all about it in the last class letter."

"I guess I didn't see it. My life has been a little . . . well, complicated lately." Lindsay did not want to share any details with Cissy, on whom she could depend to be shocked by her life choices. Cissy's life had been cut to a conventional pattern that seemed as outmoded to Lindsay as something from *Godey's Lady's Book.*

"Are you going to reunion?"

"What?" Lindsay asked impatiently, wondering how to get Cissy off the phone and keep her from calling again.

"Our twentieth class reunion. It's the only twentieth anniversary I'm going to be able to celebrate," she added wistfully.

"I'm sorry, Cissy, I'm not going. I hate looking back. Besides, I can't get away." Lindsay had never attended a class reunion, and her reasons had nothing to do with John Henry or her job or anything that was happening in her life. She didn't enjoy being an alumna—it was as simple as that. To her the very word suggested someone clinging to the past. She remembered the hordes of middle-aged women descending on the dormitories as she was packing to return home for summer at the end of freshman year. They act as if nothing important has happened to them since they left college, Lindsay had thought with barely concealed contempt, watching two gray-haired women sob as they embraced each other. She vowed then that she would never be one of them. Indeed, she no longer believed that colleges should be segregated on the basis of sex and had said so rather bluntly the last time she was solicited by a phone call from a former classmate for a donation to the annual building campaign. Impersonal letters continued to arrive several times a year explaining that matching contributions from the alumnae were required in order to secure foundation funds but none of her classmates ever bothered her again, either by phone or letter. Except for the terse Christmas cards from Meg, Cissy was the only member of their graduating class who still made the effort to keep in touch.

"I'm a little nervous about going back," Cissy confessed. "I promised myself I'd lose weight before I had to face anybody who remembered me when I was a size eight, but then Charles died and I had to move the children back home to my parents and . . ." Her voice trailed off to avoid completing the thought.

"You're living with your parents?" Lindsay was shocked in spite of herself.

"It's not permanent," Cissy was quick to assure her. "Just till I decide what I want to do. But for now it's the best thing."

"The best thing for whom?" Lindsay tried to whisper the thought she was shouting in her head.

"The children of course. I feel so much better now that I've finally given them a good home."

"But, Cissy, you've always given them a good home." Lindsay suddenly felt she had to do something to make Cissy feel better about herself before she told her good-bye. "You've devoted your life to being a good wife and mother."

Reacting to the unexpected note of encouragement, Cissy stopped trying to conceal her desperation.

"No, Lindsay, I've finally given my children a good mother. My mother. And I wasn't a good wife either. If you knew everything, you wouldn't say I was." There was a sob on the other end of the phone and then Cissy added abruptly, "Oh, Lindsay, I know how busy you are, but it's so good to hear your voice. Could we talk just a little longer?"

"Of course. It's good to hear your voice, too."

"Could you hold on just a minute? I have to get something."

Lindsay had to laugh as she put the phone beside her pillow. She knew what a glamorous life Cissy imagined she led. What would she think if she could see her now?

When Cissy spoke again, she sounded composed and sure of herself. "I'm coming into the city to shop tomorrow. I have to find something to wear to reunion. If it were only winter, I'd be able to wear an overcoat and that would hide everything. Could we have lunch? Some place small and French? You make the reservations, but I'll pay. I can come to your office around noon."

"Cissy, I'm not with the magazine now," Lindsay began hesitantly, not wanting to say more than was necessary.

"Oh, dear, you weren't made redundant, were you?"

"What?" Cissy always had a tendency toward archness but this time, Lindsay thought, she had gone too far.

"Made redundant. That's what they say in England when someone gets the sack. The English never come right out and say anything, you know," Cissy explained patiently.

"But how would you know something like that?"

"Because it happened to Stephanie Middleton. She's been living in London ever since she divorced that French journalist she met during our junior year abroad. Don't you _ever_ read the class letter?" she asked rather petulantly.

"Of course I do," Lindsay answered soothingly. "I've kept all of them. In fact, I'm thinking of suggesting that the magazine run a fictional class letter as a monthly feature. It's a wonderful way to show the changes women have been going through in the years since we graduated."

"A _fictional_ class letter?" Cissy scoffed. "Who wants to read about lives people aren't really living?" She paused then continued hesitantly, "You still have a job, then—even though you're not at the office?"

"I've taken a leave of absence—to write a book."

"How exciting! A book is just about the most permanent thing a person can leave behind. You think you're accomplishing something when you have a baby but then they grow up and you begin to feel you didn't have anything to do with any of it."

"I refuse to believe that, Cissy," Lindsay replied, afraid another round of self-pity was in the offing.

"Can you meet me for lunch tomorrow, even though you're working at home?" Cissy continued undaunted.

Lindsay replied firmly that she was working too hard to leave the house. In fact, it was just by chance that she happened to answer the telephone; if Cissy called again, she would probably get the answering machine.

"I won't be calling again," Cissy said quietly. "Good luck with the book, Lindsay." And she hung up before Lindsay could find words for the immediate remorse that flooded her.

From the day they arrived on campus freshman year Cissy had wanted to be her friend. They had been assigned adjacent rooms in the dormitory. Their roommates were from the same hometown and had wanted to room together, but it was a college policy to pair girls who had never met. Requiring a girl to share her life with a stranger on her first extended stay away from home was considered a necessary rite of passage—as much a part of what parents were paying for as anything to be learned from books or professors. However, the hometown pair ignored their assigned roommates and shared everything except the hours they were asleep. They met in the hallway each morning and walked together to the bathroom to brush their teeth. They arranged their schedules so they would be taking the same classes. They stayed in the library at neighboring desks till it closed at ten then stopped on the sun porch that had been converted into a college-approved smoking area for one last cigarette before turning into their separate rooms for the night.

To combat her sense of rejection, Cissy began to cling to Lindsay, trying to convince her that there were stronger reasons for them to be together than the fact that their roommates preferred each other. Lindsay would have been just as happy to be left alone, but with Cissy in constant attendance, she could have the security of a friendly presence close at hand without the emotional effort usually required to sustain an intimate relationship. Cissy asked nothing more than to be with Lindsay, and her constant stream of chatter never required more than an occasional nod or smile in response. Finally even Lindsay had to admit there was something restful about Cissy's undemanding affection and she would probably have drifted into a more permanent arrangement, offering no objection when Cissy assumed they would share a room sophomore year, if she had not met Meg.

But Meg at the age of eighteen already had a purpose in life, in the person of a man saving his money to marry her, and Lindsay was drawn as irresistibly as a giddy moth to the flame of her unwavering devotion. Cissy broke into tears when Lindsay told her she was going to be rooming with Meg and did not forgive her until the summer after graduation.

Lindsay and Meg had stopped in New Canaan on the last night of their coast-to-coast odyssey. Cissy was due to be married the next day. They, along with all the members of their graduating class, had received invitations to the wedding, though Lindsay had pointedly not been included in the bridal party or invited to any of the prewedding festivities. However, when Lindsay had called Cissy from the motel to say she and Meg would be coming to the wedding, Cissy began to cry and begged to be forgiven for not asking Lindsay to be a bridesmaid. Lindsay protested that no apology was necessary. She had not expected to be asked—after all, she and Cissy were never that close after freshman year.

"I know—but I wanted to be," Cissy had sobbed. "I just wanted you to make the first move. It took three years but now you finally have."

Lindsay had no idea one telephone call could mean so much to a person, but she was glad she had been able to make Cissy happy on the eve of her wedding. Then Cissy revealed that it was not just the reconciliation that was causing her to cry for joy but relief at the timeliness of it. The wedding rehearsal was an hour away and her maid of honor had just confessed she was four months pregnant. Would Lindsay take her place?

"You mean you're not going to let her be in your wedding just because she's pregnant?" Lindsay had asked, appalled at Cissy for passing moral judgment on one of her best friends.

"Oh, no, I don't care about that. I'm shocked, but I don't care. The problem is she can't zip up her bridesmaid's dress. You are a ten, aren't you?" Lindsay said yes. "Then you've got to help me. Come to my house as soon as you can. You're the only other size ten I know who's in town and not already in the wedding. Besides," she added softly, "I don't care what you think of me, I've always thought of you as my best friend."

Now it was twenty years later and their friendship was still as one-sided as ever. Oh, why couldn't I have just told her what's happened, Lindsay thought, chastising herself for the unwitting cruelty with which she had once again shut Cissy out of her life. However, another part of her refused to be reprimanded, knowing that once a door was opened to Cissy, there would be no way to close it again. The last thing Lindsay wanted from Cissy was charity. At the same time, she knew that feeling sorry for people was the only response with which Cissy ever felt truly comfortable. She had been at her best in the dormitory comforting someone who had just been dumped by a boyfriend or flunked by a professor. Cissy was always there, strong, encouraging, cheerful, secure in the knowledge that what had happened to them had never happened to her and though she had not really succeeded at anything, at least she had never publicly failed.

Lindsay gave a shudder at the thought of the unquenchable sympathy that would flow from Cissy on learning of her condition. It oozed into her voice every time she asked after John Henry. With what maudlin response would she greet the news that Lindsay was pregnant by a man who had raped her? She knew from past politicizing within the paragraphs of the class letter that Cissy was militantly antiabortion. But in Lindsay's place even she might have considered it a viable alternative. Oh, no, Lindsay thought resolutely, as desperately as she wanted Meg to come, she wanted Cissy to stay away. And, unfortunately, Cissy had to be hurt in order to keep her at bay.

Lindsay was asleep the next day when Mrs. Blayne approached her bed in some confusion and reported that someone who said she was an old friend was waiting in the living room with a picnic basket and a bottle of wine. Lindsay, disoriented, asked her to repeat what she had just said, but by that time Cissy was already in the doorway.

"Lindsay, what are you doing in bed?" she cried, hurrying to her anxiously and bending down to kiss her.

Lindsay was amazed to find her eyes filling with tears and she held Cissy's hand in both of hers as if she never intended to let go.

She told Cissy as much as she dared—that she was pregnant, outside wedlock, by a man she never wanted to see again. However, she did not reveal that anything had happened against her will.

Cissy's immediate reaction was relief. "Then you're not writing a book after all? You're having a baby instead." Lindsay nodded and Cissy began to laugh with a sense of release that approached hysteria. "All these years I've thought you were so much smarter than I was. Not a day went by I didn't envy you for your ambition. But now, for the first time since I've known you, you're not doing any more with your life than I've already done three times." She laughed again.

Lindsay wanted nothing more than to call Mrs. Blayne— quiet, inarticulate Mrs. Blayne, who kept her troubles to herself —and tell her she did not want to be disturbed for the rest of the day. But it was too late. Cissy had already begun to spread the contents of her picnic basket on the bedside table.

She had hoped to persuade Lindsay to leave her work long enough for a picnic in the park, she said gaily, uncorking the bottle of wine and quickly downing her glass, trying to find in it the courage necessary to accept Lindsay as her equal.

To her surprise Lindsay found as she began to eat and Cissy began to talk that she was really quite hungry, not just for the food Cissy had brought but for the details of her life. Her own predicament had absorbed all her emotion for too long, and she was suddenly exhilarated at the possibility of escape into someone else's life.

"Your husband's death must have come as such a shock. You're both so young."

"Young? I stopped thinking of us as young years ago. He was only young when it came to dying."

"How did it happen?"

"He'd just gotten another promotion. We'd been in San Jose the requisite three years. I'd never loved any place quite like San Jose—it was the first time in six moves and nearly twenty years of marriage I didn't feel like a stranger. Everyone in San Jose had moved there from somewhere else and felt as displaced as I did. Charles opened the traditional bottle of champagne that night— to celebrate our move to Boston. I refused to drink with him and went to bed. When I awoke at three A.M. and he wasn't beside me, I decided he must have fallen asleep on the living room couch. But he wasn't on the couch. He was slumped at the kitchen table."

"Oh, Cissy, how terrible for you—finding him like that." Reaching for her hand, Lindsay realized Cissy had not touched any of the food on her plate. She was hungry but not for anything that could be consumed.

Cissy continued to cling to Lindsay's hand as if an invisible transfusion were taking place. "It was terrible for *him.* I'm still alive." And then as an afterthought, "Though I don't know why."

The doctor who came in response to Cissy's call said it was a massive cerebral hemorrhage, but Cissy knew better. Charles had died from massive disappointment. At the moment of his greatest success, his wife had turned her back on him, made him feel he had, if not failed her, never succeeded in pleasing her.

"You mustn't blame yourself," Lindsay tried to comfort her. "You didn't even tell him what you were thinking."

"So he probably imagined a lot worse." Cissy could not be comforted. She got up and began to rummage through the picnic basket.

"I thought I brought two bottles of wine," she said, "one for you and one for me."

"I stopped drinking when I found out I was pregnant," Lindsay said, "so there's no need to open another bottle." But then she saw that Cissy had finished one bottle of wine by herself.

"I feel so guilty when I'm with the children," Cissy confessed, ignoring Lindsay and opening the second bottle of wine, then refilling her glass. "First I deprive them of a father then I bring them home and turn them over to my parents. I just don't know what I think about anything anymore, so how can I be expected to set them a good example, teach them right from wrong? I thought my mother would be better at it than I am. Even though she only had one child, she always strikes me as an authority on the subject. I've had three, but I never seem to know what I'm doing." She paused to refill her wineglass then continued with a sigh. "Sometimes I wish I'd died instead of Charles. The only thing that keeps me going is the feeling that I never really got to live my own life. The only life I got to live was his."

"Cissy," Lindsay said impulsively, "how would you like to stay here with me for a while? I think you need a change—and a rest. I can't offer you a private room—Mrs. Blayne is using the study—but you can sleep on the couch in the living room."

Cissy crossed a little unsteadily to Lindsay's bed and knelt beside it. Suddenly she buried her face against Lindsay's shoulder and sobbed.

"Wait till I tell my mother that somebody wants me."

"Cissy," Lindsay said gently. "I'm not sure it's such a good idea for you to go to reunion. It's a hard trip, and I'm not just talking about distance. I wouldn't be going, even if it were safe for me to travel."

"I didn't want to go," Cissy confessed, curling up in a chair at the foot of Lindsay's bed. "I just had to get out of the house and I didn't know where else to go. But I'd rather be here with you than anywhere in the world." And she closed her eyes and went to sleep.

Twenty-five

When Cissy called her mother in Connecticut to say she was staying with Lindsay instead of going to reunion, Mrs. Mason appeared delighted—and told her not to worry about the children. "Your father and I love having them here," she insisted. "We're making up for all those years you lived too far away to visit."

Then her father took the phone and asked Cissy if she had enough money. She insisted she did, but he asked for the address anyway and said he would put a check in the mail in the morning. "Take your friend out to dinner and to a show," he said expansively. "You're entitled to have a good time occasionally, sweetheart." He hung up before Cissy could explain that Lindsay was confined to her bed, so they wouldn't be going anywhere.

The days quickly fell into an agreeable pattern. Cissy was invariably the first one awake. She had gotten into the habit of getting up early with her children. As they got older and slept later, Cissy had continued to wake at dawn—without an alarm clock. She would plug in her electric hot rollers, make the coffee, read the newspaper, then curl her hair while she bathed. When Charles and the three children came down for breakfast, she would greet them already dressed for the day and feel at that moment that she was exactly where she belonged, doing what she did best. However, no matter what time she woke them, they always seemed to be late for wherever they were going and she would find herself alone at the breakfast table eating the popovers no one else had time to compliment, let alone consume.

Several years before he died, Charles confessed that he had a hard time sleeping once she got out of bed and said he would happily skip breakfast to keep her with him. After that she lay beside him until his alarm rang at seven thirty, but her eyes were always open by six, no matter how hard she tried to drift back into sleep. Now that she was alone, she missed having his arms around her when she fell asleep, but it was exhilarating to be able to get out of bed as soon as she was awake.

She would quickly fold the covers on the couch and clear away all evidence that she had spent the night. Though Mrs. Blayne had made no comment about Cissy's extended stay, her disapproval was evident. However, as long as Lindsay appeared to be enjoying her company, Cissy had no interest in returning to people to whom she was related only by the chance circumstance of birth.

She remembered reading a book on families a few years back. The author, an unmarried woman, said there were two kinds of families—families by chance and families by choice. Her book was devoted to the second category, describing different support systems people devise to overcome their individual isolation. Cissy had created a family by choice only once—when she married Charles and committed her life to him. Now she was left alone with her parents and her children—her family by chance. But it was Lindsay whose company she preferred, and for the moment at least the choice appeared to be hers.

Every morning she would hurriedly use the bathroom off the hallway, which she shared as inconspicuously as possible with Mrs. Blayne, and get dressed in something from Lindsay's closet. Lindsay had offered Cissy free access to all her clothes when she invited her to stay. After all, she had laughed, she would not be needing anything but a nightgown for the next few months. Actually she had insisted Cissy would be doing her a favor, keeping the clothes aired and the moths unsettled, by going through her closet and wearing whatever appealed to her.

For Cissy it was a nostalgic reminder of freshman year, when she found Lindsay's wardrobe—her compensation for a summer spent on the college board of a suburban department store—so much more interesting than her own. She borrowed freely from it and enjoyed coordinating separates and choosing accessories much more than Lindsay, who often wore the same skirt and sweater several days in a row. Cissy kept begging Lindsay to borrow some of her clothes occasionally so she wouldn't feel so indebted but Lindsay just smiled and said she had more clothes than she would be able to wear in four years of college.

The morning after she arrived at the apartment with her picnic basket, Cissy tried on everything Lindsay owned. As she modeled each new outfit, she asked endless questions about the occasion for which it had been bought and all the places it had been worn since. She would look wistfully into the mirror and imagine herself going all the places Lindsay had gone wearing those clothes and doing all the things she had done in them.

Even though she only left the apartment to go to the store or the branch library or an occasional afternoon movie, Cissy dressed up every day as if she were leading Lindsay's former life. "After all, I'm living in the heart of the most sophisticated city in the world," she told herself. "I can hardly dress the way I did in San Jose."

Only at night, making her bed on the couch, would Cissy allow herself to wonder how long she could continue to take refuge in Lindsay's life—wearing clothes she hadn't chosen, living in an apartment she hadn't rented, anticipating the arrival of a child she hadn't conceived. The only antidote to these thoughts was the white wine she kept chilled in the refrigerator.

Cissy had hated the taste of liquor since the age of four when she woke up one morning with a hangover after one of her parents' cocktail parties. She remembered her mother and father laughing as she lurched from guest to guest, begging for the maraschino cherries from their drinks. But they stopped laughing when she suddenly vomited into the lap of a startled guest. Her mother rushed her off to bed and at their next party she hired a baby-sitter to keep Cissy amused in her room—and away from the guests.

Even after her eighteenth birthday, when her parents began to treat her as their equal, inviting Cissy to join them for a drink before dinner, she refused anything with a cherry in it. But the year she lived in Paris, sharing the home and habits of a French family, she began to drink wine with her meals and somehow it never seemed like the other kind of drinking—the kind that made you sick and ashamed in front of people. It was just part of the meal—it made the food taste better and the words flow faster. Only when she was *à table* did Cissy feel the least bit bilingual. She had not returned to France since her marriage and she could no longer conjugate an irregular verb, but she continued to drink wine with dinner and to have fascinating thoughts as she drank, though she had long since stopped speaking them aloud, even in her native tongue.

When she moved to California, she forsook red wine in favor of a Napa Valley Chablis, which she bought by the half gallon and drank with ice and club soda to make it last longer. She would make the first drink in the afternoon before the children got home from school—unless it was her turn to drive the car pool. On those days she waited until her charges were delivered and the car safely parked in the garage before stretching out on a lounge chair with her spritzer, pretending she was making herself available to help the children with their homework. She would fix her last drink just before she went to bed and often fell asleep sipping it.

Lindsay had stopped drinking when she suspected she might be pregnant and after that first picnic lunch Cissy made a point of not drinking in front of her. In fact her life since she moved in with Lindsay had become so full, or at least full of possibility, that she often forgot about fixing a drink until after dinner when she was alone with her thoughts.

After a glass or two of wine she would find the courage to call her parents and ask to speak to her children. It usually took a while for her mother to round them up from whatever they were doing and then the conversations were terse and unsatisfying. Cissy couldn't tell whether they missed her or not.

But then one night when she had been with Lindsay almost a month, the phone rang as she was taking her folded covers from the linen closet, preparing to make her bed on the couch. The answering machine was connected to the phone beside Lindsay's bed, but Cissy picked up the extension in the kitchen to check on the call.

"I'm trying to reach my daughter," she heard her mother say irritably in response to the recorded message.

"I'm right here, Mother," Cissy said quickly. "Just hold on a minute while I cut off the machine."

She hurried into Lindsay's bedroom and gave a whispered explanation as she disconnected the recording. "She can't hear you from here," Lindsay laughed but Cissy was already on her way back to the kitchen phone.

"When are you coming home?" her mother asked in an anxious tone that gave the lie to her cheerful insistence when Cissy first called that the constant presence of her three grandchildren was keeping her young.

Home? Cissy thought to herself. The place her mother called home had ceased to exist as anything but a memory for her from the day she married and moved with her husband halfway across the country. When she came back to visit, alone at first and then with her children, she felt like a tourist passing appreciatively through a historical home that had been meticulously restored and trying to imagine what it must have been like to live there. Nothing in the house seemed to have any connection with her life as a wife and mother.

When she and Charles bought their first house, her mother offered to ship the contents of her girlhood bedroom to them. Cissy declined the offer politely, saying she preferred to leave things where they were. Her mother assumed she was just trying to spare her the inconvenience of packing and shipping so many things and Cissy never told her otherwise. However, the truth was Cissy could not bring herself to confront on a daily basis evidence that she would never again belong anywhere as clearly as she had belonged in that room under her parents' roof.

And yet when Charles died and she returned to it, she felt like a stranger—and was glad to be sharing it with her fourteen-year-old daughter. The room still looked just the way it did when she left for college—the books she cherished as a child filling the shelves, the mirrored dressing table with its starched white organdy skirt displaying the silver vanity set her grandmother had given her as a confirmation present. Though overnight guests occupied it from time to time, her mother never referred to it as a guest room. It was always Cissy's room. To everybody except Cissy.

"Don't you worry about your children?" her mother's voice came over the telephone to reclaim her, and Cissy realized she had not been answering any of her questions out loud.

"I never worry about them when they're with you. Besides, they're about to leave for camp."

"Well, don't you want to kiss them good-bye?"

No, thought Cissy, she didn't. She'd tried too many times to reach out to them, to hold them again as she had when they were little, only to have them pull away embarrassed, or, even worse, bored, by her open display of affection.

"Can't you leave me alone?" Muffin had asked one night after Charles died when Cissy heard her crying and crawled in bed beside her. Feeling rejected and foolish, Cissy had crept quietly back into her own bed. As a child, Muffin would beg her mother to stay and snuggle like spoons after she turned off the light. Sometimes Cissy even fell asleep holding her. Then Charles would come looking for Cissy, angry that she couldn't stay awake long enough to go to sleep with him. But now Charles was gone and the children held her responsible for uprooting them from their comfortable life in California.

"You kiss them good-bye for me," she said quietly—but inside her head she was screaming, How dare you sit in judgment on me! You've been married for almost fifty years to a man who gave you everything you ever wanted in return for your company. You never wanted anything different for yourself than he wanted for you. You've lived in the same house your whole married life surrounded by friends you met when you were young who've grown old beside you. My life has been nothing like yours—starting over every few years and leaving a town with nothing to show for my time there but a few addresses of people who promise to write but don't even remember to send Christmas cards.

She was sobbing now, not caring if her mother heard, when suddenly a voice asked, "Are you still mad at me, Mommy?"

Cissy choked back her sobs. "Is that you, Muffin?"

"Don't call me Muffin. Daddy always called me Muffin."

"It was *my* name for you," Cissy protested. "You used to sit in the kitchen with me while I cooked dinner and pretend to make muffins. You learned to count to twelve using a muffin tin, don't you remember?" She was pleading now, daring her daughter to contradict her.

"Anyway, I'm too old for that name now. Everybody here calls me by my real name."

"Madelyn Mason?" Mason was Cissy's maiden name and she

had always imagined she would pass it on to her first son as his first name and thus preserve it for another generation. But she was overruled by her husband, who wanted to continue his own name. So when their daughter was born, Cissy announced she was naming her Madelyn Mason. This time Charles had no objection beyond the comment that it didn't make much sense to give a girl a middle name since it would be supplanted by her maiden name once she married.

"Not Madelyn Mason, Mother. Nobody calls me by my whole name. Just Madelyn."

"I love you by any name, darling," Cissy said appeasingly. "And of course I'm not mad at you. I was never mad at you." And then hesitantly, "Do you miss me?"

"No, I'm still mad at you," Madelyn Mason Clark continued, with the unassailable authority of an indulged adolescent. "Daddy told me the next time we moved I would get a horse. And we did move and I didn't get one."

"Darling, you know your grandparents don't have a place for a horse. But you'll have a horse at camp."

"I don't want to go to camp. If I had a horse at home, I wouldn't have to go to camp. Daddy was going to buy a house with a stable when we moved. If he'd lived, he would have, too. I miss him so much. I bet I miss him more than you do."

Cissy waited for her only daughter to ask when she was coming back to her.

"I miss him too, darling," she said finally. "More than I had any idea I would," she added in a whisper. "But what about me, Muffin? Do you miss me? Do you want me with you?" There was no answer and Cissy began to sob softly. "You mustn't blame me for his death. I never told him how much I hated the way we had to live. He never knew I didn't want to move back east with him. You've got to believe me—and stop blaming me."

But the phone was dead. There was no one on the other end to grant absolution—or even to pay attention.

Blinded with tears, Cissy stumbled into the kitchen to open another bottle of wine. When she returned to the couch, she did not bother to spread out the sheets and blankets with which she had been carefully making her bed for the past month. She fell asleep with her arms around one of the couch pillows, rocking back and forth and singing the song with which she had rocked all three of her children to sleep:

Sweet and low, sweet and low,
Wind of the western sea.
Low, low, breathe and blow,
Wind of the western sea.
Father will come to his babe in the nest,
Silvery sails all out of the West.
Blow him again to me,
While my little one, while my pretty one sleeps.

Cissy was sleeping soundly in an upright position, the pillow still clutched to her chest, the bottle of wine lying at her feet, a damp spot on the rug attesting to the fact that its contents had not been completely consumed, when Mrs. Blayne entered the living room on her way to the kitchen to fix breakfast. She stared down at Cissy in disapproval, then picked up the empty wine bottle and carried it to the trash. She didn't understand what was happening here. The employment agency had told her a man had called about someone to take care of his wife until her baby was born. But there was no man at the apartment when she arrived, and the only husband the young woman acknowledged lay critically ill and completely helpless, unable to move or speak, in a hospital somewhere outside the city. Mrs. Blayne had no more idea this morning than the afternoon she agreed to take the job who had fathered the unborn child. Now a second young woman had arrived—and seemed to have no intention of leaving.

Mrs. Blayne made the coffee, then on the notepad hanging on the wall beside the kitchen phone left her message.

I didn't agree to all this. I don't have to work. I can move in with my married son and his wife. Hope the baby will be okay and you too.

Yours truly,
Mrs. Frank Blayne

Twenty-six

When Cissy awoke later that morning, she was surprised that it was already eight o'clock. She smelled the fragrant aroma of freshly brewed coffee and felt guilty. She was usually the first one awake and took it upon herself to make the coffee—though it wasn't expected of her. Nothing, in fact, was expected of her here.

The past month had been the first time in twenty-four years, since the carefree summer before she started college, that she had felt there was no one counting on her for anything—good grades, balanced meals, clean clothes, undemanding sex. Lindsay just seemed to enjoy the fact that she was there. But talking to her daughter on the phone the night before, Cissy had felt once again the familiar pull of need. In the form of rebellion this time: her daughter needed someone to blame for the fact that her father was dead and her life disrupted. Her anger interlocked like gears with Cissy's guilt, setting the intricate mechanism of family into motion again.

Cissy washed her face then dressed quickly in the floral print shirtwaist and linen blazer she had been wearing the day she arrived. She had been a visitor in Lindsay's life long enough. It was time to return to her own clothes, her own children, her own life.

Now, in the sober light of morning, she could admit to herself that she had been a coward to stay away. She had to find the courage to confront her children even if it meant allowing them to hate her. For finally the greatest service a parent can render children—far greater than providing food, clothing, or shelter—is to give them someone to blame for whatever unhappiness they are feeling, someone to whom they can say terrible things without risking the relationship. This is the only time in their lives, Cissy thought, that they will be able to say everything they feel to someone who they know loves them enough to listen and not hate them back. No one will ever love them again as much as I do, she told herself, remembering all the thoughts she had been so careful to conceal from her husband—and still she had lost him. So fragile, she knew now, the love that connects a man and a woman. For those you have chosen to love you can choose later not to love. But you are connected for life to your family by chance. Because you did not choose to love them, how can you choose not to love them?

Cissy was no longer the confused, helpless creature she had been when she arrived, as afraid of her past as she was of her future. She was no longer a wife, but she was and would continue to be a mother for the rest of her life. She knew now that her children needed her. It didn't matter whether they knew it or not.

She decided to have a mug of coffee before she woke Lindsay and told her she was leaving. As she was sipping her coffee, pacing the small kitchen and wondering what had happened to Mrs. Blayne and breakfast, she saw the note. She read it slowly, but her decision was immediate. Her children would have to wait. She could not leave Lindsay alone.

Suddenly she knew what had brought her into the city that

day—and what had kept her when there was no apparent reason for staying. She was the only person in the world Lindsay could count on. Lindsay needed Cissy more than her children did. In fact for the first time since they had met in college, Lindsay needed Cissy more than Cissy needed Lindsay.

Humming under her breath, Cissy tiptoed to the door of Lindsay's bedroom and saw that she was still asleep. Hurrying back to the kitchen, she quickly assessed the contents of cupboard and refrigerator and planned her menu. When Lindsay awoke, Cissy would surprise her with the kind of breakfast Mrs. Blayne had neither the time nor the inclination to prepare.

While popovers were swelling in the oven, she wound strips of bacon around pineapple rings and put them under the broiler.

"This looks wonderful," Lindsay said in pleased surprise as Cissy set down the breakfast tray decorated with a pot of African violets. "What's the occasion?"

"I've decided I'm going to take care of you until the baby is born," Cissy announced. "No one can do it better than I can."

"I don't doubt that," Lindsay laughed, "but what about Mrs. Blayne? I'm paying her to take care of me, you know."

Cissy took the note from her pocket and handed it to Lindsay without comment. Then she pulled a chair over to the bed and began to butter a popover. "What would you like for lunch?" she asked. "I've planned menus for the next week, but if there's something special you'd like, just tell me. My menus are always tentative until I get to the store and see what the specials are and what's in season."

Lindsay looked up from Mrs. Blayne's note, which she had read several times trying not to feel hurt. She realized Cissy was waiting expectantly for her to sample the array of food on her plate.

"Lunch? I don't know how I could eat lunch after all this. But, Cissy," she continued. "I can't let you wait on me the way Mrs. Blayne did."

"Why not? She wasn't a trained nurse. She wasn't a trained

anything. She was just a widow like me. I know how to do everything she did and I'm a much better cook."

"I can't argue with that," Lindsay said, attacking her breakfast with obvious enjoyment. "My mother used to bring me trays like this when I was a little girl and stayed home from school sick. A few years before she died, I suggested that the food editor do a whole color spread on eating in bed. I told her about some of the ways my mother used to decorate my trays. Of course, there was no mention of my mother in the article, but she was as proud of it as if she'd gotten a by-line. When she died, I found that issue of the magazine in her bureau drawer, with my baby pictures and all the letters my father had ever written her."

Lindsay was suddenly silent, as if she had forgotten the subject under discussion.

"I've always felt I had more to give than anybody in my family ever wanted," Cissy said slowly. "I've waited a long time for you to need my friendship as much as I've always needed yours. Please let me stay. I want so much to be here when the baby is born."

"But, Cissy, what about your children?"

"I was on my way home to them this morning when I found the note. I'd begun to feel I was in hiding. There didn't seem to be any reason for me to keep staying here. But now there is. You need me more than my children have in years. And they'll be at camp the rest of the summer anyway."

She cleared away the breakfast tray then spread a towel over the bedside table and began to prepare Lindsay's bath. As she sponged her back then patted it dry, Cissy felt her fingers respond to the familiar pleasure of physically caring for someone who expects nothing and thus is grateful for everything. How she had adored bathing her babies! Then carrying them to her big double bed, which she always left unmade till late afternoon, spreading out a towel and tenderly massaging their tiny limbs with lotion. Kissing their fingers and toes, talking to them endlessly and listening delightedly to the noises they made in response. She was never closer to her children than she was before they learned to talk. As long as they were only touching, communication was total.

She never again experienced such total physical intimacy with another human being. She used to long for it with her husband, but even when sex was the most satisfying, it was never the fusion of two separate identities into a single entity that she imagined it would be when she married. And often, when it was over, she felt lonelier and less loved than she did before it began. Whereas when she bathed her babies then lay down beside them on the big bed where they were only daytime visitors, they seemed connected to her by myriad invisible, unbreakable threads.

And now with Lindsay depending on her, she felt connected again, needed, essential. "Oh, Lindsay," she whispered, bringing her a fresh nightgown from the bureau drawer. "I'm so glad you invited me to lunch that day." Lindsay smiled—and decided not to remind Cissy that the invitation had come from her.

"Now settle back," Cissy ordered, fluffing the pillows on the bed then removing the bath accessories from the bedside table. "I'm going to give you a manicure just the way I used to do every Sunday night after chapel. Remember?"

"I remember," Lindsay laughed. "I also remember what I had to do for you in return."

"I never would have made it through that first year without you," Cissy said earnestly, squeezing the hand Lindsay was holding out to her to manicure. "I keep reading about women our age going back to school and actually being excited about it," she shuddered. "I can't imagine how they find the courage."

She could still feel the way her stomach muscles had knotted when their humanities professor had written the first assignment on the blackboard: a fifteen-hundred-word paper due the following week answering the question "Does God Exist?" The paper was not to be researched, he emphasized. The rest of the year would be devoted to studying the ways the question had been answered through the ages. But for this first assignment no outside sources were allowed. The students were to come to their own conclusions, based on their own observations and ideas.

That evening, as Lindsay was putting on her stockings and high heels for dinner (required dress for on-campus dining), Cissy came to the door and announced she was going to the infirmary. She looked pale.

"I think I'm going to faint," she said, suddenly clutching Lindsay's arm. "You've got to go with me."

"What's wrong? You look like you're dying," Lindsay said, taking Cissy's overnight case in one hand and putting the other around her waist to guide her along the petunia-bordered path that wound behind the hockey field past the Shakespeare garden, planted with all the varieties of flowers mentioned in his plays, to the infirmary.

"I hope I am dying and I hope it happens before next Wednesday," Cissy finally confessed.

"Next Wednesday?"

"I'd rather die than have to write that paper."

"But all you have to do is say what *you* think—and why. Nobody knows the answer, so nobody can say you're wrong."

"But I don't know what I think," Cissy protested, "and besides I don't like thinking about it." Then while Lindsay unpacked her suitcase for her, she climbed docilely into bed and allowed the nurse to take her temperature.

"A hundred and two degrees," said the nurse. "I'm afraid we'll have to keep you here a couple of days."

"Thank goodness," Cissy replied gratefully.

The next night after dinner Lindsay arrived at the infirmary to visit Cissy, bringing her mail, a hot fudge sundae from the snack bar, and a neatly typed paper with ten passionately argued proofs of the existence of God.

"You've done your paper already?" Cissy asked. "Oh, Lindsay, I wish I were you."

"Look at the name on the paper," Lindsay said.

Cissy stared at the paper in disbelief and began to cry. "I've always wanted to be you, but I never imagined that you'd be willing to be me."

"I've missed you at dinner the last two nights," Lindsay said, taking Cissy's overnight case from the foot of the bed and beginning to pack. "Come on, roll up your pajamas and put your raincoat on over them. Let's get out of here. You're going to be fine."

When they got back to the dormitory, Lindsay left immediately for the library to study. While she was gone, Cissy gathered up all Lindsay's laundry and took it to the basement to wash and dry. Then she made a plate of fudge and left it on Lindsay's desk.

"Actually, putting myself in your place to write that paper allowed me to go on believing in God," Lindsay said, lying back against her pillow, spreading out her fingers for the polish to dry. "I'd argued against his existence in my paper—because I couldn't prove it intellectually. But writing as you, I relied on faith. I was terrified I wouldn't get away with it, though—I mean being both of us, having it both ways."

Lindsay still remembered how nervous she was the day the papers were to be returned. When she got to class, she looked around for Cissy, seeking the comfort of someone who knew everything she knew, someone with whom she could at least exchange glances. But even though Lindsay had made Cissy read the paper through carefully several times so that she would be prepared to defend any points the professor challenged, Cissy was clearly not equipped to answer for anything Lindsay had said in her name—and cut class.

Instead of handing out the papers immediately, the professor announced he intended to discuss one in detail—as an example of what was wrong with all of them. He began to copy the paper Lindsay had written for Cissy on the blackboard, dissecting it sentence by sentence. When the bell rang, he asked the author of the paper to stay after class. But no one approached his desk. Suddenly he called out Cissy's name. Lindsay, feeling sick at her stomach, explained in a frightened whisper that Cissy was absent.

"Too bad," he said. "I wanted to congratulate her personally on the best freshman humanities paper I've ever received."

Lindsay hurried back to the dorm to tell Cissy, assuming she'd be pleased at the success of their deception, but instead she fainted.

"I'll never be able to live up to that paper," she said helplessly when she revived. "You're going to have to write all my papers for the rest of the year."

Lindsay laughed and told her she was being ridiculous but when the next paper was assigned and Cissy begged her for help, she looked at the pile of dirty clothes accumulating in her closet and reconsidered. She told Cissy to stop crying and promised to write all her humanities papers for the rest of the year. In return, Cissy agreed to deal with all the domestic facts of dormitory life —sweeping and dusting both rooms, doing the laundry, buying groceries for snacks between regular meals in the college dining room and for late breakfasts on the weekends. She even threw in a weekly manicure.

"It seemed like an even exchange then," Lindsay laughed, "but you don't have any papers due now."

"Thank God," said Cissy. "I was so frightened that first year. When I realized I wasn't capable of abstract thinking, I was afraid it might handicap me for the rest of my life. But the truth is once you got me through humanities and I decided to major in French, all I ever had to do was translate. Then I got married and I never had to think abstractly again."

"But how can I allow you to stay here and take care of me without doing anything for you in return?"

Cissy's eyes filled with tears. "I haven't felt as though I were doing anything that mattered for anybody since my children were babies. I want to make a difference in someone else's life, Lindsay."

"I have to admit I do love having you here. But if you stay there is one condition: I insist on paying you what I was paying Mrs. Blayne—if you think it's fair, of course."

"But I don't need the money," Cissy protested. "Charles had a lot of life insurance."

"That's not the point. If you weren't here, I'd have to pay someone else. It's only fair I pay you."

After a week of working for Lindsay, Cissy took her paycheck —the first she had ever earned—to the bank Lindsay used and opened an account in her own name, Cynthia Mason Clark. She made out a deposit slip for the full amount then hesitated at the window and asked the teller to cash the check instead. He replied curtly that that wasn't possible with a new account. It took at least ten days for the initial check to clear so the account could be activated.

"But I'm opening the account with a check from another account at this same bank." Cissy for once in her life felt irrevocably in the right and resolved not to leave the bank until she had gotten what she wanted. "It wouldn't take you a minute to look up the account and make sure there's enough money in it to cover the check."

The teller shrugged. What she was asking was against the rules, but it finally made more sense to agree with her than to argue. "You'll have to put at least a hundred dollars in the account to open it, but I can give you the rest in cash."

"Do you have a hundred-dollar bill?" Cissy asked impulsively. "I've never seen one. I don't even know whose picture is on it."

He handed her the bill. She touched it respectfully, studying the compassionate features of Benjamin Franklin. Of all the Founding Fathers, he had always struck her as the most human. She wanted to keep him close to her. "You may give me the rest in small bills," she said. "I'm keeping this."

The teller watched her exit. She was an attractive woman, and he admired her shapely legs as she walked briskly through the revolving door. She shouldn't be carrying that much cash, he thought. He hoped she would get home without being mugged. New York City was no place for a woman with a hundred-dollar bill in her handbag.

Twenty-seven

In the face of Lindsay's refusal to reveal any of the facts concerning the father of her child, Cissy had constructed an elaborate fantasy involving a passionate love affair with a tragic ending. But out of it a love child was going to be born. Even flat on her back, Lindsay seemed to be living a more exciting life than Cissy ever would. Just by being around her, Cissy hoped to share in the drama she sensed taking place.

"I'm the only person in her life with any kind of past connection," she tried to explain to her mother when she called to say she was going to stay with Lindsay for a while longer—she didn't dare say how much longer. "She doesn't have anybody but me. Her parents were killed in a plane crash and her husband is an invalid and . . ." She stopped abruptly, knowing her mother could not possibly absorb the information that a contemporary of her daughter's, with the same privileged and overprotected upbringing, was pregnant by a man whom—for reasons Lindsay continued to keep from Cissy—she never expected to see again. "So don't you see, Mother," Cissy continued, "I have to stay until . . . I mean as long as she needs me."

It was the absence of a father that Cissy found most fascinating about the drama she was being allowed to share. Lindsay was the independent woman Cissy had never dared to be. She had not even allowed the existence of an invalid husband to deny her the opportunity to fulfill her birthright: the right to reproduce.

Now that she had a vital role to play, Cissy was determined to stay till the baby was born, to witness the miracle of a woman living alone—without any visible male support, physical or emotional—re-creating herself at midlife, just before that privilege was lost to her forever. She envied Lindsay the prospect of having a baby all to herself, of not having to please anyone but herself. When her children were young, Cissy had always enjoyed being with them during the day but around four in the afternoon she would start getting tense about having them ready for inspection when Charles came home for dinner. She would try to have them bathed and fed by six, praying he would find them appealing enough to play with, or at least watch them play, so she could cook his dinner without interruption.

And even though it had been years since the children interrupted her sleep, she still found herself waking at intervals during the night, listening for noises. Cissy had continued to breast-feed her babies after they started teething just to keep them from crying and disturbing Charles. When she was alone with them, their crying never bothered her as long as she knew there was no reason for it. But when Charles heard one of the children cry, he always sent Cissy to stop it, as if it were somehow her fault. And so she rocked and suckled and sang until they began to bite her so hard she had to stop.

It was at those times—doing things she would never have done if she had been alone with them, just to convince Charles she was a good mother—that she began to resent them. She wouldn't admit it, even to herself, until the dentist told her she had to stop grinding her teeth. How unfair, she realized now, to burden children with all the unexpressed and often unacknowledged anger a woman feels toward her husband. If only she could have a second chance—just to be a mother, without trying to be a wife at the same time. She had a feeling she would be absolutely wonderful at it, and her children would adore her and want her to be with them always. Sometimes she wondered if Lindsay knew how lucky she was.

However, when they talked, it was not about children. Their conversation was more often about the past than the future, usually centering around the girls they had known at college and what had become of them.

Reading the reunion issue of the alumnae bulletin with Cissy seated beside her interspersing comments, Lindsay began to wonder how much the girls in their graduating class had changed since she last saw them—or worse, how little. Maiden names capitalized in the middle of one-sentence summaries of a year's activities evoked long-forgotten faces and a chorus of highly distinctive voices:

There was Sue PARKER, the butt of everybody's jokes freshman year. Her gung-ho enthusiasm for everything an eastern college had to offer a girl raised on a ranch in Arizona made her suspect in the eyes of her prep school–educated contemporaries, who had learned with adolescence that to appear sophisticated it was always safer not to seem too interested in anything or anyone. She never acquired this uninterested facade and after freshman year, when roommates were assigned, could not find anyone to share her room again—though she asked everyone. Her enthusiasm undiminished by unanimous rejection, she decorated her small single room with travel posters and announced at graduation that she was going to join the Army and see the world. The reunion issue of the alumnae bulletin contained the news that Sue PARKER would be honored with an Alumna Achievement Award in recognition of the fact that she was now the highest-ranking female officer in the United States Army.

Medora HAYDEN Mills, who had been a member of the May Queen's court beginning freshman year and brandished the scepter herself as a senior, wrote that her "life had come full circle" this spring when her oldest daughter was elected May Queen and wore her mother's dress, which, Medora reported, "still fits me like a glove. My greatest accomplishment at forty-one," she wrote proudly, "is that I still wear the same dress size I did at twenty-one."

The accomplishments of their other classmates lay somewhere between these two. A handful had embarked on careers _before_ they were divorced, taking low-level jobs after graduation, interrupting a laborious ascent up the ladder of success to stay at home until their children were school age, then timidly venturing back into the professional world, hoping their absence would go unnoticed.

The majority, however, seemed to become more defensive each year, as the women's movement gained visibility, about the validity of their original choice to function as the sturdy axis on which the movement of husband and children depended.

There was, for instance, Liz BAKER Robinson, of Americus, Georgia, to whom Lindsay had lost the editorship of the college newspaper senior year. Lindsay had ended up replacing her at midterm, however, when Liz resigned in tears after an editorial she wrote quoting in full a letter from her father in support of racially segregated schools provoked an angry rebuttal from their faculty sponsor. As Lindsay recalled, what upset the faculty most about the whole uproar was the realization that even after four years of college education, students still allowed their fathers to have the last word. Liz had now become militant in her defense of needlepoint as a daily occupation—with occasional forays into the kitchen to make granola from an original recipe. "I'm tired of being told by a lot of selfish, unhappy women who couldn't get married or stay married that I'm wasting my life," she concluded in an open letter to the college paper that she urged the rest of her classmates to sign. It was entitled "Thoughts from an Angry Alumna on the Occasion of Her Twentieth Reunion."

As her classmates sprang to life before her eyes, their angers and achievements passing in review, Lindsay felt like Betty Friedan compiling the results of the Smith College alumnae questionnaire that led her to write *The Feminine Mystique* in an effort to come to grips with "the problem that has no name."

But here it was almost two decades later, the problem had been named and a whole movement launched to deal with it, and feminine unrest seemed greater than ever. The movement appeared to be threatening the very people it was supposed to support and encourage.

Lindsay made a note in the special book she kept on her bedside table. In the weeks she had been confined to her bed, her mind had never been more active, as if to compensate for the inactivity of her body. Ideas, thoughts, connections, crowded her head, and she had gotten into the habit of jotting things down as they occurred to her. Sometimes she thought fate was calling her bluff, forcing her to write the book that had begun only as the excuse for her year's leave of absence from the magazine. Of course, she couldn't tell Cissy what she was doing. Cissy had been too relieved to learn that the book was only the cover for a last-chance pregnancy. She would feel threatened to think Lindsay was contemplating both. So Lindsay told her she was making notes for future articles for the magazine. The class letter had given her a marvelous idea for a multipart series, she said. She was thinking about calling it "Women on the Move—the Ones Who Don't Know Where They're Going." Cissy was thrilled to think the class letter she had compiled could inspire an article in a national magazine and asked Lindsay if she could help research it.

But Lindsay was reading the class letter again, looking for the one name whose life still had the power to affect hers. "Why isn't there anything about Meg?" she demanded.

"She was the only one who didn't reply. Nobody seems to know anything about her. I guess you're the only one who's kept up with her."

Lindsay shook her head, confessed how little she knew of Meg and her life since graduation. "I asked her to come—to be with John Henry—when I found out I was going to have to stay in bed. But she had jury duty—apparently she doesn't feel any more connection with him now than she does with me or with any of us."

To Lindsay's surprise, Cissy began to laugh. "To think all these years I've felt excluded from a friendship that no longer exists."

Somehow, hearing Cissy laugh, Lindsay was forced to acknowledge a truth she had not been able to face. Meg was never going to come. Lindsay could not count on her, could not count on anyone, to take her place with John Henry. She had to go to him herself—to see him at least once before the baby was born and tell him what was happening to her, what was happening for both of them.

She waited till the next morning when Cissy left for the grocery store to get dressed. It seemed strange putting on street clothes; for six weeks she had worn nothing but a nightgown. She was almost frightened to step outside her building, into the street, into the world. Cissy had woven such a tight and comforting cocoon around her and the unborn life she was nurturing, Lindsay had almost succeeded in forgetting the men whose lives had shaped her present circumstances—John Henry, defying his doctors by clinging to an existence that had long since lost all meaning for him; the still-unidentified assailant who had fathered the only child she would ever have; and Todd, the only one who could actively love her. However, only one of these lives had any continuing connection with her, and in the absence of anyone who could act in her place, she had to get to him.

If she had been able to go straight to a taxi, she could have reached the train station before anyone stopped her and arrived at John Henry's bedside, abandoning both her lives—her own and the one she was carrying—to whatever providence was sustaining him.

But when the doorman saw her get out of the elevator looking pale and disoriented, he insisted she take a seat in the lobby while he hailed a cab. Then he quickly called the number Cissy had left posted in case Lindsay ever called down for help in her absence, and kept Lindsay talking until Stephen Presnell arrived.

"You didn't have to get dressed and come downstairs," he said, putting an arm around her. "I've got an ambulance with me. They would have brought you down in a stretcher."

"Ambulance? What are you talking about? What are you doing here?" Lindsay protested weakly, as he took her outside and helped her onto the waiting stretcher. He said he was taking her to the lab for an amniocentesis—to make sure the baby was developing normally.

"I don't care about the baby. I have to go to John Henry," Lindsay sobbed. "He doesn't understand why I don't come, why nobody comes. The baby isn't even a person yet. I have to put John Henry first."

But later in the lab, watching in wonder as ultrasound waves showed her the shape of the fetus, praying that the amniotic fluid being extracted from her womb would not reveal any abnormalities, Lindsay was overwhelmed with the human potential she was nurturing. It was no longer a question of choosing between John Henry and the baby. Lindsay was now radiant with the conviction that she would sacrifice her own life if necessary to save this child, the outlines of whose tiny body she had seen with her own eyes. For she carried inside her the chance for a perfectly realized life, the redemption of all her failures, her future, her salvation, the ultimate meaning of her own life.

Twenty-eight

When the foreman of the jury pronounced the defendant guilty of murder in the second degree, the defense attorney burst into tears. Though Meg agreed with the verdict, she could not help being impressed with the obvious passion and sincerity with which the young lawyer had defended her client. She knew Mark would ridicule the tears and make some comment about women lawyers and the excessive emotion they introduced into the courtroom, but Meg saw in the attorney for the defense what she had once hoped to become.

The convicted murderess, amazingly calm at least on the surface, was reaching over now to give her lawyer a pat on the knee. Still sobbing, the young lawyer allowed her client to comfort her until she grew calm. A passerby, if asked which woman had just been pronounced guilty, would not have hesitated to point to the attorney.

Meg jotted down the lawyer's name in a notebook she carried

in her purse. She wanted to be armed with the name of an advocate if Mark threatened her with legal action when she told him what she was about to do.

It had been five weeks since Lindsay had called and asked her to come to New York. All that time, sitting in the courtroom, listening to the lawyers debate the motives of the patrician, impeccably coiffed woman accused of murdering a man she had loved for a decade and swore under oath she loved still, Meg debated within her conscience what she owed to people she had once promised to love forever.

She had kept Lindsay at a polite distance since they parted after graduation—not returning her phone calls, not answering her letters, not even letting her know when she accompanied Mark on business trips to New York. For she could not think of Lindsay without thinking of John Henry and feeling that if she had only kept her promise to marry him, the accident would not have occurred. But while Meg tried to forget Lindsay and all the roads not taken that she represented, Lindsay continued to press the claim of their college friendship. And even though Meg pretended that Lindsay belonged to a closed chapter of her life, she knew in her heart that the bonds from those four years—only a fraction of her life as measured by the calendar—were forged in an intensity of experience unequaled by anything in her life as a suburban matron. Meg did not mind the physical evidence age was beginning to inflict on her appearance—she never considered frosting her hair to camouflage the gray strands now apparent even without her glasses and steadfastly refused to punish herself when the scale registered a few extra pounds—but she never ceased to lament the loss of passion that passed for maturity.

Today, leaving the courtroom and returning from downtown Los Angeles to her beautifully landscaped home in Brentwood, she sensed a chance to recover that loss. With mounting excitement she called the airline for a reservation on the late-night flight to New York. She seemed to be making her biggest decision since leaving law school to marry Mark. And yet now as

Life Sentences

then, she reflected ironically, her journey was an act of love undertaken on behalf of a man in need.

Mark had wanted a wife at his side when he left family and friends behind in Texas to accept an offer from a California law firm. Meg, too, had left everything behind, including any ambition for a career of her own, and helped him make a name and place for himself in a community where neither of them had known anyone on arrival. She had even joined the Lawyers' Wives and had not thought until now, imagining how she would explain to Lindsay what she had done with her life since college, how ridiculous it was for wives to assume a common purpose and assemble on a regular basis simply because their husbands had chosen the same profession.

She might never have questioned her choices if Lindsay hadn't suggested an action that could absolve her or at least alleviate the tight knot of guilt inside her stomach that had kept Meg from ever successfully completing a pregnancy. The doctor had recommended a hysterectomy after her fourth miscarriage caused a depression that required electric shock treatments to cure. Meg refused, feeling that her failure to reproduce life would hardly be ameliorated by making it permanent. But Mark said he was not emotionally equipped to survive another miscarriage and refused to sleep with her again until she agreed to the operation.

Meg moved into the room that had been designated as a nursery when they bought the house and never again asked Mark where he was going when he left the house or what time he would be back. When he wanted to have dinner at home or invite company, he gave her ample notice to buy groceries and plan a meal. When he didn't say anything, she didn't expect him and waited until she was hungry to look in the refrigerator and make a modest meal out of whatever was available.

Once she had her own room, she began falling asleep as soon as it got dark. She didn't like being awake when Mark got home and wondering if he would come in to kiss her good night. Or occasionally when he'd had too much to drink at dinner, forget his oath and crawl in bed with her. What happened then was not what Meg called lovemaking—or even sleeping together. When it was over, he would stumble back to his own bed. Meg would close her eyes and try to sleep but was usually awake again before dawn. She would get out of bed eagerly, knowing that for the next few hours the world belonged to her alone. When it was not too cold, she would go out to her garden and start working in the dark, sensing just by touch what needed doing and watching the world re-created by sunrise.

It was the garden she would miss most, Meg thought, standing in the doorway. Only there, amid the jonquils and the jasmine, did she have any sense of renewal taking place in her life. But she turned quickly and went into her room to pack her suitcase. There was at last another life depending on her—one for whom her presence might possibly make the difference between life and death. She had spent twenty years trying not to think about John Henry. Now all she wanted was to put her arms around him and tell him to stay alive, that his life even now was precious to her.

"What was the verdict?" Mark asked, entering the bedroom.

"Guilty," said Meg, opening her suitcase and removing the clothes she had brought home.

"I missed you," he said, putting his arm around her. "Would you like to go out to dinner?"

"I can't stay," she replied. "I just came home to get some clean clothes."

"What do you mean? The trial's over, isn't it? You won't have to serve again. At least not for a long time."

"I'm leaving you, Mark," she said calmly. She thought of the woman convicted of killing her lover comforting her lawyer after the verdict was announced. Meg was suddenly grateful to her. Her crime had led to a trial that had given Meg a chance, during her sequestered weeks as a juror, to pass judgment on her actions of the past twenty years. The crime had cost the defendant her freedom but had given at least one of the jurors who convicted her the courage to reclaim hers. With the same objectivity that allowed her to weigh the evidence and pronounce guilty a woman with whom she identified so completely, Meg passed sentence on her own life.

"What grounds?" Mark demanded angrily.

"Infidelity."

"I stopped making love to you because I couldn't let you risk another miscarriage," he argued. Neither of them referred to the occasional nights that had nothing to do with love.

"The risk was mine."

"You left me no choice," he said finally.

"I gave you every possible choice. I always have. But I'm not talking about the other women in your life. That's your concern. I'm talking about me. I'm the one who's been unfaithful."

"You?" He was shocked into silence, a reaction Meg had never seen before. Finally he found words for his immediate concern. "Who with? How many? How dare you?"

"I haven't been unfaithful to you, I've been unfaithful to myself, to everything I started out to be."

"I never asked you to give up anything for me. If law school meant so much to you, why didn't you stick it out?"

Stick it out? How dare he imply a failure of will on her part? Had he forgotten how he had begged her to marry him so he wouldn't have to move to California alone?

"I was in the top quarter of my class," Meg said quietly with a pride she had kept hidden all the years of their marriage, along with a fact she had never admitted knowing until now. "And where were you at the end of your first year in law school?" she challenged in a tone of quiet contempt.

"When did you find out about that?" As a lawyer it was his habit to answer a question with a question.

"The day I told the Dean I was leaving law school to marry you."

"Dean Caldwell. Of course. She would."

Something about the way he said "she," as if that let him off the hook, enraged Meg, and quiet contempt gave way to tearful indignation. She confronted Mark with the knowledge she had carried inside her like a secret weapon ever since she left law school to marry him.

"Would you ever have admitted to me that you flunked your first year of law school?" But her outrage could not be contained long enough for him to answer and she continued, "Your father had to buy your way back in, admit it."

Mark remained silent until he could think of a question for an answer.

"If you knew that, why did you marry me?" he asked finally.

"Because I loved you. I didn't want to live without you. I thought it would be enough just to be part of your life. I didn't want a life of my own if it didn't include you."

In the silence that followed, they said more to each other than they had at the dinner table in all the years of their marriage. Then at last the lawyer became the judge and pronounced sentence. "You should have fought for what you wanted. I never asked you to make any sacrifices for me."

"It didn't seem like a sacrifice then. It does now."

"Where will you go?" he asked finally.

"I'm going to stay with Lindsay. She needs me."

Mark sat down on the bed, resting his hand on her suitcase as if somehow that could prevent her from leaving. Meg sat beside him, patting him on the knee, as she had seen the convicted murderess do earlier to console her lawyer for a verdict a higher authority than either of their individual consciences had just pronounced. Despite the fact that he had stopped making love with her, Meg continued to find herself attracted to Mark, but this was the first time she could remember feeling physically aroused by pure compassion. He seemed so abandoned and alone. She even wondered briefly how he would get along without her. Then she forced herself to remember how little she had done for him in recent years, how little he had allowed her to do for him. Slowly she unbuttoned her blouse, then reaching for the hand that rested protectively on the suitcase, placed it on her breast.

"I'm not leaving you to be leaving you, you know," she said gently. "I'll always love you. I have no intention of ever marrying anyone else. I just don't think I can live with you anymore. But I probably would have stayed forever if someone else hadn't needed me more than you do."

"What difference does it make why you're leaving? I'm going to end up alone." Suddenly he threw the suitcase on the floor. "I won't let you leave me," he cried. "You made your choice. You can't go back and start over."

Meg saw no point in trying to explain that you can have the sensation of going backward when you witness forward motion from a stationary position. Instead she put her arms around him and pressed his head against her shoulder. He pushed her back onto the bed, and they made love in the space where the suitcase had lain open, surrounded by piles of clothing waiting to be packed.

Afterward she knelt beside the bed to repack. Mark, usually the first to accuse her of complicating sex with emotion, was stunned.

"You're not still going?" he demanded.

When Meg said nothing had changed, he accused her of being in love with Lindsay.

"I do love her," Meg replied, "but I'm not in love with her. It's just that she's always expected more of me than anybody else. More than my parents, more than you, more even than I ever expected of myself. I've disappointed her for twenty years. I'm not going to disappoint her again. A friend has as much right as a parent or a husband to make demands. And right now Lindsay needs me more than anybody. And I need her."

"If you go," Mark said ominously, "I won't answer for anything I do while you're away."

Meg was genuinely puzzled by this threat and intended no sarcasm when she replied, "If you don't, who will?"

Mark walked out of the bedroom and out of the house. Meg heard the car leaving the garage, so she called a taxi to take her to the airport. When the "red eye" landed in New York at dawn the next day, her eyes were not red, despite tears and lack of sleep; they shone like displaced stars that had finally been readmitted into the galaxy.

Twenty-nine

It was not until her plane landed at Kennedy that Meg understood why she had traveled across the continent—and where she still had to go.

She disembarked carrying her one suitcase (wondering how many women would walk out on home and husband with only one suitcase) and briskly crossed the terminal to the taxi area. "Grand Central Station," she said as automatically as if she were a daily commuter.

She remembered her first trip to New York. Her parents had flown with her from Amarillo for a holiday in the city before college began sophomore year. Lindsay met them at the Plaza for lunch then insisted Meg come home to Larchmont with her for the weekend. In that taxi to Grand Central, Meg made no effort to conceal her excitement and asked wide-eyed questions about everything they passed. Lindsay, distracted and embarrassed by her friend's enthusiasm, underestimated the tip when she paid the driver. Muttering obscenities about ignorant tourists who ought to stay home, he hurled the coins after them as they scrambled out of the cab and into the comfortingly anonymous crowds of Grand Central.

On the train to Larchmont, Lindsay had lectured Meg about the protective armor a person had to develop to move freely and unobtrusively through the city. "Never make eye contact with anyone or appear interested in anything," she had warned. "When you walk down the sidewalk, pretend you're inside your car, driving, with the doors locked and the windows closed. Look preoccupied and in a hurry and no one will bother you."

Meg could still hear Lindsay's advice from long ago ringing in her ears as the taxi took her across the Queensboro Bridge into the city. Apparently she had absorbed it because the driver merely grunted when she told him her destination and attempted no further conversation. When he stopped at the station, she quickly calculated a fifteen percent tip, added it to the charge, then told the driver how much change to give her from the large bill she handed him. She marveled at her own calm and efficiency as she took the time to count her change before getting out of the cab and felt triumphant when the driver actually held open her door then handed her the suitcase.

As she walked into the station smiling to herself, she began to think that even if she had not come a long way in the last twenty years like the confident, smiling woman advertising cigarettes, she had at least acquired some small sense of who she was. And loose change was no longer thrown in her wake.

At the hospital Meg was informed that John Henry was not allowed visitors. She asked to see his doctor and told him she had come all the way from California.

"Does Lindsay know you're here?" he asked immediately.

"No," Meg replied. "She asked me to come—but she doesn't know I'm here."

Craig Sanborn asked no further questions, just said, "I'm glad you've come." Then, assuming by her presence that Meg was strong enough to share the burden that had been his alone till she arrived, revealed that Lindsay had left her bed the previous day and tried to come to the hospital. Fortunately the obstetrician taking care of her was alerted by the doorman and no harm was done to her or her baby.

"He's an old friend of mine—since medical school. I sent him to Lindsay, but now he's asked me to do something I don't think I can do." Craig got up and walked to the window. Meg waited for him to continue. "He wants me to tell Lindsay that John Henry is dead. He says it's the only way to keep her from trying to come to him—the only way to save the baby." He paused and looked at Meg, hoping she would say something that would make his decision easier, but she remained silent. "I wish I could do something to help her, but I can't do that."

"Do you think he's going to die?" Meg asked finally.

"I didn't expect him to live longer than a few months after the accident. That was nineteen years ago last night."

"You remember the exact date?"

"I didn't until I found out Lindsay had tried to come to him. Then I remembered."

"I don't want him to die," Meg said with a sudden intensity that surprised her more than it did the doctor. "Not before he forgives me," she added in a low voice—then was ashamed of her self-interest, or at least of allowing it to show.

"You'll have no way of knowing. You're never going to know how he feels about anything."

"May I at least see him?"

"I should ask Lindsay."

"Please don't. I'm not sure I can go through with it and I don't want to disappoint her any more than I already have."

Craig nodded in silent acquiescence then led the way down the corridor. She stood in the doorway while he crossed to the moving bed. There seemed to Meg nothing human about the figure being mechanically propelled in a rhythmic pattern of perpetual motion. How could it possibly make any difference to this machine with human features who came or did not come? Who stayed by his bed or stayed away? None of this had anything to do with the man she had once promised to marry. Why had Lindsay wanted so desperately for her to acknowledge his existence? What difference could it possibly make to anyone except herself that she had left home to come here? The exhilaration she had felt the night before, flying from west to east, was gone now and she was filled with apprehension at the hidden costs of the journey. The sense of commitments acknowledged, of allegiances owed—her justification for leaving home—had been overshadowed by her growing excitement at being given an unexpected second chance, but now loomed large and inescapable.

"I can't come any closer," she said in a whisper that was the beginning of a muffled scream as Craig walked back to where she was standing. He touched her elbow to reassure her and felt her tremble. "I can't go in yet," she confessed, starting back down the hallway. "Not until I know what to say to him."

Craig suggested she wait in his office. He had rounds to make, so no one would disturb her, and there was a couch if she wanted to rest.

"I haven't slept since I left Los Angeles," she admitted, stretching out on the leather couch facing his desk. "If I could just lie down awhile, then I'm sure I'll be able to do whatever . . . whatever has to be done."

Thirty

When Meg awoke, it was dark outside. Her cheek was sweaty from lying against a leather pillow. She turned on a light and looked at her watch. Seven P.M. Was it possible she had slept through a whole day? How kind of the doctor to allow her to rest undisturbed in his office, she thought as she stood and straightened her skirt. She wasn't sure where she was going, but she couldn't stay alone in his office any longer. And she had to find a bathroom. After that she would think about what to do next.

She started down the hallway, carrying her suitcase, looking for a nurse who could direct her to a rest room. The long corridors appeared deserted and she found herself retracing the steps that had taken her to John Henry's room that morning. Hesitantly she stepped through the doorway until she was within his range of vision.

"Do you know who I am, John Henry?" she began, but then

she saw that his eyes were closed. He seemed to be sleeping peacefully. She felt a sense of release. Whether he lived or died had nothing to do with her. She could leave now without guilt. What would it accomplish to let him know she was here? She would go into the city and see Lindsay, do anything that needed to be done for her, then look for a place to live, get a job, allow life to happen to her again. After today she would never be afraid of her friendship with Lindsay. Meg could finally afford to feel close to her without risking a judgment that would confirm her failure.

As she turned to leave, she saw Craig Sanborn coming toward her. He smiled triumphantly and said he had just gone to his office to get her.

The fever had finally broken and he felt hopeful that John Henry was going to survive this crisis. "Now maybe Lindsay will believe that whether he lives or dies has nothing to do with her," Craig said.

"Or with me," Meg added. "He doesn't even know I'm here."

"I told him this morning that you were asleep in my office."

"Oh, no," Meg cried, starting down the hallway in a panic, desperate to escape the implication that she was in any way connected to John Henry's fate.

When Craig caught up with her and tried to take her hand, she pulled away. "I have to fix my hair," she said quickly to cover her confusion. "I can't let him see me like this. Not after all these years."

Still holding her suitcase, she hurried to the ladies' room and was barely inside the stall when she began to vomit. She had not eaten all day, so there was no relief in the aftermath of the upheaval, just the feeling that she was being propelled as mechanically as John Henry in his oscillating bed down a road from which there was no turning back.

Holding the faucet with her right hand so the water would continue to run full force, she awkwardly washed her face with her left hand. She could not hear the knock at the door into the hallway then Craig's voice asking anxiously if she was all right. She dried her face with a paper towel then began to sponge off her dress. Slipping off the wet dress quickly, she opened her suitcase to find something else to wear. She was standing in her slip when a movement in the mirror caught her attention and she realized Craig had just come through the door.

"When you didn't answer, I was afraid something had happened to you," he said quickly, to hide his embarrassment.

"No, I'm all right," Meg answered, rolling up her wet dress and hiding it in the suitcase, hoping he would not realize she had been sick. "I just wanted to change." She continued to dress as if there were nothing unusual about his presence in a ladies' rest room, and he seemed reluctant to leave her alone again.

"I'll drive you back to the city whenever you want to go," he volunteered suddenly. "Will you be staying with Lindsay?"

"I don't know," Meg admitted helplessly, turning to face him as if he knew the answers to all the questions ahead of her. "Buying the plane ticket was such a big decision. I haven't thought beyond that."

He reached behind her and zipped up her dress, as if she were a child getting ready for her first day of school. "I'll be in my office," he said. "Let me know when you're ready."

As soon as he was gone, Meg took out her makeup case and carefully began to apply foundation lotion. She took the time to apply all the knowledge she had acquired along with the expensive Laszlo cosmetics she had agreed to use exclusively as a condition of their purchase. When she was finished, she smiled approvingly at her image in the mirror, closed her suitcase, and started down the corridor toward Craig's office.

But she couldn't pass John Henry's room without stopping, even though the door was now closed. He knew she had come. She had to face him—to let him see her.

Taking a deep breath, she opened the door. The bed was not

moving and she thought for a moment she was in the wrong room. Then she realized that the nurse bending over the motionless bed was bathing John Henry.

"No visitors allowed now," the nurse said sharply.

"I have permission from the doctor," Meg lied. "I'm family."

The nurse shrugged and pulled the sheet up to John Henry's shoulders. "Call me when you're through. I'll finish later."

When the nurse had left, Meg moved cautiously to the bed and sat in the chair beside it. Not until she was seated did she have the courage to look at John Henry. His eyes gazed at her steadily, without shame or sentiment. Suddenly there seemed no need to apologize or explain. Meg was struck by how young his face appeared, though his inability to move his facial muscles and change expressions gave him an intensity that was alien to all her memories. She remembered him smiling, joking, laughing when she talked about wanting to see more of the world before she settled in Texas. But he was not laughing now. His eyes seemed to devour her and Meg knew he would listen and believe anything she said and remember it for the rest of his life.

"You gave us all quite a scare," she said, smiling, bending over to touch his cheek with her lips. Then, avoiding his eyes, she reached for the sponge the nurse had left on the bedside table and began to squeeze it between her fingers.

"I wish I could finish what she was doing," she said hesitantly, "but I'm afraid of doing something wrong."

She thought she saw him tremble and she quickly pulled up the blanket that was lying folded at the foot of the bed and tucked it around his shoulders.

"I'm going to see you every day, John Henry," she heard herself promising. "Until Lindsay can come again." Hastening to answer the anxious question in his eyes, she took his hand and pressed it to her cheek. "She's going to be all right. She just needs to rest. I'll be staying with her, so don't worry. She'll have everything she needs. And so will you. I promise."

She rang for the nurse then bid John Henry a hesitant good-bye. She told Craig she could easily take a train back into the city but he insisted on driving her.

"I'd invite you up," Meg said hesitantly as Craig stopped his car outside Lindsay's building, "but she's not even expecting me. I should have called and let her know I was on the way."

"You wouldn't have been able to talk to her. She doesn't answer her phone anymore. You have to leave a message on her machine and then if she wants to talk, she'll call you."

Suddenly Meg was frantic at the thought that she was outside Lindsay's building with no way to reach her.

"We'll tell the doorman who you are. That may work," Craig laughed, parking his car and escorting Meg to the front of the building.

The doorman listened dubiously but left them standing outside while he called upstairs on the house phone. He reported that Lindsay was already asleep and could not be disturbed.

"Who did you talk to?" Craig demanded.

"The lady who's taking care of her," the doorman explained. "She decides everything."

"I'm afraid there's nothing you can do till morning. I'll help you find a hotel," said Craig.

"No, I came to see Lindsay and I'm going to stay till I do."

Craig returned to the doorman and persuaded him, with the help of a twenty-dollar bill, to let Meg wait inside. Walking back to his car, he spotted a pay phone. He deposited a dime and dialed Lindsay's number. He waited while her recorded voice asked the caller to leave a message, then told her who was calling and the time. "Your friend Meg is waiting downstairs to see you."

He hung up, got in his car, and drove back to New Rochelle. As he drove, he wondered who out of his past would come to him if he needed help.

Thirty-one

Cissy put down the phone and began to cry. How could she have done that to Meg! She would have to face her in the morning and then what would she say? Oh, why couldn't Meg have just stayed in California, remained part of Lindsay's past? Now that she was in New York everything would change. Given the choice, Lindsay would want to be with Meg, just as she had sophomore year.

However, nothing would change tonight. Cissy turned off the light in the study and closed her eyes. Suddenly the sharp ring of a telephone pierced the darkness. Thank goodness Lindsay always turned down the volume of the phone beside her bed before she went to sleep, Cissy thought, picking up the extension in the study to see if the caller was leaving a message. She heard a kind male voice whom she could easily identify from previous calls as Craig Sanborn saying that Meg was waiting downstairs.

Waiting? Oh, why couldn't she have just left? Returned to

Lindsay's past where she had taken such stubborn refuge for the past twenty years.

Cissy slowly replaced the receiver and turned on the light. She had no choice. She had to let Meg into the apartment. What happened next would be up to Lindsay.

Cissy dressed quickly then took the elevator to the lobby. Meg was seated in a chair, her hands resting quietly in her lap, her eyes wide open, gazing appreciatively at some private landscape. She seemed to be awaiting an audience that had been arranged long ago—one that she had no doubt would be granted.

Cissy was filled with envy at the quiet confidence Meg seemed to exude, the certain knowledge that once Lindsay knew she was there, she would want to see her. Even though Lindsay was paying Cissy to take care of her, Cissy never returned from a trip to the grocery store without wondering if Lindsay had changed her mind, if she still wanted her to stay.

"Meg," Cissy spoke shyly, hesitant to violate her mood. "It's Cissy Clark. Cissy Mason, I mean. At least I used to be."

Meg stood and looked at her curiously, then suddenly wrapped her in an embrace. "Cissy, is it really you? I haven't seen you since your wedding. You look just the same."

"Really?" Cissy beamed with pleasure. "Well, I'm not the same, but I'm glad it doesn't show." She stepped back to get her breath. The excitement of having her past catch up with her so unexpectedly was almost too much to bear. She continued to hold Meg's hands in hers. "You're beautiful, Meg. But then you always were."

"What are you doing here?" Meg asked. "I thought you lived in California."

"I moved back to Connecticut last year—after my husband died. I wrote all about it in the class letter. Don't you ever read the alumnae bulletin?"

Meg shook her head. "I'm sorry, Cissy. I save them—I keep them stacked in the magazine rack by my bed—but I haven't had the courage to look at one in years."

"You never answered any of my postcards or letters either," Cissy said, suddenly petulant with neglect.

"I never had any news," Meg replied matter-of-factly, refusing to offer an apology. "Are you staying with Lindsay?"

Meg leaned down to retrieve the suitcase that had been stored out of sight beside her chair. She started toward the elevator without waiting for Cissy to answer.

"I'm taking care of her until the baby is born," Cissy said in a proprietary tone, pushing the button for the eighth floor as she eyed Meg's suitcase suspiciously. "She didn't think you were coming."

"Neither did I—until last night."

"Then you're planning to stay?"

"For the first time in my life I don't have any plans at all," Meg said, following Cissy into the apartment. "I'll do whatever Lindsay wants."

"She's asleep now," Cissy said quickly.

"I know. The housekeeper told the doorman she couldn't be disturbed. I thought I'd probably have to wait in the lobby till morning. If I'd known you were staying with her, I would've asked to speak to you. How did you find out I was here anyway?"

"There was a call from the doctor. He said you were waiting downstairs." Cissy quickly changed the topic. A confession would require at least a pretense of contrition and Cissy was still too threatened by Meg's unexpected arrival to apologize for trying to keep her away. "You must be tired. I'll make a bed for you on the couch."

Meg shook her head. "No, I'm not tired at all. I just want to see Lindsay. I promise not to wake her."

Cissy opened the door into the darkened bedroom. Meg entered, shutting the door behind her.

Cissy stood outside for a moment not knowing what to do. If she had any pride, she thought, she would leave now, but she had never had any pride when it came to Lindsay. If she had, she wouldn't have arrived for lunch uninvited. But then she wouldn't have been here when Lindsay needed her. If she left now, she would never know when Lindsay might need her again. And above all, she would never discover the secret of a friendship so strong it could survive twenty years of silence. She wanted to share in it, even if it just meant standing on the outside, looking in.

So she decided to stay. She had a lot to look forward to—and a lot to learn. She also decided to keep the study. After all, she was here first.

Thirty-two

Meg sat in the darkness beside Lindsay's bed and watched her sleep. She had never been inside this apartment before, though she had sent a Christmas card to this address almost every year. It was just the way she imagined it, just the kind of apartment she and Lindsay had talked about getting after graduation. How many times had she wondered what her life would have been like if she and Lindsay had lived together while they were going to graduate school and starting out on their separate careers. If they had continued—once they came of legal age—to share each other's lives as closely as they had in college, would she fear Lindsay's judgment at midlife as she did now?

The room was too dark to distinguish any details or to see what toll age and events had taken on Lindsay. Though she lay somewhat awkwardly on her side, she appeared to be breathing easily, taking long, deep breaths and releasing them slowly, as if she were connected at the core of her being to the rhythm of the tides and the seasons.

Meg found herself settling into the same pattern and as their breathing became synchronized, she felt an extraordinary sense of release, as if she had let go all at once of her separate destiny and allowed her individual will to merge with the life force that seemed to dominate the room.

She was overwhelmed by the sheer courage the three of them—Lindsay, Meg, even Cissy, sleeping alone in the study— had demonstrated simply by surviving their separate lives and reuniting all these years later to acknowledge the claims of their friendship. She had realized the moment she entered the apartment that there was no housekeeper. Cissy was clearly in charge here. It was Cissy who had told the doorman that Lindsay could not be disturbed. How threatened she must have been by Meg's unexpected appearance to resort to such an easily proved lie. Meg would reassure her in the morning, make it clear she had no desire to displace her. Indeed the very fact that Cissy was already here, taking care of Lindsay, made it easier for Meg to stay.

Impulsively, Meg crossed to Lindsay's bed, leaned over, kissed her cheek, and said gently, "It's Meg, Lindsay. I'm here."

"Meg?" Lindsay's eyes opened abruptly. "Oh, Meg—you've come. I was so afraid you wouldn't. How long can you stay?"

"As long as you need me," Meg promised, answering the question for herself as well as for Lindsay. "Now go back to sleep. We'll talk in the morning."

Lindsay reached for Meg's hand and cradled it against her chest. She closed her eyes and continued to keep Meg's hand so closely pressed to her that Meg could feel the beating of her heart. When Lindsay's breathing became deep and regular again, Meg tried to withdraw her hand, but even though she was now sleeping soundly, Lindsay would not let go. Finally with her free hand Meg pulled her chair closer to the bed. She leaned her head back and closed her eyes. She was not tired, there was just nothing to see until morning.

When Meg opened her eyes again, the sun was shining and Lindsay was smiling at her. "How long have you been awake?" Meg asked.

"Not very long. I still think I must be dreaming."

Then Meg confessed the reason she had kept her distance all these years. She had never been able to lie to Lindsay and yet she couldn't bear to admit the truth—that she had failed at everything since she graduated from college with honors. She had done nothing with her life after leaving John Henry. She had nothing to show for her marriage, not even a child.

Lindsay sat up in bed and held out her arms to Meg. Why hadn't Meg called or at least written and told Lindsay what she was going through?

"I didn't think you could possibly understand what a baby would have meant to me."

Meg's statement, spoken in innocence, struck Lindsay with the weight of an unexpected judgment. "I had an abortion," she said dully.

"When?" Meg asked. Whatever pain and guilt from past failures, real or imagined, that she had brought with her into the apartment suddenly seemed irrelevant in the face of Lindsay's confession.

"I called you. I wanted you to come and be with me."

"And I told you I was getting married."

"So I didn't ask. But it was better for you not to know. I hoped you were going to be happy. Happy enough for both of us."

Meg got up and walked to the window. When she turned back to face Lindsay, there were tears in her eyes. "I'm sorry, Lindsay. I haven't been. I haven't even been happy enough for one of us. That's why I'm here. I wish there were some strong and noble and unselfish reason for coming to you after all these years, but the truth is you gave me an excuse to do something I didn't have the courage to do on my own—leave my husband."

"It doesn't matter why you came," Lindsay said gently. "All that matters is that you're here."

No one who knew only the facts of their friendship, thought Meg, could possibly understand the hold she and Lindsay still had on each other after twenty years apart. What amazed her was that the friendship continued to mean as much to Lindsay as it did to her. Each seemed to be the mirror in which the other saw her true self reflected—a wiser, stronger self than appeared to other people. In Lindsay's presence Meg dared to be the kind of person she was afraid to be alone.

They were embracing when Cissy entered with a breakfast tray.

"I'm so sorry," she said apologetically. "I didn't mean to intrude."

"Cissy, come back here," Lindsay laughed. "How could you be intruding? You live here too."

Cissy quickly pulled a table close to the bed and began to set two places. "Cissy—aren't you eating?" Meg asked, helping with the silverware.

"I ate in the kitchen while you were still asleep."

"You always get up while I'm still asleep but you always wait and have breakfast with me," Lindsay said sternly.

"To keep you company. But now you have Meg." The strain of trying not to feel sorry for herself was showing on Cissy's face.

"It's not like college, Cissy. We don't have to choose roommates, you know. There's room for all three of us in the apartment, as long as we're all three happy with the arrangement. Now go get your mug and at least have coffee with us."

After breakfast Meg helped Cissy clear the table and offered to do the dishes, but Cissy refused, explaining that Lindsay was paying her to take care of the apartment. "Well, you're not being paid to take care of me," Meg insisted. "I have no intention of making it harder on anyone by being here. Please let me help."

"I guess you've figured out there's no housekeeper," Cissy said, fiercely scrubbing a skillet, not daring to face Meg. "I was the one who tried to keep you away."

"It's okay. I understood. You thought I'd be taking your place with Lindsay. Don't worry, Cissy, I can't even cook. I've always had full-time help."

After the dishes were done, they bathed Lindsay together then Meg helped Cissy change the bed and take the used linens down the service elevator to the laundry room. While the clothes were tumbling in the coin-operated machines, Meg and Cissy swept and dusted the apartment, mopped the kitchen, and cleaned the bathrooms. Meg left Cissy alone to prepare lunch and returned to Lindsay's bedside.

She told Lindsay that she had seen John Henry. Lindsay listened calmly, as if the actions Meg was recounting were somehow inevitable. "Craig Sanborn called while you and Cissy were doing the laundry. John Henry's out of danger. They still don't know what caused the fever but it's gone."

"Please don't make it sound as if I had anything to do with it," Meg begged.

"It doesn't matter whether you did or not. At least not to me."

"I promised him I'd come every day—till you could start coming again."

Lindsay squeezed her hand. "You didn't have to make any promises."

"I know. I guess I wanted to prove I could keep one."

Thirty-three

Two weeks had passed since Meg's arrival and Cissy still found it hard to believe that she was finally included in a friendship she had envied for so many years.

But it was true. Beyond her obvious usefulness—which even Cissy with her faltering sense of self-esteem had to admit was considerable—they valued her company. Not that the three of them were always together. They were often alone at their separate tasks, then they would pair and re-pair in different combinations. Cissy continued to wake up ahead of the other two and have breakfast waiting. They shared all their meals seated at the table beside Lindsay's bed. After the first morning Cissy did not protest when Meg offered to help with the housework. And none of it seemed like work with the two of them doing it together.

Listening to them laughing and talking above the roar of the vacuum cleaner one morning, Lindsay reached for the notebook beside her bed and jotted down a note for a future magazine piece on communal housekeeping and child care. She wondered why more housewives didn't make a habit of banding together to overcome their individual isolation. Of course, Lindsay had to admit to herself with a smile, it was easy for her, lying alone in her bed, to imagine solutions to problems she had never experienced. Still, the idea intrigued her. What if five women with young children met each weekday morning at a different house? They could work together entertaining the children as they cleaned, polished, washed, then share lunch, take their children home for naps, and have their afternoons to themselves.

The meals they shared were a source of great joy and satisfaction to Cissy. From the day she took over the cooking, Lindsay had encouraged her to experiment freely, saying that for the next few months food was the only area in which adventure was possible for her. And Cissy thrived on the challenge—making elaborate menu plans and trying at least one new recipe at every meal. She had never had the courage to try new recipes on her husband. But with Lindsay and Meg she wasn't afraid to fail. If they didn't like something she served, they just laughed and told her not to worry.

For lunch she made quiches or crepes or soufflés, accompanied by unusual salads—hearts of palm, celery root remoulade, asparagus vinaigrette. As a wife, Cissy had never given a thought to the noon meal, since Charles was not home to share it. She made her lunch out of whatever was left in the refrigerator from dinner the night before. It never occurred to her to fix something new just for herself; neither, on the days when her small appetite would have been satisfied with a piece of fruit or cheese, did she feel right not clearing some space in her perpetually overcrowded refrigerator by reheating the contents of at least one plastic container.

However, Lindsay looked forward to each meal as a new experience and encouraged Cissy to throw away anything that was left after they ate.

After lunch every day, while Lindsay rested, Meg and Cissy would leave the apartment together. Cissy would turn off at the bank or the grocery store. Weather permitting, Meg would walk the twenty blocks to Grand Central then take a train to New Rochelle, where she would spend the afternoon with John Henry.

This was the first time since Meg left law school that she had a destination each day—a place where she was expected and her absence would be noticed. She embraced the sense of purpose the hospital visit gave to her life. The very routine imposed a welcome structure on her day and gave her an incentive for hurrying through the morning housework. She usually fell asleep on the train and woke up on arrival some forty minutes later, refreshed and exhilarated, feeling that an adventure disguised as an obligation awaited her.

She liked the fact that the nurses had begun to greet her by name, and Craig Sanborn often stopped by the room and asked her to have coffee with him before she took the train back to the city.

When she was with John Henry, all the years and events that had come between them evaporated and Meg felt again like a girl of eighteen. She told him that when they first met, he was like no one she had ever known—so sure of himself, of what he wanted and how to get it. Never needing anybody. But then suddenly she was part of his life and it was just understood they were going to get married and she was expected to want everything he wanted.

"It wasn't you I was running from that summer, John Henry," she was finally able to explain—to herself as much as to him. "It was marriage. If we could have just had a chance to know each other, to be together without making plans, how different both our lives might have been."

Meg was always back in the apartment by seven, in time for dinner. Stephen Presnell, stopping by to check on Lindsay, occasionally joined them. Cissy loved having four for dinner—Lindsay in her bed, Stephen seated across from her, and Cissy and Meg on either side. She had never had such an appreciative audience for her culinary efforts and basked in their praise.

"You really should open a restaurant," Meg said.

"Or cater parties," Stephen suggested, savoring the last bite of a chocolate mousse cake Cissy had tried for the first time that night.

But it was Lindsay who said what Cissy wanted most to hear. "I just want her to keep on doing what she's doing right now." Cissy was quite content taking care of Lindsay and now Meg. And with Stephen providing a male presence at dinner, without any accompanying obligation, Cissy felt completely fulfilled.

They had been waiting anxiously for two weeks for the results of the amniocentesis. Finally one night Stephen arrived with a bottle of champagne. He kissed Lindsay and announced that she was carrying a healthy baby girl.

"A daughter?" She was suddenly hesitant and shy. Until now the idea of a baby had been so abstract. "What will I say to a daughter?"

"None of the things our mothers said to us—that's for sure," Cissy responded with a ferocity that surprised all of them. "They had all the answers. We have none."

"We have answers." Lindsay was becoming more confident, already imagining a child in her arms. "We just don't know ahead of time what they are."

"Have you thought about a name?" Stephen asked.

"Claire," Lindsay said suddenly, as if someone else were speaking through her. "I've always loved that name." She hesitated a moment, trying to grasp the elusive thread of recognition that was just beyond her reach. But then it no longer mattered from which dark recesses of her consciousness the name had surfaced. She understood why she had chosen it. "Claire," she repeated with serene authority. "Claire will light the way for all of us."

Meg raised her glass of champagne. "To Claire—the daughter of us all."

Thirty-four

Cissy knew, of course, that once the baby was born, everything would change. The study she now occupied would become a nursery. Lindsay would be able to resume her daily visits to John Henry, and Meg would probably go home to her husband, even though she never mentioned him.

But Cissy had a plan. In the two months she had been staying with Lindsay, she had become a confidante of the superintendent of the building. Lindsay had a hard time remembering the name of any of the other tenants; Cissy knew their life histories. She was particularly attentive to the elderly couple on the floor above Lindsay. They were retiring to Spain in the fall but reluctant to relinquish the lease on their apartment in case the Costa Brava failed to live up to their expectations. The rules of the building prevented them from openly subletting their apartment, but the superintendent hinted that if Cissy were willing to pay a slightly higher figure than their monthly rent, they would be allowed to claim her as a visiting cousin.

Cissy calculated quickly. The apartment was furnished, so aside from utilities and groceries, she would have no foreseeable expenses. With the interest from her savings account plus the salary Lindsay was paying her, she could just about manage it. Of course, there was always the money from Charles' insurance policy, which her father kept invested for her in money market funds. But in her mind Cissy had reserved that money for her children. Even though she had followed Charles wherever his work took him, taken care of his house, provided his meals, and raised his children, she never felt any of the money he earned, either by his life or by his death, belonged to her. The money Lindsay paid her each week was the first Cissy had ever felt free to spend.

It was now August. The couple was sailing for Barcelona aboard a freighter in October. The baby was due in January. Cissy didn't tell anyone what she was planning, least of all Lindsay, but at night, falling asleep in the study, she would try to imagine what it would be like to live alone. Of course, Lindsay would be living on the floor below and Cissy would spend her days looking after her just as she did now. The apartment was designed like Lindsay's—so there was a place for her children any time they wanted to be with her.

She wrote long, individual letters to each of them at camp every night before she went to bed, but never got more than an unsatisfying postcard in reply. Sometimes in the early morning, when she tiptoed out to the mail chute beside the elevator and sent the three letters, each in a separate envelope, tumbling down to the ground floor pickup, she would wonder if any of the three even bothered to open the letters, let alone read them. Then she would resolve not to write again until she heard from at least one of them. She would put all thought of the children out of her mind as she started her daily routine, but when she told Meg and Lindsay good night and retired to her room, she could think of nothing else. She would pour out her thoughts on paper, staring at the three pictures on the desk, kissing each after she sealed the envelopes.

One afternoon the superintendent arranged for her to meet the elderly couple and agree on the terms for the apartment. Cissy, demonstrating an unexpected ability to deal with the intricacies of life in the big city, offered to pay a month's rent in advance to hold the apartment and slipped the superintendent two twenty-dollar bills as he was getting into the elevator.

The phone was ringing when she returned, elated, to the apartment. On the other end her daughter was crying.

"Muffin, what's wrong?" Cissy asked frantically. "Why aren't you in camp?"

"I didn't want to stay for the second half, but Grandmother says I have to go back because we already paid."

"Of course you don't have to go back if you don't want to. Oh, Muffin," she continued happily. "I've got such good news. I've found an apartment for us in New York."

"Please come and get me," Muffin begged. "And don't ever leave me alone again."

"Darling, the apartment won't be vacant till fall. By that time you'll be away at school. But you'll be able to spend all your vacations with me. And I hope the boys will, too. I want more than anything for us to be together again."

"I don't want to go away to school. I don't want to go away anywhere. I just want to be with you. And I don't even care about a horse anymore. The ones at camp were mean and stupid. I tried to give one an apple and he bit me."

"Muffin, I'm coming home tonight," Cissy announced decisively. "Tell your grandmother I'll be there in time for dinner. And don't worry. I won't leave you alone again."

Cissy dressed quickly in the flowered shirtwaist and linen blazer she had been wearing the day she arrived with her picnic basket. Only the bankbook in her purse revealed how much had happened to her in the intervening months.

She left a note for Meg attached to her menu plan for the week then quietly opened the door to Lindsay's room.

"It's all right, Cissy. I'm awake," Lindsay said, sitting up in bed. Then noticing Cissy was dressed, she remarked, "Where did you get that outfit? You look beautiful."

"It's mine. Don't you remember? I was wearing it the day I invited myself for lunch."

"What would I have done if you'd waited for me to invite you? I couldn't have gotten through the past two months without you." Lindsay reached for Cissy's hand, but to her surprise Cissy turned away.

"I have to go home for a while, Lindsay. I just talked to Muffin. She misses me. She actually misses me. I'm so excited."

Lindsay hugged Cissy. "I don't know how to thank you for everything you've done," she began but Cissy quickly interrupted.

"Oh, you don't understand. I'll be back in October. I'm getting my own apartment—right here in the building."

Lindsay listened with undisguised surprise as Cissy explained that she had arranged to sublet the apartment directly overhead. Though Cissy was wearing the same outfit, she was not the same person who had arrived for lunch two months earlier, so frightened of facing her college reunion—and equally frightened of contemplating her future choices.

"You've come a long way, baby," Lindsay grinned as Cissy leaned down to kiss her good-bye. "See you in October. I'm glad we're going to be neighbors."

Thirty-five

In the long days of the longest summer he had ever spent, Todd could find no relief from the oppressive heat and his memories of Lindsay. She pursued him wherever he went. But he was determined not to call her.

On his return from California he had buried himself in his work—staying late at the office, soliciting new clients, welcoming out-of-town meetings. And then one day when he was at his busiest, his thoughts furthest from Lindsay, his secretary buzzed to say that there was someone on the line wanting to speak to him on a personal matter. Lindsay! She was calling at last. So for a moment he couldn't even place the voice, despite its familiarity. And when he did realize it was Laura, he assumed she was calling long distance.

"No, no, darling," she laughed. "I'm practically around the corner. Can we have lunch?"

There was a pause—not too long but enough that they both noticed it before he said, "Yes, of course."

When he walked into the restaurant, he smiled. She was clearly the most attractive woman there. Had she always been that lovely? Had his mind tried to make her less attractive?

She rose to embrace him, and he felt the loveliness of her body once again. She had lost weight. It was becoming, yet he missed it.

She continued to hold his hand as they sat. "What are you doing in New York?" he asked. Did his voice have an edge to it? He hoped not.

"I'm on my way to Paris with Paul. Business," she smiled.

Todd breathed audibly. The marriage was better. Why didn't she let go of his hand?

"I don't want to go," she continued softly.

"To Paris?"

"I want to stay here. With you. Will you let me?"

"Jesus, Laura."

"Is that a 'no'?"

He saw the pain flood her face. What was he doing? What had he done? This lovely woman, halfway to Paris and ready to abandon her husband for him. For how long? Forever? Why couldn't the call have been from Lindsay? Why couldn't this be Lindsay? Jesus Christ, he must be losing his mind.

Then as suddenly as she had called, she stood.

"Where are you going?"

"To Paris. Where else?" And finally she let go of his hand.

He watched her leave the restaurant. So did other people. My God, she was beautiful. To keep from following her, he ordered a full meal and ate it.

After lunch he decided to call her hotel, then realized he didn't know where she was staying. He couldn't help being relieved. And yet he felt a sharp stab of loss. Laura was the only woman he'd known since Lindsay. How could he let her go so easily? Had Lindsay made it impossible for him ever to love anyone else? Would he have to live the rest of his life alone?

Then he remembered the letter his mother had sent him last spring. Instead of returning to his office, he hurried back to his apartment. He found the letter, reread it quickly, then stuffed it into his pocket. His mother had been careful to include a current address as a subtle reminder that some gesture was expected from him.

When he arrived at his destination, a small town on the Hudson River, he had no trouble finding the house. A ten-minute walk from the station was a small white-frame cottage on a street that led to the river.

He stood staring at the front door for several minutes before ringing the bell.

"Todd?"

"Hello, Sarah."

"What are you doing here?"

"I came to say how sorry I am—about your husband."

"That was six months ago."

"Yes, I know. I suppose I should've sent flowers."

He continued to stand in the doorway, satisfied just to be in her presence. Finally she asked if he wanted to come in.

"Are you alone?"

"I'm always alone now," she replied simply, "even more alone than when I was married to you."

"I never married again," he said as if in apology.

"I know. Your mother told me. I hoped you'd be able to find someone who would make you happy."

He did not admit that he had never been able to make anyone else happy either. Starting with Sarah. Why had it never been enough for him just to sit in a room with her, as they were sitting now?

"May I take you to dinner?" he asked suddenly. "Are there any good Italian restaurants around here?"

She smiled—and he could see how pleased she was that he remembered.

"You do still like Italian food?" he asked.

"Once I like something, I never stop."

During dinner she told him she wanted to open an antique store but was afraid of the risks involved. Todd offered to help with the business side—happy that she needed something he was able to give. When he took her home, he promised to return Saturday and spend the weekend helping her find a location.

But in the middle of the week Sarah surprised him at his office in the city. She had found the perfect setting for her store—across from the local train station—and wanted him to look over the papers before she signed the lease.

They went out to dinner to celebrate. He could not remember ever seeing her so happy. Certainly not while they were married. She asked where he lived. Could she see his apartment? He said it was a mess—he was planning to move as soon as he could find a new one. He took her to the train. She did not seem surprised when he sat down beside her. As they pulled out of the station he wondered why he'd resisted so strongly taking her to his apartment. But that night in her bed, with her arms enclosing him, he slept soundly for the first time in months. However, in the crowd of commuters pouring out of Grand Central the next morning, he passed three women who looked like Lindsay.

He spent the rest of the summer commuting between his office in the city and Sarah in the country. Evenings and weekends they devoted to the store—renovating, repainting, driving around the countryside looking for farmhouses with antiques for sale. Occasionally they would meet in the city for a play and though it would have been more convenient to spend the night at his apartment, they never did.

By the time the store opened, Todd and Sarah had become something marriage had never allowed them to be: friends.

A month after the opening Sarah declared the store a tentative success—and in her next breath asked Todd when he was going to move.

"What?"

"You said you'd been looking for another apartment."

"Not in the last few weeks."

Sarah smiled. Did he want to give up his apartment and move in with her?

It made such sense Todd could not refuse. But when he returned to his apartment that evening to pack, he was surprised to find Sarah waiting.

"I had to see it just once," she said.

Outside his window a siren was screaming, flooding his mind with images of the night he sat beside Lindsay in the ambulance, terrified that she was dying. She had lived but he had still lost her.

"I can't move in with you, Sarah."

"I know. That's why I came. I could tell you were living with someone else. I thought I might find some trace of her."

"I haven't seen her since June."

"But you are still living with her?"

"Yes."

He knew now he could never let go of this apartment, any more than he could let go of Lindsay. It didn't matter where he lived—or with whom. No one from his past or in any possible future could lessen the hold Lindsay had on his mind and heart.

"I've been unfair to you, Sarah—again," he started to confess, but she put her hand over his mouth.

"I was as lonely as you were," she smiled, and then kissed him to prevent further apology. "Please don't think you've taken advantage of me. I always grieved that we never got to say a proper good-bye."

They undressed slowly, knowing it was for the last time. In one night they tried to make up to each other for all the hurt they had inflicted over the years of their marriage from understanding so little of what love required.

When Todd awoke, he was alone.

Thirty-six

Cissy had been gone a month when it occurred to Meg that she too might be pregnant.

However, she decided not to tell Lindsay. She had come to take care of her, not add to her burdens. And yet Meg knew she was running a risk. With her history of miscarriages, she should be taking precautions herself. If only Cissy would come back to take care of them both. Then Meg could stay in bed, except for the daily trips to John Henry. But that might not happen—she had to face the fact that Lindsay's fate, as well as her own, was in her hands alone for the next few months.

After a month of cleaning and shopping and cooking, she had begun to feel used, to resent Lindsay's dependence on her. What right did Lindsay have after so many years to ask her to come and when Meg did respond to her plea, to expect her, in Cissy's absence, to assume full responsibility for the physical well-being of her and her unborn child? Admittedly Meg had at first been grateful to find that the spontaneous bonds of friendship still held firm, despite years of silence and small betrayals. And she knew that if she were to admit her exhaustion from all that she was doing, Lindsay would answer without hesitation that she understood and hire someone to take care of her, never letting Meg know how much she had disappointed her. But Meg would know—just as she had known the day she told Lindsay she was leaving law school to get married. Even as she accepted her congratulations that day, Meg had felt Lindsay relegating her to the long-distance friendship of the formerly intimate whose actions no longer affect each other for good or ill.

And so Meg said nothing and continued to care for Lindsay and to visit John Henry every afternoon. Lindsay looked forward to Cissy's return in October, when they would all be together as they had been before. Meg smiled and kept to herself a growing suspicion that Cissy would not be back.

Meg's first loyalty was to Lindsay, but what was going to happen to her once Lindsay had her baby and no longer needed a twenty-four-hour companion? The baby would have the room where she was sleeping now. Would Lindsay expect her to share it in return for around-the-clock child care? And even if she did, could Meg live like that, allowing Lindsay's choices to shape her life? There was only one way it would make sense for Meg to continue sharing Lindsay's life: if she had a baby of her own.

Finally one night when dinner was over and Stephen Presnell had examined Lindsay, Meg asked to speak to him privately. She took him into the study, which had become her room when Cissy left, and told him she suspected she was pregnant. He asked her to come to the office the next day so that he could examine her with a nurse in attendance. But she said she had to have an answer tonight. He confirmed her suspicions—and gave her the advice she had anticipated. With her history of miscarriages, if she really wanted to have this baby, she should take as many precautions as Lindsay.

"No," she answered firmly. "Every other time I learned I was pregnant, I made it the whole reason for my existence. And then when I lost the baby, there seemed to be no reason to go on living. I can't go through that again."

"Do you have doubts about having a baby? At your age you're entitled to a few, you know."

"I don't want an abortion, if that's what you're asking." Even though she didn't know where she'd be living when she left Lindsay—or with whom—she wanted the baby. However, only if it were strong enough to survive on its own. She said she didn't have the strength to try to will yet another human being into existence. "I've tried and failed at that too many times. I want a baby that wants to be born."

He looked at her quietly and wrote out a prescription. "These are vitamin supplements. You should start taking them right away."

"That's all the advice you're going to give me?"

"You don't need advice from me or anyone. It's your body, your life, your decision."

"Please do me one favor. Don't tell Lindsay."

He agreed. "But just remember, you're my patient now, too. And I expect to see you in my office in a month."

When Meg told her good night, Lindsay looked at her curiously. "Is everything all right?"

"You're the only one who can answer that," Meg replied with a smile.

"I'm fine—I'm worried about you. With Cissy gone, I feel I'm asking too much. Let me hire someone to come in during the day."

Determined to be everything Lindsay thought she was, Meg assured her she didn't need any help. She was managing just fine. And, she added, neither of them wanted a stranger intruding on their lives.

Lindsay seemed relieved. She said she had never felt closer to anyone than she did to Meg since she had come back into her life. But Meg now felt irrevocably separated from Lindsay by the knowledge she was determined not to reveal.

"You must promise to let me know if it gets to be too much for you," Lindsay said as Meg kissed her good night. She nodded, then connected the answering machine and turned down the phone so it would ring silently. Often now days would go by without a call but there were still occasional wrong numbers or business solicitations. Lindsay had talked Meg into recording a new message, identifying herself and explaining she was staying in the apartment while Lindsay was away. Only Craig Sanborn, who called every morning from the hospital to report on John Henry's condition, and Stephen Presnell, who stopped by the apartment every night, knew it was not true.

Meg was alone in the study watching television when the phone rang. Hungry for human contact, she answered it on the first ring.

"Lindsay," a man's voice began.

Frightened, she allowed the answering machine to intercept the call, but continued to listen on the extension. This was a voice she did not recognize, speaking with a passion and urgency for which she was unprepared.

Ignoring Meg's recorded message, he said, "I know you're there, Lindsay. And I have to see you. I'm going to keep calling till you talk to me."

Confused but also fascinated, Meg fell asleep trying to imagine who the man was, why he hadn't called earlier, what he wanted now.

The next morning Meg awoke to the sound of voices coming from Lindsay's room. She discovered Lindsay listening to a long message on her machine.

"Who is he?" Meg asked, when the recording ended.

"His name is Todd Newman. He's been part of my life for a long time. He didn't know about John Henry until after I'd been"

—she hesitated, searching for the words that would make the experience bearable—"until after the rape. Then I told him everything."

"And he went away?"

"No. He wanted me to move in with him. When I refused, he began to follow me everywhere. Even after he found out about the baby he was willing to stay and take care of me, but I didn't think it was fair to him. I told him I never wanted to see him again."

"He still loves you."

"I know."

"Are you going to talk to him the next time he calls?"

Lindsay shook her head. "I can't let it start again."

"You're a fool, Lindsay."

In response Lindsay unplugged the machine. "From now on, just let it ring," she ordered. "I don't want any more messages."

"What if something happened to me," Meg protested, "and I couldn't take care of you? What would you do then?"

"If you can't stay, I'll understand. Really."

"I won't leave you," Meg heard herself promising. "But to turn your back on a man who loves you, who knows everything and only wants to go on loving you—I can't let you do it, Lindsay."

"It's not your decision," Lindsay said.

But finally it was.

The phone rang again at one, just as they were finishing lunch. Without looking at Lindsay, Meg went into the kitchen to answer it.

Lindsay picked up the extension by her bed and heard Meg agreeing to meet Todd for dinner. She replaced the receiver while Meg was still talking and closed her eyes so that if Meg looked in on her again before she left for the afternoon, she would think she was asleep.

Meg heard the click on the line but continued talking. She was usually shy on the telephone, not being gifted at small talk, but now to her surprise found herself confiding easily in this man she had never met.

She decided to dress for dinner before she left to visit John Henry. Lindsay, hearing Meg singing in the shower, buried her face in a pillow to muffle her sobs.

Thirty-seven

Meg realized as she entered the darkened restaurant that she had not dined alone with a man other than her husband since leaving law school. She was wondering how she would recognize Todd when she felt a hand touch the small of her back. "You have to be Meg," he smiled.

She responded first to the touch, which revived in her the memory, long since obliterated by the habits of marriage, of being cherished as a woman, someone separate and unique. She turned to see a tall man with a face made more attractive by age, and surprised herself by reaching for his hand and holding it for a moment without speaking.

"Thank you for coming," he said as the maître d' led them to a table at the rear of the restaurant. Meg realized from the nod of approval Todd gave him as he seated them that his reservation must have included a request for privacy.

The presence of a sympathetic stranger across the table acted on Meg like some mind-expanding drug, heightening every perception, until she felt, as she seldom did, irresistibly immersed in the present moment. To have her every thought and feeling engaged in the event at hand was a rare experience, and it was by comparison to this moment that she later measured how much had been missing from her life during the years when she allowed marriage to provide the sole purpose for her existence.

She was amazed at how easily the conversation flowed. Lindsay had told her almost nothing about Todd, so Meg had many questions, and each seemed to lead inevitably to another. And when he questioned her in return, she, who had so often remained silent throughout entire meals with Mark's business acquaintances, marveled at the wit and ease with which words came to her.

When Todd asked about Lindsay, Meg said she was in good health as far as the doctor could determine and would be giving birth to a healthy girl soon after the New Year.

"A girl," Todd said. "I always wanted a daughter."

"Claire," Meg murmured.

"What?" he asked, startled.

"That's the name she's chosen. Claire. I don't know where it came from."

"It was my grandmother's name."

"Oh. Then she—"

"I doubt it. We talked very little about our families."

When they left the restaurant Todd, reluctant to end the evening, asked Meg if she felt like walking for a while. She had not been outside Lindsay's apartment after dark since she arrived and it was with a real sense of physical pleasure that she tucked her hand inside his elbow as they crossed the street, heading into the evening breeze.

They did not mention Lindsay again, but her separate relationship with each of them set limits to what was beginning to happen between them. Like what has become known in this nuclear age as a limited war, a limited friendship between a man and a woman can make use of techniques considered highly effective in earlier times but rendered obsolete by the totality with which the twentieth century engages in both sex and war.

Meg had not had a true friend of the opposite sex since kindergarten. Her first best friend was a boy—Sammy Rogers—who came to her house every afternoon to continue the games they started that morning in school. They built freight trains out of orange crates, camped out with their teddy bears in a tent made of two lawn chairs and a bedspread, and created their lunch together out of whatever the refrigerator had to offer (even as an adult Meg found few desserts to compare with their favorite: a banana dipped with each bite into a jar of chocolate syrup).

But when her serious education began in the first grade, her mother enrolled her in a private girls' school, feeling along with many of her academic betters that girls had to be educated separately from boys in order to remain their intellectual equals.

At the time all Meg understood of the move was that she was losing Sammy. Her mother consoled her by saying she could still see him, and she did call and invite him over after school on one occasion, but they had become strangers to each other. He even said he had stopped liking bananas. After that, though Meg sometimes saw him playing on the asphalt-covered playground of the public school in their neighborhood, they never spoke again.

Once, though, in the sixth grade just before he graduated from elementary school and went into a junior high school across town, she stood at the edge of the playground and stared through the cyclone fence, hungrily following his every move as he taught a friend how to execute a perfect hook shot. Her overwhelming sense of loss was only partially assuaged by the fact that the friend who had replaced her in Sammy's affections was a boy.

That night she begged her father until bedtime to put a basketball backboard on their garage. He was amused at the irony of the request. No athlete himself, he had hoped by having a daughter to escape the responsibility of encouraging athletic activity in the family. However, his daughter's request was made with a passion that, though he did not understand, he had to respect. The backboard was erected within the week and for the next six years, through junior high and high school until she went away to college, when Meg came home in the afternoons, she would quickly shed the gray skirt and tailored white shirt that were required dress at the private school she attended, slip into blue jeans and a sweat shirt, and practice her hook shot.

Sammy was the only member of the opposite sex who had ever entered Meg's life solely and simply as a friend—someone whose company she preferred over that of anyone else. All those who followed him played a functional role: father, pediatrician, dentist, professor, lover, husband, gynecologist, minister.

Until Todd.

Walking with him along Fifth Avenue, stopping in front of lighted store windows seductive with promise, Meg felt they would always be interesting to each other. She did not know whether Lindsay would agree to see him, but she was already looking forward to being with him again—and resolved not to allow the evening to end without setting a time for a second meeting.

However, Todd spoke first.

"Do you have to be back by a certain time?"

Meg shook her head. Then, looking at her watch, "Lindsay's probably already asleep."

"Then why don't we stop by my place? I have an espresso machine."

Meg decided not to tell him that she had never acquired a taste for the bitter brew Italians prefer over an honest cup of coffee. Besides, she had ordered sweetbreads for dinner at his suggestion —after avoiding them scrupulously for the first half of her life —and they had proved to be delicious. Possibly her tastes were changing at midlife, along with other elements of her body chemistry. It was an interesting possibility to contemplate, so she accepted his invitation—and decided at least to consider anything else he might propose.

Todd lived in an old, once-elegant building just west of Central Park completely lacking the conveniences of the new high-rise apartments. There was no intercom and if the doorman decided to take a break, visitors and delivery boys had no choice but to wait patiently for his return if they hoped to gain access to the building. The sole elevator broke down at least once a month, usually at sundown on the Friday preceding a long holiday weekend.

It was out of order when Todd arrived with Meg. He asked if she objected to taking the stairs. She said she preferred them, but after four flights she had to stop for breath. Todd apologized for not telling her his apartment was on the sixth floor.

"Why do you put up with this?" she asked in a tone more hostile than she intended as they finally reached his apartment—but when he opened the door, she saw the answer.

Todd lived on the top floor of the building, in what must have been called the garret in the days when the irregularly shaped rooms with the slanted eaves were occupied by all the servants required to maintain the elegant mansion below.

Meg slipped off her shoes as she settled onto a couch that seemed to be made entirely of down. No framework of any kind could be seen or felt, but none seemed to be required. The couch yielded completely to the shape of its occupant—the secret, Todd said, of its durability. He had bought it eighteen years ago, when he moved into the apartment, and never even had it re-covered.

"I went to this lecture once—on mind-expanding techniques," Meg said, pulling an afghan over her stockinged feet. "The one technique I remember was to create and furnish a room in your mind—and to live in it mentally for part of each day. The room could be any size as long as you occupied it alone."

"The same room?" asked Todd. "What's the point of a fantasy if it takes you to the same place every day?"

"The room is not the fantasy. It's just the starting point. It's a place where you go to feel safe and private and comfortable —a setting you can control completely. Your only conscious, rational act is to create the place and imagine yourself in it. Then the mind is free to go anywhere."

"Where did your mind go?" he asked, handing her a demitasse of espresso garnished with lemon peel.

She laughed. "I loved my room so much I never left it. I never wanted to go anywhere else."

"What was it like? Can you describe it?"

"I tried to tell my husband about it once but he thought I was describing a room I wanted to add on to our house." She paused, but then continued, bravely determined not to be evasive. "He said since we didn't seem to be able to have children, what we needed was a smaller house, not a larger one."

She got up from the couch and crossed to the two gabled windows cut into the eaves, each of which had a window seat outlined with pillows. She curled up on one and looked out at the city.

"I don't have to describe my room to you. This is it. It has everything I imagined—window seats, slanted eaves, fireplace, and a couch so comfortable you could fall asleep and not wake till morning."

"I often do," Todd laughed. "Nobody who lives alone needs a bedroom."

"But you do have one?" she couldn't resist asking, glancing curiously at the closed door.

"Oh, yes," he said, opening the door opposite the front entrance to reveal a narrow hallway leading to a bedroom that looked like a companion piece to the living room—a smaller fireplace, one window, and booklined shelves on every wall.

"I never expected to live alone," he confessed as they moved back into the living room.

"I can't imagine what it would be like," Meg said, "being able to fall asleep whenever you're tired or to stay awake till dawn if you're not, to eat only when you're hungry and not just because it's time for dinner. Sometimes I think I would love living entirely alone, not feeling anyone needed me for anything."

Todd was listening to her attentively but without any understanding of what she was saying, as if she were a recently arrived immigrant from some uncharted country. She realized she was describing a way of life that had become abhorrent to him and remembered the despair in his voice on the answering machine the previous night. The intensity of his need for a human connection was as alien to her now as her hunger for solitude was to him. Had she ever felt for anyone as he felt for Lindsay? The two men in her life—John Henry and Mark—had fallen in love with her and she had merely acquiesced to their feelings.

"I can't thank you enough for what you've done for me tonight," he said, putting another log on the fire then bringing a brandy decanter and two glasses to the coffee table.

"What I've done for you?" she laughed. "I haven't had an evening like this ever—in my whole life."

Meg sighed contentedly as she sipped her brandy—she could actually feel her responsibilities slipping away from her, like a laborer who dares not admit how heavy his load is while it is still on his shoulders.

She closed her eyes but continued to see the room's every detail in her mind. How many times had she come here before, to a room she had furnished mentally but, even with all the resources of imagination at her command, had failed to endow with the comfort and warmth of this very real retreat. She felt so right being here that she could accept completely the one element that had never been present in her imagined garret—the comforting presence of a man beside her who expected nothing more than to watch over her as she fell asleep.

Careful not to wake her, Todd turned off all the lights in the living room, removed the down comforter from his own bed and laid it gently across Meg as she lay nestled on the couch, then went back into his bedroom and stretched out fully dressed to wait for morning.

He must have fallen asleep finally, for the next time he opened his eyes the sun was shining. He thought for a moment he might have dreamed the night before until he saw that he was still wearing his clothes.

Meg was sleeping soundly on the couch, oblivious to the sunlight streaming through the garret windows. The down comforter had slipped to the floor but she lay with both arms flung above her head as if she would never again need a comforter of any kind.

Todd hesitated only briefly before reaching into his pocket for the key to his apartment. He wrote a hurried note to explain what he was doing, then quickly searched Meg's purse until he found what he wanted.

The sound of the front door clanging shut woke her. The first thing she saw was the key on the coffee table and the note beside it.

> This is the only key you need for this apartment. Stay here as long as you like. I'm going to Lindsay. I've taken the key from your purse. Call if you need anything.
>
> Thanks for everything,
> Todd

CHAPTER
Thirty-eight

Lindsay had been convinced, listening to Meg make plans to meet Todd for dinner, that she was bluffing in order to get Lindsay to agree to see him. Meg came of age in an era when a woman could only prove her existence by being attached to a man, Lindsay reflected, and was probably not even capable of imagining that there were women who might prefer to live alone. But Lindsay had summoned strength from sources she was not even aware she had—and closed her mind to the possibility of Todd's reentering her life.

Not since the early months of her marriage had she been as happy as she was now that Meg was living with her. Stephen Presnell had presented her with a stethoscope of her own so she could listen to the fetal heartbeat as often as she liked, and she had grown to feel warm and secure in a world of her own making. Meg was there to represent her past, she carried her future safely enclosed inside her, and the present was its own reward.

From the time she moved into the city and entered graduate school, Lindsay had measured her life in terms of tangible accomplishments—deadlines met, by-lines printed, money earned. She realized for the first time lying in bed, the stethoscope in place, listening for hours on end to the rhythmic assurance that her unseen daughter was alive and well, that by these standards she had done nothing with her life since being confined to her bed. And yet she awoke each morning with an overwhelming sense of accomplishment that had nothing to do with what she was beginning to realize were male-imposed values.

She was coming to the conclusion that the universe was organized according to two often opposing principles: male and female. There was a basic tension between existence and essence, product and process, doing and being. To lead a full life it was necessary to acknowledge both forces, for both were present in everyone. Lying in bed, the heartbeat echoing affirmation, Lindsay felt it was all so clear—and yet she knew that what she was just beginning to grasp was a truth that her generation may have been the first to acknowledge. For her mother life was all process —cooking food that would disappear within a day, planting flowers that would bloom and die, going through nine months of agony to give birth to a daughter who would grow up believing her mother had done nothing with her life. It was her father Lindsay had admired—he could point with pride to tangible accomplishments. His efforts had resulted in buildings, shopping centers, whole communities where before there had been only unproductive land.

From the time she was old enough to count, her father had made Lindsay his assistant when it came time to prepare his income tax return. Every year he would set up a card table in his study and collect all his receipts for the previous year. He would give her figures to add and, as she grew older, taught her to use his adding machine. He got extra tax forms so she could practice filling in the blanks for herself, and the year she was sixteen she calculated his taxable income faster than he did. He had kept a copy of his returns from the time he got a social security card and every year after he had computed what he owed he got out his old returns to see how his income had increased since the year he received his first paycheck. Lindsay, seated beside him at the adding machine, shared his sense of accomplishment.

Now that she was having her first child, Lindsay missed her mother terribly. How she wished she could share what was happening to her now—though of course without revealing the circumstances. Sometimes she felt the presence of her mother and her father merging inside her in the form of her unborn child, and she knew they would be part of her life now in a way they had never been when they were alive. And be united in a way that was beyond the power of sexual intercourse to accomplish. Her daughter was going to begin life a giant step ahead of Lindsay on the evolutionary scale, for she would encompass at birth the masculine and feminine forces Lindsay had grown up believing were meant to be separately embodied in a man and a woman.

Her child had been conceived in a union of extremes—the active male in its most radical act of assertion, rape; the passive female in a surrender so total that it even embraced the consequences, pregnancy. However, it was not an androgynous society Lindsay envisioned her daughter joining but a world in which men and women, no longer strangers, would at last be able to love each other completely, recognizing in each other aspects of themselves.

Lindsay smiled, listening to the heartbeat. This was her triumph over the man who had entered her life against her will— a triumph more total than if she had kept a gun by her bed and been able to kill him. She had not only saved her own life without taking one in return, she had allowed a new life to form inside her—and with it a future not only for herself but for her husband, who had lost his along with everything else except his life.

From her window she watched the sun set—and waited for Meg to come home from the hospital. Surely she would return to fix dinner for Lindsay before going out with Todd.

Then she saw the tray beside her bed—a plate of sandwiches, the crusts delicately trimmed, covered with Saran Wrap so they would stay fresh. It was too early for dinner but Lindsay decided to eat anyway. What did it matter since she would be eating alone? She ate all the sandwiches—too quickly, not tasting any-thing—and wondered where Todd would take Meg to dinner. She knew she was irrationally jealous. In coming to her rescue, Meg seemed to be replacing her with both men in her life—first John Henry, now Todd.

After she finished the sandwiches, Lindsay opened the book she was reading—an optimistic appraisal of the future of the family —and tried to read. But she couldn't concentrate. She kept thinking about Meg and Todd. She wondered if he would come back here with her after they had dinner. Suddenly she was convinced that was his plan. She reached for the cosmetic tray she kept on the bedside table, combed her hair, powdered her nose, and put on lipstick.

But then it was ten P.M. and then eleven and still no one came. She fell asleep waiting.

When she awoke, it was dawn and she was still alone. She thought for a moment Meg had come home late, after she fell asleep, but the empty sandwich plate was still beside her bed.

She called out, hoping Meg might have been too tired to check on her when she came in. "Meg," she cried again, her irritation increasing.

She got out of bed to go to the bathroom, wondering if she should try to do something about breakfast. But she wasn't hungry and was determined not to endanger her baby by disobey-ing the doctor's orders.

She climbed slowly back into bed and made a decision. She

would never again be dependent on any one person. What if Meg
didn't come back? What if she decided to move in with Todd?
She had set her course by a man from the time Lindsay met her.
Though she seemed to be happy for the moment staying with
Lindsay, she was apparently not as strong as she appeared. Being
with Todd probably made her miss Mark. Perhaps she had even
flown home to California.

"I can't be left alone indefinitely," Lindsay thought. But who
could she call at six A.M.? Then she smiled and picked up the
phone. Cissy answered on the first ring.

"I've missed you, Cissy," Lindsay began—and was surprised
to realize she meant it. "When are you coming back?"

"I'm not," Cissy replied hesitantly.

"What happened? Did you lose the apartment?"

"No, I've asked them to return my deposit."

"Oh, Cissy." Lindsay made no attempt to conceal her disappointment. "Didn't your daughter want to live in the city?"

"It was my decision," Cissy said slowly. "I'm sorry, Lindsay.
I know you were counting on me, but you have Meg. You'll be
all right."

"Cissy, I'm not all right." Lindsay couldn't believe how weak
and dependent she sounded, like the kind of helpless, whining
woman she despised. But she couldn't prevent herself from adding, "I'm all alone."

"Where's Meg?"

Somehow not being able to see her, to watch her reaction,
made it easier for Lindsay to tell Cissy about Todd.

"Oh, Lindsay, if you wanted a baby, why couldn't you have
had one by him—by a man who loved you—instead of by, by
—" And then Lindsay knew why Cissy was not coming back.

"Meg told you I was raped?"

"Yes. And I don't understand what you're doing, I don't
understand any of it. How could you want this baby—after what
happened?"

"I didn't plan it, Cissy. But I have a chance to make something good come out of it. Please come back. Please help me. You can bring Muffin. You can both stay with me."

"No." And then after a long pause, "But if you really need me, Lindsay, I will be your neighbor—if that apartment is still available."

"I'll call right now and find out."

"Lindsay, it's six thirty in the morning."

"All right. I'll wait till seven."

"And, Lindsay, if you need me today, I mean if Meg for any reason . . . Well, just call me, I can be there in an hour."

Lindsay was dialing the number of the apartment above her when the front door opened. She didn't realize anyone was in her room until she saw a shadow across her bed. She screamed into the phone—and then fainted.

Thirty-nine

Lindsay felt her face being covered with kisses. Her mind was a montage of unrelated images rapidly superimposing themselves—John Henry helpless in his moving bed, the father of her child forcing himself into her. She started to scream again but now there was a voice whispering in her ear. "I didn't mean to frighten you. I took Meg's key. I thought you'd still be asleep."

"Todd . . ." she murmured, opening her eyes and smiling. "I'm so happy to see you."

"I'm not leaving you again, Lindsay." He continued to caress her.

"Where's Meg?"

"I left her sleeping at my apartment."

"You spent the night together?" The question was out before Lindsay remembered that she prided herself on not exacting or even allowing promises from Todd.

He seemed amused at her interest. "She was exhausted. She fell asleep on the couch."

When Todd told Lindsay he was going to fix her breakfast, she did not protest. She had done everything in her power to keep him from loving her, from ever having to feel responsible for her. But now that he was here, she was as powerless to prevent him from doing what he had come to do as she had been to resist the man who raped her.

He watched her as she ate. "Aren't you hungry?" she asked.

He shook his head. "Do you realize I've never been with you before without knowing I would have to leave?"

Suddenly Lindsay felt tears flooding her face and heard herself saying words she had sworn she would never say again. "Stay. Stay with me. I don't ever want you to leave."

Todd's face was against hers and their tears merged and bound them like a blood pact. He held her in his arms until language was again possible between them.

Later that morning, Todd bathed Lindsay, sharing her excitement over her changing contours, cherishing the only physical intimacy their circumstances allowed. He realized he was more in love with her now than he had ever been before—or ever believed he could be. And not just spiritually. He was physically in love with the swelling body he could not even claim.

Lindsay did not question Todd about his time away from her, but she knew by the way he touched her now how much had happened to him since the night he reclaimed her after the rape. She had ceased to think of herself as a sexual being in the aftermath of that night, but now, feeling his fingers tracing the length of her back, knowing he asked nothing in return except to be allowed to go on loving her, Lindsay felt her life as a woman was just beginning and a world of new experience was waiting for her along with the responsibilities of motherhood.

Forty

In the late afternoon Meg returned to Lindsay's apartment to pack
the one suitcase she had brought with her from California. Todd
invited her to stay for dinner—he had called his favorite neighborhood restaurant to deliver a five-course meal—but she declined, as did Stephen Presnell. They left the apartment together
as a waiter arrived and began setting a table beside Lindsay's bed.

"Are you taking care of yourself?" Stephen asked, carrying
Meg's suitcase as they walked to the elevator.

"Yes," she answered, smiling at the thought of the unoccupied
apartment that awaited her.

"I have to be at the clinic in an hour, but I want to grab a
bite to eat first. Will you join me?"

But Meg wanted nothing more than to be alone in the apartment that was hers for as long as she cared to stay.

"Thanks," she said, "but I'm awfully tired. I think I'll just go
back to the apartment and sleep."

"As your doctor, I can't object, but I'll miss your company."

He helped her into a taxi then looked at his watch and headed for the subway. He wasn't hungry enough to eat alone, so he decided to go on to the clinic.

Alone in the apartment Meg discovered she wasn't tired at all. She made a cup of herb tea, then curled up in a window seat to watch the lives reduced to miniature proportions passing in review below.

Now that she had a place of her own to await the birth of her baby, she dared to hope it might actually happen this time. She knew now that if she finally had a baby to hold in her arms, she would want to share the triumph, not with Lindsay but with her husband Mark. She began to visualize the scene. She would send Mark a telegram telling him she was coming home, asking him to meet her plane. Nothing more—just a flight number and time of arrival. Then she would step off the plane with the baby in her arms—the baby he had not even known was on the way. It was the only homecoming she could imagine—the only way she could go back to him without explanation or apology.

Cissy moved into the apartment above Lindsay within a month after Todd arrived. Her two sons had gone away to school as planned, but Muffin was as excited about the move as her mother. Cissy resumed her former routine: doing Lindsay's housework and cooking lunch every day. Lindsay invited Meg to join them for lunch too, along with Stephen Presnell, who continued to check on her daily. Meg and Cissy always left together after lunch, Cissy to run errands, Meg to visit John Henry, just as they had when they were living with Lindsay.

When she returned to the apartment, Cissy would prepare something for dinner that Todd could heat in the oven when he came home from work, but she always made sure she was finished before Muffin came home from school. She would never feel safe in the city again after what had happened to Lindsay, but she loved being needed and looked forward to sharing the experience of a new baby. Gradually, the danger of attack from a stranger began to take its place alongside all the other dangers that Cissy knew existed but had never experienced. Still, she was determined to take every possible precaution to lessen the risk and did not allow her daughter to stay alone in the apartment or walk unaccompanied through the streets.

Meg had been afraid to confess to Lindsay how much she still loved her husband and wanted to bring a baby home to him—something to show for her life, to confirm her choices. So she had no one to share her loss when she awoke one morning in a pool of blood. The triumph had been hers alone to imagine. This final failure was hers alone to bear.

She could not face her friends. When she finally found the strength to bathe and change the sheets on the bed, she got back in it and called Cissy to say she wasn't feeling well, not to expect her for lunch. Then she called Stephen Presnell and told him what had happened. He insisted on coming right over but she had accepted her fate before he confirmed it.

"Please don't tell Lindsay. Ever," she begged. "This affects no one but me."

"Don't punish yourself," he urged. "Stay in bed for the next few days. Don't try to go anywhere."

"Thank you," she said, without promising to follow his advice.

When he left, she fell into a deep sleep, not knowing where she would go when she woke up, what she would do—or if she would go anywhere or do anything ever again.

It was dark when she opened her eyes and she sat up in bed with a start. Suddenly she was aware that her despair had vanished, along with her indecision. There was only one place for her to be now: at John Henry's bedside. Even though she had again and for a final time proven incapable of carrying a baby to term, she still had within her the ability to sustain life, the life of the man she had once promised to marry. Though he could not speak or even smile, she knew by looking into his eyes that she was keeping him alive just by acknowledging his existence with her presence. And because it mattered to him that she was alive, it had to matter to her. She dressed hurriedly and took a taxi to Grand Central.

The next day at lunch, seated across from Lindsay and Cissy, pretending nothing had happened since she had last seen them, Meg sensed a plan forming in her mind. The larger purpose behind the curious communal existence they were sharing suddenly seemed clear. Lindsay was having this baby to take the place of the one she had aborted—but there was no real place for a baby in her life. She had her work and a man who loved her unconditionally, a man who had no claim on her child. Just by the simple act of giving birth, she would pay whatever debt she owed society—or herself. But it was Meg whose life had been geared to the raising of children, Meg who wanted a baby to hold and to love and most of all, to present to her husband, thereby regaining his respect. Of course she wouldn't tell Lindsay her plan until the baby was born. For the moment it was important, in fact essential, for Lindsay to believe she really wanted this baby she was making such a sacrifice to bring into the world. But once the baby had been safely delivered, Meg would plead her case, explaining to Lindsay how much it would mean to her to be able to adopt the baby and take it home to Mark as their own.

During the months that followed, Meg began to plan for the baby as if it were hers already. She bought books on child care and read them avidly in the privacy of her apartment, making copious notes in a new notebook she had bought exclusively for that purpose. Once she had read and absorbed each new book, she would present it casually to Lindsay.

As the stack of books on her bedside table grew taller, Lindsay began to joke that she was going to be the best-prepared mother in the history of the world.

"I envy you, Lindsay," Cissy said wistfully. "I was too busy being married to enjoy my children. This baby is a second chance for me."

"It's my only chance," Meg said, then turned away quickly before Lindsay could see how serious she was.

The next day she began shopping for baby clothes. She bought blankets, a hooded towel, tiny stretch suits. But she didn't show them to Lindsay. She kept them neatly folded in a box under her bed, and every night before she went to sleep, she would take all the clothes out and try to imagine a living creature small enough to fit inside them.

A month before the baby was due, Lindsay suggested at lunch that perhaps it was time to think about transforming the study into a nursery.

"Oh, no," Meg cried out. "Please no." Suddenly she broke into tears and excused herself from the table.

When she returned from the bathroom, Lindsay took her hand. "I'm sorry, Meg. I wasn't thinking."

Thinking what, Meg wondered. Lindsay couldn't have guessed that Meg was crying because she saw any chance of adopting the baby slipping away from her. Lindsay would never consider letting her adopt a baby that already had a fully furnished nursery waiting for it.

"I wasn't thinking about what you've had to go through," Lindsay continued, "how many times you must have had a nursery waiting."

"Only the first time," Meg said, realizing she was exploiting Lindsay's sympathy to her own advantage but not letting that stop her. She assured Lindsay there would be plenty of time to get the room ready after the baby was born. After all, most new mothers don't have their two best friends standing by, with nothing more important to do than help with the baby.

Then Cissy became an unsuspecting ally, explaining how few needs a newborn infant has—contrary to what magazine and specialty stores would have the anxious expectant mother believe. She told Lindsay that she and her husband were living in a one-bedroom apartment when their first baby was born. The only equipment they had for the first six months was a portable bed that could go from car to bedroom to living room—with the baby often sleeping through every move.

"Keep the study the way it is. You're going to need a room to work in. Don't let the baby disrupt your life any more than it already has," Meg advised. "Besides, Cissy and I will want to help all we can—we'll be keeping the baby with us a lot of the time."

Meg was seated beside John Henry a month later when Craig Sanford came hurriedly into the room. "You have a phone call," he said. Once they were out of John Henry's hearing, he told her Lindsay was in labor.

"I'll drive you into the city," he volunteered, as he had when she arrived from California. "I feel responsible somehow— though I don't know why."

There was no one in the waiting room when Meg and Craig arrived.

"Are you family?" the nurse asked Meg when she inquired about Lindsay.

Meg nodded.

"Her husband and sister are already with her," the nurse said as she led them into the labor room. "Usually we don't allow more than two visitors at a time, but Dr. Presnell said this was a special case."

The delivery was accomplished with an ease that mocked the long months Lindsay had spent in bed waiting for it.

"Hello, Claire," Lindsay smiled at the baby the nurse handed her, then looked quickly at Todd to see if he heard.

"Why did you decide to name her Claire?" he asked.

"Can you think of a better name for your daughter?" Lindsay replied, knowing how much she was giving him. In the months since he had moved into her apartment to take care of her, Todd had never once mentioned marrying her or adopting her child. And because she knew he would never ask, she wanted him to have what only she could give him—a family.

Meg saw her last chance at the role she had once imagined to be her birthright disappearing. How foolish she had been to think Lindsay would let her adopt this baby. Now she would never be able to return to Mark in triumph. And so she would never return.

Dr. Presnell kept Lindsay and her new daughter in the hospital for a week. When Todd was finally allowed to bring them home to the apartment, Meg and Cissy were waiting to greet them. Meg had set up a small portable crib in a corner of the study and cleared a bookshelf for the clothes she had been keeping under her bed.

"This is all she'll need for the first few months," she explained, then offered to take the baby so Lindsay could rest.

Lindsay said she never thought she would lie down in the daytime again after having spent so many months in bed, but she was surprised to discover how exhausted she still was.

Cissy led her into the bedroom, reminding her of what an extraordinary ordeal she had been through, and Todd gratefully handed the baby to Meg.

"I'll come every day—and stay as long as you'll let me," Meg promised. "There's nothing I'd rather be doing. And, besides, I owe you for the apartment. You won't let me pay rent. At least let me help with the baby."

"Because of you, I'm where I want to be—with the woman I love and a baby I'm going to be allowed to love as if she were mine. I'm completely happy—and you made it happen. The least I can do in return is provide an apartment."

It seemed natural to Meg to nap that afternoon on the couch in the study where she had slept before Todd moved in with Lindsay. The baby was asleep in the portable cradle beside the couch, so Meg could reach over and rock it without even having to open her eyes. Lindsay was resting in the bedroom, Todd had gone back to work, and Cissy was walking Muffin home from school. A soft crying from the cradle woke Meg. She reached sleepily over to rock Claire but the crying continued.

"It's not time for you to be hungry again," she chided gently. "Besides, your mother needs to rest."

She tiptoed down the hall to Lindsay's bedroom and opened

the door. Lindsay was sleeping soundly, just as Meg had suspected. She hurried back to the baby, lifted her out of the cradle, and held her in her arms, singing in a low voice. Suddenly she felt a nuzzling against the folds of her blouse.

"Oh, my goodness," she laughed. "We're all the same to you, aren't we? I'm sorry," she said, shifting the tiny head to her shoulder. "I can't give you what you want."

This was met by a disconsolate cry. "You're not even supposed to be hungry," Meg said, a note of panic in her voice that betrayed her lack of confidence at communicating with this less-than-rational creature.

Then almost furtively, trying to believe her only purpose was to keep Lindsay from being disturbed, Meg carried the crying infant into the bathroom and shut the door. As Claire began to wail in what appeared to be a tone of total deprivation, Meg slowly unbuttoned her blouse.

"I'm not who you think I am," she said. "You're not going to get what you want."

But to her surprise the baby grew quiet immediately and was soon asleep again, making contented sucking sounds.

"Well, if you don't know the difference," Meg smiled, putting Claire back in her cradle, "who am I to tell you?"

CHAPTER

Forty-one

The special-delivery letter arrived one afternoon while Lindsay was nursing the baby.

"Please take Claire and put her to bed," Lindsay said to Meg as she opened it.

When Meg returned, Lindsay was in the bathroom. The shower was running full force, but Meg thought she could hear choking sobs behind the door. She knocked but there was no response. When she tried to open the door, she discovered it was locked.

"Lindsay," she cried, pounding on the door. "What's wrong?" The sobbing ceased abruptly—or became indistinguishable from the sound of the shower.

Meg looked curiously at the envelope torn open on the bed. She hesitated only briefly before reaching inside to examine the contents.

It was a cashier's check for twenty thousand dollars made out to Lindsay. There was no other name on the check. Meg was examining the envelope when Lindsay emerged from the bathroom.

"You're not going to find a name or address," Lindsay said flatly.

"Then you know who sent it?"

"He sent a basket of food the first time—after the attack. Then flowers when I found out I was pregnant. Now this."

"How can you be sure it's the same man?"

"Who else could it be?"

"What are you going to do?"

"I gave away the food and the flowers."

"How can you give this back? You don't even know his name."

Lindsay had not left her apartment in the week she had been home from the hospital. The rigidly confined existence forced upon her by her pregnancy had provided a structure on which she had come to depend and she was hesitant to venture outside it. But now there was something she had to do. She dressed and went down to the lobby. At the entrance to the building she stopped abruptly.

"Can I get you a cab?" the doorman asked.

"No, thank you," she said, walking decisively out the door. She kept walking until she reached the Park Avenue bank that had issued the check. Taking her place in line, she waited for a teller.

"I'd like to know who sent this check," she began. "It's made out to me but there's no other name."

"You mean you don't know?" the teller asked in amazement, looking at the size of the check.

"I have no idea."

He disappeared into an office at the back. When he returned, he was accompanied by an older man, who asked Lindsay to follow him to his desk.

"I'm sorry. The information you want is confidential."

"If I don't know who sent this check, then how can I return it?"

"You can't."

"What am I to do with this money?"

"May I suggest you open a savings account while you decide."

"Actually, it's not my decision. I mean I'm sure the money is meant for my daughter."

"How old is she?"

"Two weeks today."

He smiled indulgently and Lindsay could guess what he was thinking: the money was being offered in compensation for some unsanctioned liaison that had produced a child. Well, he wasn't entirely wrong.

He suggested that, since Lindsay seemed to have no immediate need for the money, she open a long-term savings account in her name as custodian for her child under the uniform gifts to minors act.

"With the interest we're paying now, if you let it accumulate, you won't have to worry about your daughter's college education."

Lindsay filled out the necessary forms but as she handed the check to the bank officer, she had a sudden thought. "I know you can't tell me who sent the check, but somewhere in your files you must have a name and address."

He nodded. Lindsay quickly wrote two words on a piece of paper. "Could you see that this gets to the person responsible?" She folded the paper and handed it to him.

He put it in an envelope and sealed it. Lindsay smiled gratefully at his discretion and repeated the two words she had just written. "Thank you."

She was fine until she left the bank but, once on the street, her knees suddenly buckled and she had to take a cab back to her apartment.

When Todd arrived home that night, Lindsay was waiting for

him in the living room wearing a low-cut jersey dress that outlined her figure in becoming folds.

"Do you know how long it's been since I've seen you in a dress?" He crossed to her and enclosed her in his arms. "You're beautiful."

"I thought you might like to take me out to dinner. Meg is happy to stay with Claire."

"I've been waiting for you to ask. I know it's hard, but you've got to stop being frightened of what's out there. I'm with you now. You don't ever have to be afraid again. And you don't ever have to go back to the office. You can stay home and take care of the baby and write in your spare time—you know, free-lance articles, maybe even a book."

"No," Lindsay said firmly. "No. I can't just keep hiding at home. I have to go out. I have to go to John Henry and tell him about the baby."

"One step at a time," Todd cautioned. "Tonight dinner. To-morrow, if you're up to it, John Henry."

She pressed her lips to his. "Thank you, Todd. Thank you for being here."

Lindsay felt safe at last.

Forty-two

A tall, dark-haired man was arguing with the doorman when Todd and Lindsay got off the elevator to go to dinner.

"She's my wife, damn it! Just tell me which apartment!"

Relieved to see Lindsay, the doorman asked her to settle the dispute. "This man says his wife is in your apartment and he wants to see her."

"You must be Mark," Lindsay said, extending her hand. "I'm Lindsay and this is my friend Todd Newman."

"I'm here to see Meg," he said, reluctantly shaking her hand.

"Did she know you were coming? She didn't mention anything to me."

"She hasn't written or called or communicated in any way since she left California. So why would she know or care where I am?"

"I'll go up and tell her you're here," Lindsay said quickly, wanting to avoid an argument.

"No, Lindsay," Todd interrupted with unexpected authority. "I'll give him my key. If you ask her, she may say no. You did. If it hadn't been for Meg and her key, I would never have gotten back into your life. The least I can do is return the favor."

"Thanks," Mark said curtly and disappeared into the elevator.

As soon as Todd and Lindsay had left the apartment, Meg undressed and slipped on a soft pink kimono. Then she took Claire in her arms and sat beside the window in the bentwood rocking chair she had bought at Bloomingdale's the day after Lindsay came home from the hospital. She looked down at the people below, moving in corridors of self-imposed isolation along the crowded sidewalk. She felt the baby at her breast and knew that at last a bridge had been formed to other human lives. She didn't dare look into the future to see exactly what her place would be among these lives to which she was joined by neither law nor blood—Lindsay, Todd, John Henry, Cissy, Claire. All she knew was that she was where she wanted to be and she had never once in the months since she had answered Lindsay's call felt the aching loneliness of living in the same house with a man who barely acknowledged her existence.

Her back was to the door, but she knew suddenly that someone was in the room with her. Guiltily she separated the baby from her breast and pulled her kimono tightly around her. A wail of sudden and total deprivation ensued.

"A baby—my God," a familiar voice said in a tone of unfamiliar tenderness. "I never guessed this was the reason you were staying away. When was he—"

"She," Meg corrected him. "Claire." She could not bring herself to correct his larger mistake. Mark believed this child was his—and he was not entirely wrong. A child had been conceived in their last act of lovemaking, Meg thought, justifying her deception.

"Why are you here?" she finally remembered to ask.

"I came for you. And now for the baby, too. We're going home, Meg."

CHAPTER

Forty-three

The plane was on the runway, waiting for a signal from the tower to take off, when the pilot got the message.

Meg was seated beside Mark, the baby in her arms. As the plane turned around and taxied back to the terminal, she knew that Lindsay had found her note too soon. She saw the stewardess coming toward her and smiled to reassure her that she was neither insane nor violent.

It had been an impulsive decision, yet her reasons seemed so sound when she put them in writing that she honestly believed Lindsay would not object when she came home and found the baby gone.

> You thought it was your life you were saving by deciding to have Claire, but it's really mine. Having a baby makes it possible for me to have a husband again. I

can't risk another pregnancy. I was pregnant when I came to you, though I didn't know it then. I lost the baby—and never told anyone except John Henry and Stephen Presnell. If you really want a baby, have one by Todd, a man who loves you. John Henry will understand. Don't be afraid to make it a choice.

Think ahead. Who will you tell Claire her father was? This child could have been mine. Let Mark believe it is. You'll be going back to work soon. You don't have time to be a mother. Even if I were to stay here with you, I'd be the one taking care of Claire—let me do it in my own home, with my husband to help and love us both.

I'll bring her to New York as often as you like and stay as long as you say—and when she's older, I'll send her to stay alone with you.

By the time you read this, I'll be airborne, so it will be too late to stop me. There will be nothing for you to do in the next few hours except think about what I've said. Please try to look at it from my point of view — or, better still, from Claire's.

Your call for help saved my life. Whatever happens, I will always love you.

Meg

But Meg had not counted on Cissy, who had been standing at her window folding sheets on her dining room table when she saw Meg getting into a taxi and a man she did not recognize handing her the portable cradle. Cissy used her key to Lindsay's apartment and found the note on the coffee table, then quickly reached Lindsay at the restaurant.

"What's the problem?" Mark demanded as the stewardess asked Meg to follow her—and bring the baby.

"I can't leave yet, darling," Meg said hastily, gathering up the flight bag packed with baby equipment. "You go on to Los Angeles. I'll come as soon as I can."

"Here. Let me take the baby," the stewardess offered impatiently, anxious to expedite their exit.

"No," Mark said firmly. "I don't know what this is all about, but I'm not giving up this baby to anybody."

"Mark, don't make a scene—please. Just give me the baby and I'll take care of everything. You stay on the plane."

"I'm not going anywhere without you."

The stewardess accompanied them to the door of the terminal and told them good-bye with obvious relief. Lindsay was waiting as Meg entered the terminal. "Where's Claire?" she cried—then she saw Mark with his arms wrapped protectively around the baby.

Todd was standing next to Lindsay, ready to do whatever was required. Neither, however, had any idea of what was going to happen next.

Mark hesitated a moment then, recognizing in Todd the man who had provided the key that allowed him to reclaim his wife, moved toward what he hoped was an ally.

"Do you mind telling me what's going on?" he asked.

"It's between Lindsay and Meg," Todd replied—and wished it were that simple.

Lindsay and Meg stood in silence, watching the Los Angeles–bound airliner taxi once more down the runway and out of sight. Tears were streaming down Meg's cheeks.

Lindsay smiled as she saw Todd take the crying baby from an embarrassed Mark. "I could have let Todd believe he was her father too, you know. He didn't have to know about the rape. But I'd already risked losing his respect by not telling him about John Henry. All those years I imagined that once he knew the truth, knew the reason I could never marry him, I would lose him. And all the while he was admiring me for my honesty. Oh,

Meg, don't you see how wrong I was, how falsely and unfairly I judged him. The more he knows of me and accepts, the more I'm able to love him. I want that for you. If you lie to Mark now, then your marriage is really over."

Meg did not argue or even answer. In the background the baby continued to cry as if acknowledging that she was the source of contention among all these anxious adults. Meg felt her breasts seeping in response to the cry and, looking down, saw two damp circles spreading across the front of her silk blouse. Embarrassed, she quickly slipped on her suit jacket and buttoned it.

"I think she's hungry," Meg ventured finally.

"I'll feed her in the taxi," Lindsay answered. She gave Meg a quick hug. "Have a safe trip back to California. And remember, you have a place here with us, with all of us, whenever you want to come."

Meg continued to stand at the window, not wanting to watch as Lindsay walked over to Todd and took Claire from him. When Mark started to protest, she said softly, "Meg wants to talk to you." Then, placing her arm on his elbow, she added, "I hope you can be happy"—as if it were his decision.

Mark sat down heavily as Todd put his arm around Lindsay and they walked away. He knew now that Meg had nothing to say that he wanted to hear and so he waited for her to come to him. Finally she crossed the lounge and sat beside him.

"Why did you let me believe it was our baby?" he asked in a tone of such despair that Meg's heart ached for him. She realized suddenly that there is no greater bereavement than losing something you never had—and she wept for both of them. And for their children.

"I wanted to believe it as much as you did."

"Will you still come home with me?"

"As if none of this had ever happened?"

"Yes."

"I don't want to pretend it never happened," said Meg with unexpected passion. "I can't go back to being the kind of wife I was before, Mark. I just can't."

And suddenly thoughts and feelings she had refused to acknowledge for twenty years came clamoring to life, fully formed and demanding attention as loudly as the screaming infant he had held and considered his own only moments before. It was as if she were giving birth at last—not to a child of passion, created in her image, but to a bloody afterbirth, an unrecognizable mass of unexpressed rage and resentment that instead of nourishing a new life like a placenta had poisoned it in utero. She told him she had lost twenty years of her life and the only way to recover them was to live all the years left to her with a ferocity he would only find threatening. Being with Lindsay had forced her to recall the excitement she felt at twenty-one. Waiting for the baby to be born, imagining her future, she began to feel that excitement growing inside her. At her birth Claire seemed to embody not just Meg's hopes but the unfulfilled ambitions of a whole generation of women. "It took all of us to bring her into the world," she said triumphantly. "Lindsay, Cissy, me—all of us. I had a perfect right to be doing what I was doing when you walked in on me. Claire is the daughter of us all."

Mark pulled Meg close to his chest to comfort her but then he drew back quickly. "You're wet," he said. "You're going to catch cold if we don't get you into some dry clothes."

"I have another blouse in my suitcase," Meg said, "but it's on its way to Los Angeles. Without us."

Mark pulled a cashmere cardigan out of the overnight case he was carrying and helped her remove her suit jacket. Then he buttoned the sweater around her like a cape. She quickly removed her blouse and stuffed it into his suitcase then slipped her arms into the sleeves of his sweater. "Do you have to go back tonight?" she asked.

"The next flight is not till morning. I'll have to find a room for the night."

"Would you like to stay with me?"

"In that little bedroom you share with the baby? No, thank you."

"Not there," said Meg, opening her purse and removing the key to Todd's apartment. "I have a place of my own."

Forty-four

He had begun to wonder if he would ever see her again. He had often doubted her love in the early innocent days of their marriage. He felt unworthy of her—and kept waiting for her to notice the chasm between what he was taking from her and what he could offer in return. But if she noticed, she kept the knowledge from him, and so his unease continued. Until the day when he could no longer give her anything—and she continued to love him. Even her refusal to bear the child he had fathered seemed to affirm her single-minded devotion to him. He knew there were parts of her life he could never share—and was grateful when she decided not to try. She was totally his when she was with him, and in gratitude for that, he tried never to imagine what her life was like when she left his room.

But it had been so long now since she had come to see him that he had stopped expecting her. Yet he never considered for a moment that she might have ceased to love him. For once he was no longer able to earn her love, he could accept it for what it had always been—a gift, all the more precious for being undeserved.

In the meantime there was Meg—gentle, tenderhearted Meg, who still believed she had left him, never suspecting that once he saw Lindsay it would not have been possible for him to marry anyone else. Meg had spent her whole married life feeling she had betrayed him and had come at last to beg forgiveness, but too late to achieve absolution for her unborn child, which became, like all the others before it, a sacrifice to her imagined betrayal.

It was with Meg that he felt most helpless. Lindsay brought with her an aura of acceptance that was able to still—at least in her presence—his own overwhelming anguish. But Meg stood before him utterly naked, confessing her failure to achieve any of the ambitions with which she had entered adulthood. He ached to be able to say something, do something to comfort her. All he could do, however, was be there for her—and gradually he sensed his presence beginning to make a difference. On her last few visits, especially, she seemed almost radiant, as if she had finally discovered the meaning of her life. "I'm happy, John Henry," she had said to him just the day before. "I can't tell anyone but you how happy I am. They wouldn't understand." And she had covered his face with kisses when she told him good night.

It was dark now. Where was Meg? Where was Lindsay? Was no one coming?

He must have fallen asleep, because he had to be dreaming. Lindsay was kneeling beside his bed, her arms around his neck, her face pressed close to his. "We're a family now, John Henry, and you're part of it." There was a man standing behind her, saying something about always wanting a brother and telling him the baby belonged to all of them, that he was no more the father than John Henry was. Father? Baby? But Meg had lost the baby. She had cried telling him. Didn't they know that? Was there another baby?

"Maybe we shouldn't have told him everything today," Lindsay was backing away from him.

The man seemed to agree. "Me, the baby—it's a lot to absorb."

Why were they talking to each other as if he weren't there listening to everything they said? But then the man went into the hallway with the doctor and Lindsay was back at his bedside, touching his eyelids with her fingertips the way she had when they were first married and she used to pretend she had the power to put him to sleep. "Sleep well, my darling, and don't try to understand any of this. All you need to know is that we all love you very much. I thought the only way I could go on living was to make you a separate part of my life, keeping you untouched by everything that was happening to me outside this room, and not talking about you to anyone else. But I've learned with the baby—this baby I never expected to have—that it's wrong to try to erect boundaries, to separate the good from the bad. Everything overlaps and finally you have to accept all—or none—of it. I love Todd, though not in the same way I love you. You taught me to love, my darling, and it will never be the same with anyone else as it was with us. But he loves me the way you do, and I am grateful. He also loves the baby, even though it's not his. He wants to take care of all of us. You, too, my darling." She continued to stroke his eyelids. Was it to keep him from staring at her? "I wish I knew what you were thinking," she said finally as she rose from her chair. "I've told you all I can bear for you to know just now. Please don't hate me."

She was staring at him, her eyes overflowing with tears. Suddenly the man was beside her, his arm around her shoulders. "If only I could feel that what I'm saying makes a difference to him," she said, reaching for the man's hand as they left the room.

A difference! To know that she would no longer be alone? It made a difference he was only just beginning to grasp. Relief flooded through him. He was free at last of a responsibility that had been too awesome to acknowledge. Why had it taken him so long to understand that what had been keeping him alive all these years was not Lindsay's love for him but his love for her? He had lived when it would have been so much easier to die, because he was afraid she would not have survived without him to hear her nightly confession. But he was exhausted from loving her. Thank God there was finally someone to take his place. He had amazed his doctors by continuing to live; he would not have to amaze them much longer.

When he closed his eyes to sleep, he could still feel Lindsay stroking his eyelids even though she had left the room.

Afterword

Lindsay was now waking up earlier than the baby, leaving Todd
sleeping peacefully, so she could make coffee and read the *Times*
before the demands of the day began. If Claire started to cry
before she finished, Lindsay had learned to cradle the child against
her breast with one hand, turning the pages of the newspaper with
the other. She read every page, even the obituaries, realizing that
she had fallen into her mother's habit of checking first for the age
of the newly deceased then measuring her own against it. Was
it John Henry's death that had made her so aware she was halfway
through her own life?

One morning in April—a year after the rape—a photo accompanying an obituary seemed to assault her. She stared at it for
several seconds then, recognizing the eyes, gave a sharp cry,
letting the paper slide to the floor. She had convinced herself that
she could not remember his face, but she knew now that she
would never forget anything about him. The headline over the

photo read: PROMINENT EXECUTIVE COMMITS SUICIDE. The story summarized his accomplishments, ending with the statement "His wife of thirty years died last year after a long illness. There are no survivors."

Only Lindsay knew differently.